AN AULD BED IN HAVANA

BY

JOHN MOLLOY

U.S. U.K. Digital edition first published 2014   X X
By John Molloy
Molloyjo68@hotmail.com

DESTINATION HAVANA

CONTENTS

INTRODUCTION

Cormack a young Irishman leaves Dublin for a holiday in Havana. He is trying to get over a broken romance and wants time to himself to reflect on life. He doesn't reckon on a chance meeting with the beautiful Cuban young woman Kathie, and becoming ensnared by her beauty and vulnerability.
He becomes enmeshed in a world of secrecy and deceit as he learns that Kathie is holding a deadly family secret which could cost her life. She is being pursued by a corrupt secret service policeman who knows the value of this secret. Kathie has to get out of Cuba to freedom but can Cormack find the will and a way to get her to Ireland and freedom. Will she reveal her true identity and her commitments before its too late for both of them?

Review snippets.

John Molloy has given us a whirlwind adventure full of romance and excitement.

Excellent read. Cormack and Kathie are two great characters. Great love story.

Fantastic read, great author, I have read all three books, brilliant.

CHAPTER 1

Cormack O'Gara stretched out his arm to press off the alarm button on his bedside clock. He turned back into the warm comfort of the linen sheets and coveted his usual ten minutes before rising for another busy day. Monica's shapely bum normally nudged him as she turned over for a second snooze. The realisation of her not being there took a few seconds to sink in. He stretched his legs, taking the full length of the bed and encroached into her out of bounds half of the large deliciously comfortable mattress. In his twilight zone of wakefulness he selfishly relished the absence of his bed mate as he wallowed in a freedom space he hadn't experienced for years. The thrill of their first months living together, their nakedness beneath the bed clothes, early morning sex: 'a jockey's breakfast' as the lads at work called it. He missed this part of life but he wondered could he be feeling a sort of relief or freedom. However, it was time to get out and shower, and gulp a cup of coffee before heading out into the chaotic traffic the city of Dublin's road network had become.

He arrived at work, and met his partner Derek. They were in the design and advertising business which they had successfully developed together, into a thriving upmarket company, now employing fifteen people. Derek casually remarked with a hint of concern: "No Monica this morning, is she sick?"

Cormack looked over to her empty desk: "No, she was out with the girls last night, probably traffic delay."

Derek went to his design table: "It's just we need all hands on deck for the next week to get that project for the beer ads out."

Cormack smiled his casual aureate of confidence: "We'll be on time once they approve the sketches which I'm showing to them today." He showed little concern about Monica's late morning but he secretly cast little thoughts about in his mind about her night out with the girls. A little pang of jealousy rippled his confidence as he harboured the thought of her sleeping with another man. He realised he had been neglecting her a bit of late, but put it down to pressure of business on both of them. He started work and his creative mind cast out all else, otherwise he couldn't concentrate.

It was nine thirty when Monica arrived in; she was still in her party clothes not having had time to go back to the apartment to change. She went straight to her desk, and throwing her hand bag underneath she started to work her computer. She was there ten minutes before Cormack heard Deidre asking her if she enjoyed her night out. He deduced between titters and giggles it had been a great success and enjoyed by all.

He went to her and gave her a peck on the cheek: "Did you enjoy your night out?"

She kept her fingers on the keyboard and looked at the screen: "I felt like a teenager again, you know the feeling!? The abandonment of responsibilities is like the shedding of a skin, and a vast open playing field with a team of Adonis's vying for my wanton charms."

"My god what were you drinking?"

She turned her pretty face up to him and tossed her honey blonde hair back from her face: "It's so poetic, one of the girls, Katherine, I don't think you've met her, got us into company with this fellow of immense charm and a poetic way with words. It was he who quoted the one about Adonis, actually I had to ask quietly what he was referring to, I'd never heard of this fellow Adonis."

He straightened up and touched up the tresses around her creamy pale neck: "I must go and meet our clients with the proofs of the work so I'll see you back at home later."

She nodded and didn't look up, and as soon as he was out of sight she opened her e-mail box and read a little ditty from her new admirer. She smiled to herself, clutching her guilt like a soft cuddly teddy bear.

Cormack concluded a successful meeting securing the very lucrative contract, and hoping it would be the first of many more. He phoned Derek to tell him the good news and enquired if Monica had left the office.

"Yes, great news. Monica, she went a bit earlier than usual, I suppose she had to do a bit of shopping and have your dinner ready when you get home."

"I can understand the shopping bit but not the dinner part of it. I'll see you in the morning."

It was nearly seven o clock when Cormack got home. 'No sign of the Prima Donna,' he spoke softly to himself. He felt elated at having secured the lucrative contract against what he knew was stiff opposition, making it all the sweeter. He'd decided to take Monica out for a few drinks to celebrate or a meal if she wanted. He made a sandwich and brewed up a pot of coffee. He then sat and waited for the Manchester United game against Barcelona to come on, switching through the channels from one soap opera to the next. How people could sit and view this pathetic television he felt was beyond him, two minutes of any of them was enough to make him switch again. He had to endure the panel of Irish soccer hierarchy before the action began, but the game lived up to all the hype and expectations. Manchester United was his team since he was about seven years old, and winning again tonight was as thrilling as the first game he could remember when they clinched the Premier League title. He was considering whether to go out for a jar just to celebrate the new contract when he heard the front door close. Monica came into the room clutching her post; she opened an envelope and took out a large pink card which she placed on the mantle. Then came a funny one, she giggled at, and another and yet another. She arranged the four cards and looked at Cormack who shame facedly averted eye contact. "Do you think I look my age?"

"I'm sorry for forgetting your birthday, but I suppose it's all this pressure the last few weeks trying to get that contract, but the good news is we secured it. I was going to take you out to dinner to celebrate but I suppose it's a bit late now."

"Yes I've already eaten and drunk a few so I'm only fit for bed, I enjoyed the evening."

"Who did you go with, anyone from the office?"

"No, I met some of the girls and Katherine had her fellow, you know him he was asking for you, Peter something or other."

"Yes I know Peter; I played rugby with him, decent chap."

"Katherine brought along the poetic man, the one I told you about, who talks like a Greek Philosopher. He has the most peculiar name, Uriah Cashel. His people were English landowners and held some sort of title in years gone by, he works at some stockbrokers."

He went to hold her and try to make up but she pulled away, pursing her lips in a stern pout fashion. He'd seen this look only once and remembered the soft tirade of warning.

"Do you think my petty obsession with birthdays is somehow ridiculous!?" The steady look from her violet-mauve eyes with long lashes and a soft dampness beneath them highlighted a beauty that was created for love not scolding.

"Of course I don't think birthdays are frivolous or times to be passed over without some recognition, at home we always remembered family birthdays."

"Really, well that's interesting you can remember family birthdays but not mine, but it's not only birthdays!" She paused and walked closer to him, he could smell the sweet alcohol on her breath, and she was always irresistible for sex when she was like this, anxiously purring like a spoiled cat. She put her face teasingly up to his. "Do you remember the last time we had sex?" She didn't wait for his calculated, hesitant answer. "Three weeks ago and if I remember correctly I had to initiate it, raise that flagging member to a proud and cheeky stance, like a Roman General for his brief but triumphant entry."

"My God Monica, how poetic! I never thought of that part of my anatomy as a Roman General, but I'll keep it in mind next time he's making a triumphant entry."

"I'm afraid it won't be an entry between my portals! I've decided to take a break, I'm moving in with Katherine and we'll see how things work out, what do you think?"

"Well I wasn't expecting anything like this but if you've made up your mind I'll go along, and it'll teach me a lesson to be more attentive and caring when you decide to come back."

She walked across the room towards the bedroom, stopping she turned to face him. "If, I come back, and tonight behave yourself and stay on your own side of the bed."

He sat watching the television and seeing nothing, his thoughts in turmoil of personal guilt. He moved and swerved between the programmes of love, lust, and platonic rubbish. How could one define love, just what were the guide lines for some people, it seemed for others like something they could fall in and out of with impunity. Working with Monica every day would add to an awkward situation he was not looking forward to. He went to the bedroom and saw her in a shaft of light coming through the living room, she was sleeping soundly, and as he listened he could hear a silvery ghost of lisping in her breathing. He gazed at her youthful beauty, the blonde hair spread over the blue satin pillow, and a pang of regret clutched his heart. He saw the words written in Italic lettering back somewhere in the mist of his memory; *'Beauty is the splendour of truth'* and if so she's so right and how could he have been so unseeing. He closed his grey infant eyes and clenched his mouth tight, like a child watching a miscreant parent, the muscle on his lower face pronounced on the subtly stubborn jaw. He ran his fingers through the extravagant mop of fair hair, opening his eyes he gazed at her peaceful beauty and realised how empty he felt. How could he have been taking her for granted and now be standing on the brink of despair at the thought of losing her? He went back to the living room, and like *Scarlett O Hara*; he said to himself that *'he would think about it tomorrow'*. He slept on the large settee, waking and slipping back into unreal mixed up dreams. He was glad to see seven on the clock and he left early for work, he decided not to wake Monica as she could have decided to take the day off.

She never turned in to work but phoned to ask for two days off, which she could take from her holidays. Cormack returned to a bachelor apartment, all Monica's possessions were gone, he couldn't believe the emptiness. The bathroom shelves that were filled with her lotions, creams and shampoos were now bare and empty. The clothes lying around, shoes left in corners, her see through nightie lying on the bed with the big brown teddy he'd bought her on their first holiday abroad, all gone. He left and went for a walk on the East Pier at Dunlaoghaire. The May sun was setting over the church spire and Marine Hotel, the old red brick post office building glowed in a rose hue and he was amazed at the beautiful outline of the buildings set against the crimson orange sky. He sat and observed the people walking on this popular pier, the couples young and old chatting, some holding hands, other's with their dogs on leashes striding out. Lying at anchor was the Irish Lights vessel Granuaile, sporting her splendid tinted pink rigging. He thought of Monica and how 'he never brought her here for a walk, he realised he rarely took her anywhere except to a pub and restaurant, one night at the weekend.' The poem he'd learned at school came to the fore, *'A laggard in love and a dastard in war were to wed the fair Ellen of brave Lochinvar'*, whatever about the war bit he was certainly a laggard in love.

She was only twenty four and he'd been treating her like a married woman of sixty, work, and too much work. He decided then and there to take a break and assess his life, he'd come back to Monica a new man he'd win her back. Where to go and for how long, he knew he could take time off having secured the big contract, the hard part was over the lads could complete production of the contract. He had her mobile number and he wondered should he phone her, maybe not, better just give her a little more space. A plane flying south left a trail of white as she rose to her higher altitude; I wonder where she is bound.

He arrived back at the apartment and inside the door an envelope addressed to Cormack, he opened it and a key fell out, a small note read, '*thanks for the memories*'. He was beginning to feel sorry for himself, he put on a C.D. of U.2, and this was one of her favourites also.

He picked up a travel brochure from among some magazines and he began to flip through it, a holiday on his own wasn't the most appealing option. They'd been to Bulgaria and Greece, so he looked at Spain and Portugal, he didn't want a lively commercialised place, and truthfully he didn't know what he wanted. Then he thought of his painting he hadn't put brush to canvas since his college days, yes that's it someplace nice and quiet where he could relax, swim, and paint. He moved through Egypt, Morocco, Tunisia, and Cyprus, then he saw Cuba, he'd known one friend who went to Cuba, he'd loved it and really enjoyed himself. Tomorrow he'd do some ringing around and find out the details of a holiday there. He also remembered his friend telling him never book a package holiday there but move around and see the country, its breathtakingly beautiful and the people are very friendly. He went to the closet and took out his easel and paint box and spread them out, the tubes of paint were hard but the brushes were okay, he'd replenish the paints and canvases in Cuba. He went to bed happier with a holiday adventure in sight, he wondered about vaccinations.

Next day he discussed his holiday time with Derek, who assured him they could manage without him for a few weeks. When he went to book his holiday, the travel agents tried to get him into a package holiday but he insisted on a freelance three week stay. It was compulsory to book into a Havana hotel for two nights, after that you could move around where you liked. Car hire was available regardless of what you see on television about all the old American cars, they have small cars for hire there. He was excited now he'd made up his mind and his flight from Dublin to Paris and straight to Havana in one day was attractive time wise.

He took his leave and got himself ready, he was told what to bring, things that were not readily available in Cuba or otherwise very expensive, sun block and plenty a must, and good sun hats a necessity. The temperatures could reach over thirty. He had his painting gear all ready and the night before leaving he decided to ring Monica. She wished him well and told him to send a card; she sounded non committal as to whether she cared if he ever came back. He wondered about Uriah. He'd overheard little whispers at work he wasn't supposed to hear, about her new man. He did feel jealous but he had to be philosophical it was his own doing. The adage about women and their attitude to relationships he never really thought appropriate and anti feminist but he couldn't help repeating it to himself, '*Women's behaviour with men was like monkeys, they never let go one branch until they had a grip of another one.*' He threw the last of his clothes into his case and checked his passport and flight ticket. The name of the hotel in the old city of Havana was Inglaterra; it looked nice on the brochure.

CHAPTER 2

An early flight took him to Charles De Gaulle and then on to Jose Marti airport Havana. The flight arrived at eight thirty night time and Cormack being a lone traveller had to get a taxi to his hotel. He stood at the carousel waiting for his luggage, his artist box and easel came but no bag. He stood and watched until all the bags were collected and the conveyor was empty. Just a nice way to start a holiday lost baggage, he walked on to find an information desk and surprise there was his bag left sitting on the floor space like a lonely sentinel. 'Thank goodness' he exclaimed to himself as he picked it up and made his way out to the taxi rank. The package holiday people had gone in their busses, and he went to get a taxi when he observed a man standing at a doorway. He was middle aged lean and fit looking, light skinned with an intense stare. The face over his left eye scarred and the lid drooping over a motionless eye, he stopped Cormack and asked him "Where are you going?"

Cormack was taken aback a little as he wasn't sure who this fellow was, or why he should enquire. "I'm going to the Inglaterra Hotel."

"Will you show me the booking papers please?"

"I'll show it to the taxi driver if you don't mind." He walked over and got into a taxi, the driver threw his luggage into the booth and they headed into Havana. Cormack pondered the man and wondered was he a pimp, when he said to the taxi driver, "why did that man ask me where I was going?"

"What did you say to him?"

"I told him I'd show you the name of the hotel I was booked into but not to him, is he a pimp or what?"

The taxi driver laughed "no, no, he is not a pimp he is a special branch, I think you call them agents or detectives. He watches all the people coming off the planes, and he asks anyone he might think is not on a package holiday where they are staying. You were lucky sometimes they can be nasty and insist on seeing where you are going. But lately with tourism so important to Cuba they have to be nice and polite with people, in case there is a complaint and it could prevent people coming here."

Cormack looked out at the dimly lit streets as they were approaching the city, "I thought all that 'cloak and dagger stuff' was a thing of the past."

"Well not completely finished, there are still a lot of police on the streets here, which is good because crime is low and tourists can feel very safe. But behind the scenes you have all those special agents trying to keep their jobs, so they have to justify their existence by stopping people and trying to invent subterfuge and intrigue."

Cormack was surprised at the command of the English language this man had, "you speak very good English."

"Yes I am a professor of languages especially English but I have no job at the University so I drive this taxi, I earn more money doing this than teaching." He turned and handed Cormack a card, "if you want to go anywhere or if you need any advice about your travels just ring this number." He pulled into the kerb, "here is your hotel now."

Cormack slept fitfully, and rose to a brilliant sunny morning. The cobalt sky seen through the big old colonial window of his room was bleached from the relentless heat of a scorching sun. He enjoyed a plentiful breakfast but was distracted by the young coffee coloured waitress, whose charming smile revealed gleaming white teeth between full ruby lips; she pampered him with her warm bountiful attention. He couldn't help following her liquid movements as she walked to the serving hatch, her figure in a tight fitting cream cotton skirt was hugely sensuous, and she flaunted it. He realised he hadn't looked at a girl with such thoughts as such since he'd started living with Monica. It was a new experience, a kind of renaissance of youth he liked the feel of it.

He felt like a prime tourist as he slung the camera over his shoulder, donned his panama hat, adhering to the advice from the travel agent about the strong sun especially morning and early afternoon. The view from the front steps of the hotel was beautiful. The bright sun shone on the magnificent statue of La Manzana de Gomez standing high in the open park, surrounded by majestic palm trees and water features. There were marble benches set around shaded by the trees where people sat out of the hot morning sun. He turned left to walk down the Prada; this paved avenue was set between two roads one on either side and adorned with larges leafy trees. The low walls had entrances with figures of reclining lions on both sides, sculpted from marble. To his surprise he was in the midst of paintings and artists sitting on small stools before their easels, with paintings near finished and some just started. The sight of half a mile of art on both sides of this Prada under the shade of the trees was a view of splendour and colour. He strolled among the many people, a mixture of native and tourist, scrutinising and bargaining but also buying some of the artists work. The locals were going about their business and some stopping to ask "where are you from?" their friendliness was warming sometimes shy. He stopped at the end of the Prada where he observed the Malecon stretching along the seafront for as far as he could see. The sparkling ultra marine blue water of the Caribbean was enchanting, with the ancient Morro Castle lighthouse standing sentinel over the entrance to the harbour. He walked back and admiring a painting of a horse he spoke to the artist. "How much do you want for this painting?"

The young man, around his own age of twenty five or so, with very Spanish features and dark bronze colour, welcomed him with a broad smile. "I would want fifty pesos and I can get you a permit, this is no problem."

"Why do I need a permit?"

"You cannot take a painting out of the country without a permit but it is no problem and costs very little, I will arrange it for you."

"Well I have just arrived and will not be leaving for a few weeks but I will take it from you. I have not changed any money into Pesos yet, I have only Euro."

The artist smiled and laid down his brush, the dark haired maiden he was painting would have to stay on hold. "I will take Euro! One International Peso is one Euro, but Cuban Pesos are twenty four for one International Peso, so be careful when you buy, sometimes you can pay too much."

Cormack fished in his pocket and peeled off a fifty Euro note. The young Cuban gasped at the sight of the roll of notes.

"Here in Cuba five Euros would be one week's wages for one man, so do not take out your money like you do just now, most people are very honest but temptation can make an honest man a thief!"

"My name is Cormack and thank you for the advice."

"I'm Miguel, my job is an artist I study at the university but it can be hard to sell paintings, and there is no work. What hotel are you staying?"

"I'm just up at the top of this avenue The Inglaterra Hotel."

"I will bring the permit to you if you give me your name, here please, write it here." He handed Cormack a slip of paper and pencil. "You can take the painting and I think if I took it off the frame and rolled it up you could carry it better."

"That will be fine, I will leave it to you and you can bring it to the hotel, and I'll pay you for the permit then."

He left Miguel and walked into the streets of the old city heading towards the dock area. He was amazed at the non existence of traffic along these old colonial streets with their colourful towering Spanish buildings, Their Neo Moorish facades and beautiful Baroque balconies overlooking the shabby appearance of faded paint and cracked plaster. He came to a street called O'Reilly and wondered what this Irishman had contributed to Cuban history to merit a street being called after him. The market was a colourful place as he rounded into a square of brightly fronded sun shades and stalls with their wares set under canopies. The people moved nonchalantly around choosing their purchases in a careful slow motion. Cormack came to a stall selling fruit and he couldn't help but stand and gawk at the abundance of colour, and variety on offer. He held his hand on a roll of notes in his pocket and realised he couldn't purchase anything with a fifty Euro note. He took cognisance and realised fifty cents would buy a bag of succulent tropical treats.

CHAPTER 3

Her arm crossed over in front of him and picked up a melon, he followed the movement and her green hazel eyes caught his gaze, and like emeralds in a crystal pool, captivated his very soul.

"Excuse me for reaching," she smiled a wondrous breathtaking image of exquisite beauty.

He caught a breath and couldn't speak. She took some more fruit and paid the vendor, thanking her in a soft honey voice. Her movements were like poetry as she sorted her change and held up her bag. As she turned to walk away she looked at Cormack, her smile bespoke his muddled thoughts, about; '*the beautiful lady who could launch a thousand ships*'.

"Are you on holiday?" she enquired.

"Yes this is my first day here and I love your country so far."

"Where are you from, what country, would you like to sit awhile?"

As they began to move away from the stalls, a stone bench beneath a tree offered a place of cool repose,

"I'm from Ireland," he offered her his outstretched hand. "I'm Cormack."

She took his hand in her soft firm grip. "Pleased to meet you, I'm Kathie. Are you staying long in Havana?"

He held her hand a little longer than was normal, absorbing the blonde shoulder length hair and high cheek bone structure of her North European features. "I don't know yet, I want to do a bit of painting, a sort of therapy you might call it for a cross road relationship. I might move on out of Havana after a few days."

"That's an unusual relationship you call cross road. What do you mean by it?"

"Well, this girl who I had been living with for two years decided to take a break from our relationship. It reminded me of when you come to four cross roads and you can't make up your mind which one to travel. Each one will take you to a different destiny."

She smiled a benevolent parting of rose red lips, moistening them with her tongue through pearly white teeth. "Have you made up your mind which road you will take?"

"No I'm not there just yet but might I ask you how you speak such perfect English?"

She looked around and he thought he saw a slight sign of frailty nervousness in the perfect eyes. He noticed for the first time two policemen walking through the stalls.

She stood up beckoning to him, "You can walk with me if you like." She went on ahead and he quickly caught up.

"Yes, I would very much like to," he said, looking at her for some reaction, but she looked ahead and walked on her face expressionless. "Would you care to come for a drink," he ventured, "and we could get out of this heat for a while?" He noticed she had no wedding band so he thought he was within the bounds of etiquette.

She stopped and looked behind her then motioned to a bar, La Bodeguita del Medio. "It's a bit early for drinking alcohol but seeing you're on holidays come on."

It was cool in the small bar which boasted only one customer. "What would you like to drink?" he asked.

She sat herself down and straightened her skirt, "a beer please."

He brought back two pint glasses frosted with little rivulets of tears running down making filigrees through which to glimpse the amber liquid.

She smiled as she raised the drink to her mouth. "'Cheers', you say in English."

"Actually 'Slainte' we say in Ireland which means 'good health'."

She licked the cool liquid from her lips. "'Slainte' I must remember that, it has a nice lilt to it."

"Yes" he gave a rippling laugh, "we call that sound in our speaking a 'brogue'."

"I'm learning quite a bit about Irish today, I haven't met many Irish people. You see when tourists arrive here they stay in Habana for a few nights and are then whisked off to Varadero, to the glorious beaches and sumptuous hotels. Very few Cuban people live there, its only those working there can go to this area, it's reserved for tourists only."

Cormack was intrigued by the photographs and pictures covering all the walls, he stood up to view one on the wall behind them, it was written in Spanish.

Kathie stood and read the caption in English it was some kind of award given to Ernest Hemmingway. "You know this was the favourite watering hole of Ernest Hemmingway, and look here are the autographs of some famous people, Salvador Allende, Fidel Castro, Harry Belafonte, and Nat King Cole. We have none of these famous faces today only foreign sycophants trying to capture the Bohemian type atmosphere that once permeated this place."

Some tourists came in and Cormack deduced they were French Canadians, their language was definitely French but the pronounced Canadian accent was obvious. The two women in their late thirties dressed in shorts and revealing blouses, ordered mojito. The men saw the pints of cold beer with Cormack and Kathie. "We'll have two of those," in perfect English.

They sat at the other end of the bar and Kathie eyed them with a knowing smirk. The two women, one over weight, and the other slim and much tanned, vied for attention from their husbands who engaged in man talk to the exclusion of their spouses. They were looking at the photos of the great men scattered around the walls, some sporting the trophies of fishing competitions with huge marlin dwarfing the catchers.

Kathie understood their French and laughed at one remark she overheard. She leaned over to Cormack and whispered, "they're trying to get away from the women already and I'd say they've just arrived."

"Why do you say that?"

"One of them is asking the other how would he like to take a day out fishing for marlin, you see that is only for men and it would be an excuse to get away for a day. They've seen the young girls offering their favours around the hotels and along the Malecon, so it would be so easy to steal an hour of forbidden passion."

Cormack looked at the two men as they were viewing the photos of the great fish hoisted alongside their catchers, and all the paraphernalia of pictures and scripts on the walls. "You really think they would be interested in young girls? I didn't see any of them around the hotel."

She swallowed a large swig of beer and smacked her lips, her green eyes admonishing and tenderly mocking "you've seen them but didn't recognise what you saw."

Cormack's thoughts went back to the tempting waitress who served him breakfast, but he thought 'they can't all be advertising their sexual wares.' "There was a young woman serving breakfast with a twinkling eye and fluent movement, but you couldn't reckon on her being anything else."

"You have been here such a short time, this is Cuba." She smiled.

The bar began to fill up as more tourists came in. Cormack sniffed the tantalising aroma of roast pork; a waitress came to their table and asked would they like to order lunch. He looked at Kathie. "Would you like to stay for lunch?"

"Yes that would be nice, I'll have the roast suckling pig, I think you should try it Cormack that is if you are not Jewish."

He smiled at the waitress "I'll have the same please I left my little cap at home because I didn't want to spoil the party."

Kathie was serious when she said "are you Jewish?"

He laughingly looked through her beautiful eyes, "I'm not Jewish just joking."

She returned his stare "my ancestors were Jewish, and I suppose I still am the skull cap as you call it I knew as the "Kippah" and there were always some of them in our old home. I believe I might have one tucked away somewhere in my grandparents old trunk."

"Are there many Jews in Cuba?"

"There used to be quite a lot but religion is not identifiable anymore so it's hard to say how many there are. The wealth associated with Jews has also vanished here in our Cuban society. It is better not to speak of such things as you never know who's listening, and you can bring suspicion and trouble on yourself."

"Here's our food now and it surely smells great." He said.
The suckling pig was absolutely scrumptious and another pint of beer completed a perfect meal.

CHAPTER 4

Outside the early afternoon sun was baking the huge block masonry of the great buildings, the heat rose from the cracked and broken pavements. Kathie walked on looking around at the almost deserted street, there was one parked old Buick the lone vigil of the street.

"I live not far if you would like to come home with me?"

Cormack cheerfully replied. "Yes I would like to very much."

They walked in silence for a few minutes as Kathie strode on purposely. She turned into a street of high colonial buildings, the balconies were crossed with clothes lines decked with a colourful array of washing.

She stopped and pushed open a great panelled door its peeled paint revealing naked bleached hardwood. The dark stairway led to a first floor apartment, inside the living room had big bright windows and a high ceiling, it was remarkably cool.

Cormack was surprised at the eloquence of the large room with furniture so fine and beautifully hand carved from Cuban hard wood, and hide upholstered chairs and sofa, gilt framed oils and a crystal candelabra. He stood on the now worn Turkish rug with its beautiful hand woven pattern of horned animals standing out against the polished tropical wood floor. This room was a reminder of the old colonial opulence enjoyed by the wealthy landowners, and sugar plantation bosses before the Castro revolution.

She did a little pirouette, like a child waving an arm to show the complete room, "are you impressed with the trappings of long gone wealth?"

He crossed his arms and stood eyes admiringly for both her and the beautiful surroundings. "It's absolutely stunning to see such old grandeur still exists."

"I'm afraid it exists but stops abruptly there, I can't offer you anything to drink except coffee."

"Fine; coffee will be fine."

She went to boil the kettle and took two china cups from the ornate cupboard, "you must realise that people who come on holiday here never see the real Cuba. After a couple of days in some hotel here they're whisked off to Varadero to their holiday hotel. They're wined and dined in the finest surroundings with sugar white sandy beaches, and blue warm sea on their door step. You said you were moving out of Habana in couple of days, are you booked into some hotel in Varadero?"

Cormack went to look out the window and he spoke to her with his back turned. "No I'm not booked into any hotel. I haven't decided what I'll do, I'm just playing it by ear but I would like to travel around and see the country. Who owns the huge space at the back of the houses, it's like a jungle except for one small space that has been cultivated and is growing some kind of fruit and vegetable?"

Kathie came to stand alongside him and peered out through the dust covered window, "you see all that green area, well like a lot of property in Cuba it belongs to everyone, but in actual fact belongs to no one. The old man that tends that garden doesn't sell his produce but shares it with all his neighbours; he is a proper old gentleman I often get some fruit and vegetables from him. You see he can get seeds and fertiliser and other things for his garden free from the government co-op shops, so it helps him to grow nice things."

Cormack put his face closer to the glass, "I think there is someone over in that house opposite looking over at us."

Kathie pulled him away from the window, "don't let that surprise you, the area has lots of nosey people some would call them spies. Each area has at least one person who is a member of the C.D.R. that is short for Committee for the Defence of the Revolution, and they report anything they think is untoward or out of sync. with the party policy. I overheard a remark from a young girl prostitute lately when she was being observed by a couple of policemen, '*there are eleven million people in Cuba and there must be nine million of them police*'." She laughed at the audacious statement and noticed the incredulous look on Cormack's face. "Don't look so shocked it's not quite that bad, come over here the coffee is ready."

He sipped the hot fragrant brew and thought it tasted like no other coffee he'd ever drunk. "This is absolutely delicious it has a unique bouquet and it tastes," he sipped again, "smooth and earthy or is that a silly description for it."

She agreed she loved her coffee but had to admit it was scarce and expensive, and out of reach for most people who were living on state subsidy.

"You know Kathie to change the subject you have a remarkable command of the English language, I know people at home who are brought up speaking the language and they couldn't express themselves as proper as you do."

She took out a packet of cigarettes and offered one to Cormack. "No thank you I don't use them, but you have one yourself."

She placed them into a drawer, "I never use them and hopefully never will, I keep them for visitors who would like a Cuban cigarette. As for my command of your language, I took English as one of my major subjects. When I was twelve years old I always imagined myself in England or the U.S. and felt I should have good spoken English. Over the years as part of my learning I've read Dickens, Bronte, Shakespeare, Jane Austen, and even tried Joyce's Ulysses but without success, I just couldn't get to grips with it. So you see why I speak so well, and I might add with limited practice. I don't get to speak with fluent English speakers very often, so I appreciate your time with me."

He smiled and raised his coffee cup to her, "it's been to my pleasure dear madam you are so refreshingly beautiful and interesting, a speech taken from one of your old English masters."

She gave a little nod of her head and her blonde hair fell over her face, "thank you so kindly dear sir." They both laughed at the mock pretence.

"Excuse the inquisitiveness but do you now teach English?"

She finished her coffee and poured the remainder between their two cups, she changed from flippant to a seriousness which shaped little lines on her forehead. "If you have time and patience to listen to my boring life story I will tell you."

He settled himself comfortably in his chair and laid his two hands on the table, "I'm all ears."

"To start with I am twenty five years old and I hold a doctorate in biology from our Habana University. My grandfather came to Cuba in nineteen twenty after the Great War; his family had estates in Bohemia a part of Germany and Czechoslovakia but which no longer exist today by that name. There were two sons left alive after the war, two more were killed, so only one son could stay on the estate. My grandfather being the youngest got his fortune and left. He eventually made his way to Cuba. In terms of wealth at that time he would have been considered very rich, he bought a plantation of three thousand five hundred acres and grew tobacco and sugar cane. After a few years he went back home to see his sweetheart and ask her hand in marriage, but to his surprise she had married his brother. Her younger and more beautiful sister who was only sixteen fell in love with him, and he with her, they married and returned to Cuba."

She smiled a knowing smile and ran her tongue across her blood red lips.

"You see there was romance in those days also. My father, their last child was born in nineteen forty, a mistake by all accounts as all their family which consisted of two children a boy and girl were grown up. My father was educated and mastered in physics he was a supporter of Fidel Castro and the revolution. He never believed the country would become totalitarian and his family would lose their estate. My father's brother was shot by Batista's military for helping Che Guevara's men. My grandfather kept the plantation going with his wife and their daughter in law who was childless, and my father's sister, my aunt. He was manager until he retired in nineteen eighty four, I was very young when we moved to Havana. He gave my uncle's wife what money he could and she went to South America, Argentina I believe. We haven't heard from her for nearly twenty five years. My aunt his sister, went to Israel and we stopped hearing from her twenty years ago so we know little of her, I believe she never married. My grandfather, grandmother and my father, and mother, got a nice house here in Habana in Miramar a beautiful residential area, and my father kept his position with the revolutionaries and was sent to

Russia to study Engineering Technology. Am I boring please tell me to stop when I am."

"Your story is most interesting please continue."

"As the years passed my grandfather became very disillusioned with his life but also wasn't allowed to leave Cuba. He began to talk openly about Castro and the ruination of the country, some said it was his age and dementia but he was brought before a disciplinary committee and warned to stop his anti revolutionary ranting. He was eventually arrested and put into an asylum where he died shortly after, my grandmother died with a broken heart. My father had married a white Russian and I am the only product of their union. When the Russians pulled out and left us in poverty my mother went back to Russia and divorced my father, so there were only the two of us left. I continued with my studies and got a doctorate in biology, but my father who had spent time in Russia and was now our top engineering technologist, was now reduced to lecturing at college. He spoke with me of trying to leave Cuba, but there was no way the authorities would hear tell of it and he knew this. He was careful not to let anyone know his thoughts or he could have been jailed. He played the political cards well and got junkets to conferences abroad. He wouldn't defect without me so he constantly plotted to have the two of us leave at the same time, it wasn't going to be easy but we planned. He was okay for papers but I needed a passport, as I'd have to go on a civilian airliner possibly to The Cayman Islands."

Cormack asked could he have a glass of water.

"Just tell me to stop now if I'm boring you." She handed him the water and he took a gulp.

"It's a fascinating story please go on."

"Well where was I?"

He eagerly reminded her "you were plotting to get away from Cuba."

"Yes I needed a passport and that wasn't going to be easy as I would have to get a forged one, which is possible here but very risky and expensive. My father's contact had one stolen from a tourist staying at a hotel in Varadero, similar in age and looks except hair colour to me. Now all I had to do was dye my hair dark brown and put on plenty of makeup and I'd get through, her return flight was to Madrid. We had it arranged and the day before the flights my father got a stroke, it was devastating for him and it left him without speech, and he was partially paralysed, he died two days later. Then with the funeral and all the upset I forgot to destroy the stolen passport. The girl who stole it and passed it on to me was caught stealing again and when she was interrogated she confessed to all and to selling one to me."

Cormack leaned his two elbows on the table and spoke in a low tone. "My goodness Kathie I never realised such restrictions were still in place here."

She smiled a sad expression, "I'm afraid it gets worse. Amadeo a notorious secret service detective raided our house in Miramar and found the stolen passport so I was arrested. To make a long story short I was given six months in a correctional institution and lost my job. When I came out after serving four months I got this small apartment and I'm doing now what I'm doing." She stood up and excused herself, "I must go to the toilet."

She came back and Cormack asked "do you mind if I use your loo?"

She pointed "it's through there."

Cormack noticed as he dropped back to earth from the suspense that there were no bottles of scented spray and fancy pink toilet roll or blue flush. The long chain to the tank for flushing reminded him of his grandmother's toilet in the country when he was little, and how he had to stand on the seat to swing out of the chain to perform the noisy flush.

She was tidying away some photographs from the sideboard when he came into the room. She put a large photo behind her back turned, and put it into the drawer.

"Old family photos make me sad at times," she sat opposite him and throwing back her extravagant blonde hair from her face she said. "Now where was I?"

He sat back and rubbed his chin, "you were doing what you are doing."

"Yes." She laughed. "Now the next big episode came when my grandfather's sister left Germany with her son David to escape the round up of Jews. They sailed on the cruise ship S.S. St Louis, to a new life here in Cuba. They left Hamburg May thirteenth nineteen thirty nine and fourteen days later arrived in Havana on May twenty seventh. The ship was anchored in the harbour and all passengers were refused to land. The diplomatic wrangling went on with C. Hyman the executive director of the Joint Distribution Committee in New York, and Milton Goldsmith in Havana but they were unsuccessful in getting all passengers to land, a few were let ashore. On the second of June the St Louis departed Havana and eventually arrived back in Antwerp on June seventeenth. The day before the ship sailed, and my grandfather's sister knew what she and David's fate would be, she passed a security box over the side to my father. I knew about this famous box but never knew what it contained or where it was hidden, until a letter left to me as a type of will by my father told me where it was. I was instructed to burn this letter immediately after reading it, which I did."

She paused and a strained look on her face told Cormack that the reliving of the events was taking a toll.

"When my grandfather's sister and son David arrived in Antwerp they were sent to a work camp 'Westerbork' and then on to Belsen, we never heard about them again."

He took the liberty to put his hand over hers, "I'm sorry I shouldn't have asked you to relive all that it must be traumatic for you still, how long ago is it since it all happened?"

"Believe it or not it seems like ages but its only six months since my father passed away."

"My goodness that short time, no wonder you're still nervous." Cormack exclaimed. "Jesus Kathie their serious about people trying to leave this country. We were shown on television a lot of the people trying to get to Key West Florida on make shift rafts and anything that would float, it was a harrowing sight to see people so desperate. The lads with the old car made into a boat was a sight for sore eyes, I can't remember if they made it or not."

"What you saw was only the tip of the ice as you say, there were hundreds drown that were never reported anywhere." She walked over to a window and opened it, she stood looking out onto the street a watchfulness she'd adopted of late, and just automatically looked for any stranger standing around. She came and stood behind Cormack and ran her fingers across his brow "are you feeling hot" she pulled at his damp shirt. "You're perspiring and I have nothing cool for you to drink."

He felt a shiver run along his neck and shoulders "I'm okay I'll have to get used to this heat, come on and finish your story or is that all?"

She took her place opposite him and leaning across the table her green hazel eyes staring purposefully into his as if she could see right through him. "Do you want to hear more of my disjointed life?" She sat back licked her lips sucking some moisture from her mouth making a smacking sound. "We now have computers but not for private use, we can only get an e-mail address through a security department, and when they receive your mail they telephone you, then you can ask them to reply for you, fair censorship don't you think?"

"Now that you've mentioned it I was going to e-mail home to let them know I arrived safely, but what the hell there's no hurry." Cormack felt like she needed a friend so badly, in a country where she was born and raised yet now all alone without kin or friend. He sat back and folded his arms pursing his lips in disbelief, "how do you live and pay your rent is everything state subsidised?"

"Yes your right my rent is free and I get a small state allowance plus food tickets where I can get the basics at the state run shops. The small amount I had saved I spent for some repairs to the apartment when I moved in."

"It's a shame with such qualifications you are not allowed to work what a waste of such talent.

"There are thousands like me all over Cuba highly qualified and no work, but at least there is some work I can do to earn some money."

He looked at her relieved to hear she had some small job even if it was in the black economy, "and would the authorities object if they knew you were working?"

"They probably know but turn a blind eye, because they're so many of us there's not much they can do, anyway we're an addition to the tourist industry that they're so dependent on. It's an age old profession this prostitution and I suppose I'm lucky I'm not fat or ugly or I'd get very few clients."

Cormack was waiting for her to start laughing and tell him she was joking, but he saw she was deadly serious.

She stood up and picked up the coffee cups, she said with her back turned. "You're shocked."

He didn't answer.

"Well you needn't be, there is an English saying I think it goes something like this, '*needs must when the devil drives*' and in times of despair I think maybe I'm luckier than some, I can pick my clients and charge top rate."

Cormack stood up and caught her by the shoulders he put his face close to hers, "whatever you have to work at you're still a beautiful and wonderful girl."

She turned her face down, "thank you for that" she paused then looked up and in a whispering lisp "Cormack."

He kissed her on the forehead and brushed the strands of hair from her face. "Do you want me to go?"

She looked at her watch, it was three pm, "It's still too hot to walk the streets, I generally go for a siesta in the afternoons so you can stay and do the same or whatever."

He looked at her undecided.

She turned and walked into the bedroom if you want to stay there's a bed in that room you can use, pointing to a closed door. She shut the door behind her and he stood alone in the big room.

CHAPTER 5

The last few days seemed like a dream coming from a well organised life, and beautiful girlfriend. Now here I am standing in a strange girl's apartment in Havana. He realised it was the first time he thought about Monica since he left. He pushed open the door to the small bedroom, the single bed had spotless white linen, and a large open window let in a diffused light and some warm air. He closed the door, stripped to his shorts and lay down on the cool soft bed.

Maybe it was jetlag or contentment but he slept soundly, a soft gushing of water woke him and he looked at his watch, nearly six o clock. He pulled on his trouser and shirt, slipped into his shoes and went into the living room. Kathie wasn't there but he heard the shower stop and out she came wrapped in a blue fluffy towel, she smiled a great warm friendly smile.

"Did you sleep well?" She asked.

"Yes I never slept so soundly in a strange place, I felt so relaxed."

"Good now put on the kettle and I will make some coffee and something to eat or would you prefer to go to your hotel?"

"No I will go to the hotel later, I would like to stay for coffee, but I'm afraid I'm drinking all your coffee and it's so scarce."

She disappeared into the bedroom and Cormack pottered around getting cups and the coffee pot. When she came back out she was dressed in an above the knee tangerine cotton skirt, and cream blouse with soft orange beading around the cuffs and collar. Her drying hair hung in gold strands as she brushed it gently.

"The coffee is in that tin, put in four heaped spoons and half fill the pot with water just on the boil." She observed him as he did exactly as she said. He put two cups on the table and looked in the fridge for milk, there was no milk and nothing much else.

"I'm afraid I'm out of milk, I usually drink it black."

"Fine; black is better," he said, "It doesn't compromise the flavour."

She stood in the glow of an orange sunshine coming through the large dusty glass panes, and Cormack believed he never observed anything so beautiful before in his life. She poured the coffee and from a battered old biscuit tin she took out a packet of biscuits, shook some onto a plate and placed them on the table. "Now that's all the niceties I have on offer."

He ate a biscuit and sipped the hot coffee savouring every drop; the silence was palpable as they avoided one another's eyes. The sharp click of the coffee cups resonated as they laid them on the saucers. They reached for a biscuit together and their hands accidently touched, he caught her finger and held it. "Will I see you again after tonight?"

"That's up to you now that you know where I live you're welcome to call."

"Thanks Kathie I enjoyed today and especially your company, but I must find someplace else to stay other than the hotel. You see I have very little freedom there to do what I want, like painting, that's what I came here to do to try and get my mind off other things. You understand?"

"You can find some room to rent there are plenty of them around the city, you will see the sign on the door if they are approved for tourists. Tomorrow I will go with you and try to find someplace suitable, with good light to do your painting."

"That's very kind of you what time will I come to meet you?"

"If you are here at ten in the morning you can accompany me shopping and I'll show you the rooms to rent."

He stood up, ten o clock it is then, he glanced back as he opened the door, she was sitting at the table with her head in her hands and her eyes closed. The evening air was warm and languorous as he strolled the Malecon, he now realised what Kathie meant about the young Cuban girls offering company to tourists.

"Where are you from" the opening question, and after some broken and Pidgin English an offer to go your place. He was tempted by some of these very young and beautiful coffee coloured girls. He sat on the sea wall and watched the young men swimming and further out the lads sitting in big black tractor tubes fishing. Realisation of how poor the people were that he'd seen, but also how happy and seemingly resigned to their way of life was astonishing. A dark young girl appeared out of nowhere and smiled showing a set of pearly teeth and full ruby lips. "Hello what country do you come from?"

"Ireland, you know where Ireland is?"

"Yes I know Ireland small country, Dublin you city."

"Yes that's it I come from Dublin."

"You stay long Cuba?"

"Maybe I'll stay three weeks."

"Three weeks but not Habana you go Varadero nice hotel and swim on beach."

"No I'll stay in Havana for a week and then move somewhere else maybe Matanzas for a week."

"I been Matanzas very nice city near beach you like very much. You like come home my place, 'amour' no problem."

He saw the ring on her marriage finger and picked up her hand. "You married you have a ring?"

She smiled and squeezed his hand.

"No married my grandmother ring, I live my mother and one four year old son no husband or boy friend so no problem."

He stood down from the wall and was surprised to see how tall this young girl was. "What's your name?"

"My name is Isabelle, and your name?"

"I'm Cormack." He shook her soft gentle hand, and she smiled an inviting and welcoming twinkle in her eyes.

She held his hand and gently tugged, "you come with me."

"No Isabelle I'll not come home with you tonight, I have too much girl problems at the moment."

Her face downcast and a little curl to her lip, she gave a futile soft tug on his reluctant hand. "No money just cigarettes."

He felt a note in his pocket and crumpled it up small, opening her palm he placed the twenty peso note in her hand and closed her fist over it. "You buy cigarettes Isabelle and I hope I meet you again some evening, you are a very pretty girl," he kissed her cheek and they turned and went in different directions.

His thoughts were on Kathie as he looked at the beautiful buildings that had been renovated along the sea front, while others were literally falling down with their balconies being held in place by old rusted scaffolding poles. He hoped he might get a room in one of those with a balcony and big windows, and a view across the sea wall out over the Caribbean to the west. Where the sky was still pinkish holding the few last rays of this day's sun.

He decided not to go to a pub and went back to his hotel for a night cap. The bar of the hotel was lively as another coach load of tourists had arrived. He tried to decipher the different accents of these mixed people and came to believe they were mostly Italian. He sat alone outside and watched the night strollers pass by, young girls peering in at the men drinking on the hotel veranda and trying to attract an attention. Seemingly they were not allowed past the porter standing at the entrance.

He went to the computer to check his e-mails, and was so surprised to see such old computers; they reminded him of the old American cars he'd seen on the streets. He took a bit of time to get on line and at one stage thought he'd have to crank it up like an old car. He had a missive from his partner Derek telling him all was well and to enjoy himself. He had nothing from Monica but he really didn't expect to hear from her. He replied to Derek and told him how he was finding his way slowly and enjoying his mini adventure so far. He retired to his room feeling relaxed and looking forward to the next day, and surprisingly Kathie was foremost in his thoughts. The cool air conditioned room was welcome after the heat outside and he slept a dreamless fitful sleep.

He was early into the dining room and with only four other guests he ate a delicious breakfast. It was still only eight thirty when he passed through the foyer, and to his surprise the young artist Miguel was inquiring at the reception for him, the canvas rolled up in a tube.

"Morning Miguel I see you have my painting."

He turned, and with a beaming smile he greeted Cormack. "Yes I have your permit here it is." He handed him an envelope and the tube with his canvas.

"Thank you Miguel and I hope to see you again before I leave you may have some paintings I could be interested in".

"Yes Cormack I will take you to my house where I do my painting, I have lots of work anything you would like I will give you at a cheap price."

"Right Miguel I will see you at the art exhibition on Saturday before I leave for Ireland."

He turned to leave his eyes bright with simple happiness and a white smile of joy. "I will see you then and enjoy your holiday."

Cormack was careful to apply a sun lotion as his face and arms were sore and red after his brief time in the sun. He looked at his watch and it was past nine o clock and he decided to ramble on to Kathie's apartment. It was a beautiful hot sunny morning and he strolled under the shade of the trees down the Prada. He took a minute to find the right turn off up to O'Reilly Street, and once there he recognised buildings and familiar shops. He stood to look at the beautiful Bacardi building with its green fronted marble façade, further on was the old Woolworths store, now a multiple of state shops. He stopped at the market and purchased some fruit, he wanted to buy flowers for Kathie but could see none for sale, maybe Cubans didn't go in for that trivial extravagance.

CHAPTER 6

It was just past nine thirty when he arrived at her apartment he pushed the door open and walked up the concrete stairs. He noticed in the dim light the peeling powdery blue paint on the walls and the bare worn steps. As he moved on the short corridor the door to her apartment opened and to his surprise a middle aged man came out. He saw Cormack and held the door open to him, then without a word walked on. Cormack stood inside the large room and there was no sign of Kathie, and as he was about to make his presence known by calling out her name she came out of the bathroom naked, with her two hands above her head drying her hair with a small towel.

"Oh my God" she exclaimed and tried to cover her nakedness with the little pink towel.

Cormack turned away with embarrassment, when he looked around again she was gone.

She shouted to him from her bedroom. "There's fresh coffee in the pot help yourself."

"Thank you I will." He sat down and sipped the hot brew and looked around for a bowl to put the fruit into. He took a basket from a shelf and arranged the fruit laying it on the sideboard.

"You found the coffee?" She was standing dressed in pink blouse and rust coloured skirt, she was brushing her hair.

"Yes thank you and I'm sorry about walking in on you unannounced, but the man leaving left the door open and ushered me in."

"Oh! You met my overnight customer, that's why I said ten a.m. you see they like to stay a bit late, and usually want to get full value for their money."

He stood up and bade her sit down, "let me brush your hair it fascinates me. I think sometimes I should have been a hairdresser." He slowly ran the brush down her wet hair and watched as the dark blonde revealed the platinum highlights. He stroked the soft silky tresses gently putting his hand under it to get a brush full. She sat still not speaking holding her head straight like an obedient child. "You have beautiful hair it's so soft and silky like down."

"What's down, I never heard that word?"

"It's the soft feathers on a bird or the new hairs on a young body."

"You have a special way with words you know, you are the first Irish person I've met. Do you all speak like that?"

"I suppose it is an Irish thing they like to play with words and express themselves indirectly with metaphors."

"Now you have me again what is a metaphor? I'm beginning to realise how inadequate my English is."

"You could not be expected to know all that stuff with English being a second or third language, a metaphor is using one thing or phrase to describe something different, like a brazen sky."

"Yes I remember learning about that now, my school lessons are coming back to me."

He moved around and lifted her chin brushing back the hair from her face.

She looked at him with bright emerald eyes and her lip trembled as she spoke. "You know this is the first time anyone has brushed my hair since my grandmother, when I was a young child. She was so gentle and would tell me stories as she moved around me, her loose clothing brushing my arms and face. I can still smell her perfume it was like wild roses wafting around her like a gentle breeze from a garden."

Cormack stood back as if to admire his work. "You know you are the most beautiful of all the roses in the garden."

She blushed and closed her eyes "you say that to all your girl friends, a perfect charmer."

"I never said that to a girl before because I only thought of it now looking at you. What way are you going to style your hair? I like it hanging loose around your shoulders."

"Well today as you are my hairdresser it will be your choice."
He ran his fingers through the silky tresses and let them fall loose over her smooth shoulders. "God was in a very good mood the day he made you," he stood back a step to admire her beauty, "a master piece."

"If you flatter me anymore I may just drag you into that bedroom and we won't get to see any apartments for you, so come on before the day gets too hot for walking the streets."

They were a happy couple walking and stepping over the broken pavements, as the heat of the day began to fill the spaces between the high colonial houses, and the sun climbed higher to dispel the shadows. These back streets were quiet with very few people coming and going from houses. Only the blaring of some salsa music from a radio somewhere high up on a balcony broke the silence.

The first place she brought him to had a lovely room, but you would have to go through the living quarters of the house to get to it. He felt this would be intrusive whenever he came or went.

The next was nice but had no window only a door to a balcony and the balcony was divided by strong mesh wire about ten feet high, and you had to open a locked door to exit onto the balcony proper. It reminded him of a prison, but Kathie reminded him the people could not get a licence to let the room without meeting the security regulations.

The next room had a shared bathroom and shower and was fine and airy, but had no view through the big dusty window and no balcony.

They tried several more and he couldn't find what he wanted, he had in mind a balcony to sit and paint during the warm part of the day. After a lunch they went back to Kathie's apartment and she told him to relax and they would try again later. He went to lie on his auld bed and fell asleep.

She woke him at five p.m. and told him he snored.

"You're not the first one to tell me that, but did I keep you awake?"

"No I wasn't asleep anyway, I was just dozing and making plans and dreaming dreams."

"I hope your plans and dreams come true, and if there is anything I can do to help just ask."

"You might be sorry you made such a generous offer, I feel so frustrated sometimes I would engage the devil himself to help me."

"I may not be as prolific in the ways of the devil but I'd do my best to get you what you want."

"What I want would be just a simple holiday for you. But for me here in Cuba, it is complicated dangerous and very expensive. Never mind come and have a cool beer." She opened the windows onto the balcony and they sat out and drank from the bottles, he was seated under a small cloths line with some of her negligee drying.

"Excuse me" she said as she un-pegged them and put them into a small basket, "the only place I have for drying clothes."

"You know I sleep so soundly in that bed here, as soon as I lay on it I fall off to sleep. I feel so comfortable and homely in that room."

"Yes it is very quiet you hear no noise, like the loud radios that you can hear now coming from across the street, and the dogs barking late at night often wake me."

"The one thing you don't have to contend with is heavy traffic, there are virtually no cars away from the main roads, you only see the odd bicycle or small horse drawn cart. In Ireland the traffic on our main roads in the capital city is chaotic it could take me two hours to drive to work a distance of five miles."

She crossed her legs and threw her head back to empty the last of her bottle, her figure shaped against her flimsy clothing and the skirt rode up her smooth thighs. Cormack felt his heart miss a beat watching the grace and beauty of this lithesome girl. She stood up smoothing her skirt and noticed his look of admiration and desire. "We'll go and see if we can find you a suitable."

He cut her short, "auld bed."

"Right auld bed."

They walked the Malecon and she pointed out the high rise hotels which belonged to the wealthy Americans, "this one" she showed him 'The Hotel Capri' belonged to Meyer Lansky the Mafia boss. Now! " She laughed, "the American Government want them all back again and the land that was confiscated from them. It could happen someday. I should not talk like that if the wrong person heard me I could be arrested for counter revolutionary idealism."

They passed two policemen walking the beat casually looking at the young girls touting for tourists.

They stopped and Cormack lifted her up onto the sea wall, and sat up beside her. The smooth stone was still warm to touch even as the sun was low over the western sea.

"You see all the beautiful young girls now you realise how much competition there is to get business. The German and Nordic people prefer the dark coloured girls; they have plenty fair people like me in their own homes, so you see I have to work hard to get my clients."

"Do you bring all the clients back to your apartment?"

"No you see that building over there, come and I'll show you." She jumped down and caught his hand and they crossed the road. "You see that building there?"

"Yes the one where the girls are bringing men into." He could see the young girls some as young as sixteen pulling their clients by the hand through the entrance into the courtyard area, and as they moved closer he could see they were coming and going through the front door.

She held his hand and squeezed it in a motion to stop at the entrance. "This place is called 'The Casa Amour'; it was originally a motel of ten units with patios and sliding aluminium doors built around a swimming pool."

He could see a heavy dark woman in a loose brightly coloured dress sitting on a metal chair in a paved courtyard.

They stepped aside to let a young girl with her middle aged client pass.

Kathie smiled "business is brisk today. It was originally set up for conjugal activities between Cuban couples who couldn't find sufficient privacy at home. Now it is mostly used by tourists, inside there's an office and a register, also a selection of condoms, beer and rum tropicola. You see the Jineteras? That is what the young girl prostitutes are known as."

"Do they not go to the hotels where the men are staying wouldn't that be easier?"

She turned him away and they walked on.

He saw there were a lot of tourists in this area and the young girls absolutely stunning. Some of them walking with men in tow towards the hotels, and others chatting and coaxing middle aged men with panama hats and pink sun splotched faces.

"You see the hotels," she said looking askance at a beautiful coffee coloured girl who almost brushed off Cormack, "are well policed so most times you have to give them a few pesos to let you go in, also the porters in the hotels have to be bribed too, but the man usually pays them."

"Is it legal for the girls to work at this ancient profession?" He subtly enquired of her.

She turned him towards herself as if to show the girls she had a fine young man, not a pudgy pink faced retiring fellow with a nondescript figure. "It is illegal for girls to proposition men for sex, but not illegal for men to proposition girls for sex. So if a fellow asks a girl she is quite entitled to go with him where they like. The authorities actually encourage prostitution as it helps the tourist trade which is Cuba's biggest earner." She kissed him on the cheek. "I must leave you now will you find your own way back. I have to earn some money; if you like you can call tomorrow morning if you haven't found a place yourself."

"Thanks for coming with me I will call to you in the morning." He smiled, "it'll be after ten."

He walked the Prada and met a young girl who coaxed him to go for a drink, which he did. She took him along a dimly lighted street holding his hand as though he might escape. The bar she took him to, though scarce on lighting, he could see was patronised by Cubans, he couldn't see any tourists. Her company was refreshing and she seemed somewhat coy compared to any of the girls he'd met even Kathie. She was in her late teens, with such beautiful coffee coloured smooth skin. Her black hair like a raven's wing shimmered under the little light borrowed from dusty lanterns stained with a tawny translucence. He enjoyed her broken English and the quite happy resigned attitude to her life, which she described as poor with little prospects of ever working. They drank mojitos and followed with pints of cold beer, then a band struck up and they danced among overheated bodies on the small floor. The atmosphere was carnival, the men and girls movements on the dance floor were lavishly lascivious, and his friend Maritza twisted and wriggled to the loud drum music with wanton abandonment. His shirt was clinging to his wet body as he tried to emulate some of the rhythm with dance. It was total euphoria being carried on a wave of loud salsa music, colours and shapes of moving bodies, mesmeric through thick cigar and tobacco smoke.

It was early morning when they left and Maritza asked him if she'd come to his hotel room, but he thought 'she might not be admitted' so they parted with a passionate kiss. He pressed some pesos into her hand as a present for her delightful company. He found the hotel bar was still doing business when he arrived. He was tempted to join some English speaking group for a conversation, but after his evening of broken Spanish and tattered English sentences from Maritza, and the unadulterated joy of a Cuban experience, he decided no contest, so he declined. Tomorrow is here he thought so he decided not to get involved, I must see Kathie this morning. He climbed the stairs to his room and wondered was he getting too involved with this intriguing girl, with her web of mysteries.

CHAPTER 7

As he walked to Kathie's apartment he threw his mind back to Dublin, it was afternoon there now and probably raining. Monica hadn't sent him an e-mail, but he could visualise her sitting across from him in the office at her desk working away diligently. She sometimes winked at him a slow provocative smile creeping round her lovely face when she caught him looking her way. If she was here now he was sure things would be so different, they'd have time only for one another and he'd give her lots of playful attention, which he knew she'd wallow in like a purring kitten.

He stood before the door into Kathie's and looked at his watch it was nearing eleven, the coast should be all clear and overnight guests gone. He walked with trepidation up the shabby staircase hoping he wouldn't meet a man coming down from her rooms. It was her work, why should it bother him. The door was closed but a note pinned to it read. 'Come in and wait, Kathie.' He pushed the door open and went into the big adorable room, a note on the table read, 'help yourself to some coffee.' He made up a small brew of the delicious freshly ground beans and felt so content sitting there sipping from a china cup she had laid out for him. He saw the special coffee cup which she must only use on special occasions, was made in Japan, and when you held it to the light you could see on its base through the delicate porcelain the imprint of a Japanese girl's profile. He felt curious and wanted to look around especially into her bedroom, some perverse thought flitted across his thoughts that he could get a glimpse into her inner being from seeing her private room. He put the thought quickly away and chastised himself for thinking of such a breach of her thrust and privacy.

She arrived in with bags of shopping and threw them onto the table. "I see you had coffee, are you waiting long?"

"Thank you for letting out coffee for me, and no, I'm only here about ten minutes."

"Today is the day I get my food coupons and I try to do my shopping as all the good things are taken the first day, especially pork and chicken. If I can't get my food from the co-op shop I have to go to the supermarkets that only take International pesos, and I am hording all of them that I earn. If the C.D.R. for my area reported me doing a lot of shopping and spending International pesos, I could be asked to account for how much money I've earned. I would have to hand a large chunk over to the authorities. It's a case of being discreet and keeping a very low profile."

"Who is the C.D.R. for your area?"

"Oh she's an Old Crone who lives across the street and watches everything, I'm sure she sees who comes and goes here in my apartment, I only spoke to her on a few occasions and it was just a polite everyday chat. These older ones were born of the revolution and believe they are the savours of the modern Cuba; they also get special treatment from the higher ups and bribes from the lower downs. That's one thing I'd never do is offer her a bribe as it only confirms you are doing something illegal or on the fringes of illegality. Of course I would come in for special treatment because of my chequered family connections, as I've told you about."

She continued to pack away her shopping and Cormack hoped by coming to see her he wasn't putting her in the way of unwanted attention from the Old One.

He helped with her shopping, "would she report you, for me coming to visit you?"

"No you see I could say you were a boyfriend and not paying me any money. That's why I try to keep my business away from here as much as possible, but it's not always easy to do that. As you've noticed I have to bring some men back, it's generally always late as I pick them up in the bars and nightclubs, but she sees them leave in the morning. Well I have to keep going as best I can for some time yet, and hope my plans come to fruition. It's all about money and lots of it, and of course luck, in abundance."

He winced at the thought of how she had to resort to such a life to make this needed money. "Do you mind me asking, what do you need the money for, is it something to do with getting out of Cuba?"

"It's all to do about getting out of Cuba, you get nothing here without bribing someone in an official position, and you have to be very careful to know the person you are dealing with. There is always a go between so you never get to know the top person, the officialdom here is very corrupt, but Euros or sound foreign currency opens most doors."

He felt sorry for this beautiful girl trapped in such a hostile country and environment and struggling to break free, degrading herself to earn money the only way open to her. He felt so helpless standing over her as she bent down to put her purchases into the fridge, her blonde hair falling over her bare shoulders; she was the perfect young wife.

"Is it very hard to get a passport?"

She paused before answering in an admonishing tone. "Hard to get one?" she looked at him with a satirical smile. "It's almost impossible unless you are on official business or have got one of the special visas to enter the U.S., who take thousands of our best educated young people every year. For me it would be impossible, as my position is very tenuous and I have to be extra careful as you must realise." She stood up and gathered the plastic bags rolling them up and placing them in a holder to use later for her rubbish. She spoke to him as she looked out the big window. "Will we go look at some more places for you to stay?"

He sort of sighed and walked over to join her at the window. "Yeah I suppose so it's hard to find a place I can use to put up my easel, and feel relaxed to do a bit of painting, maybe it would be better if I moved on to Matanzas I could find a better place there."

She looked away from him a little down turn on her lip betraying disappointment. "Yes I suppose everywhere we've seen, none were suitable." She faced him a broad smile on her lips. "Are you an accomplished artist do you have the right to impose yourself on a young defenceless girl in the name of art? I suppose you can have the 'auld bed' if it's what you want."

He swung her round and gave her a peck on the lips. "Great when can I move in?"

She spoke as if it was just a formality, "immediately."

An hour later he whistled as he sorted some of his cloths in the little chest of drawers, he laid out his other few items on top and sat on the comfortable bed. He still had four days in his hotel room, he hadn't checked out. He could still use the facilities there like the computer, and spend some time out of Kathie's way if she had company. He felt so much relaxed as if he was returning to a place in a former life. He felt he had some kind of affinity with this little room and the bed with its beautifully carved headboard which he didn't take too much notice of until now. The hard native timber polished a dark umber depicting a sailing ship with fulsome sails, and handsome rigging with a strong bowsprit. Whales and dolphins adorned the waves beneath her sleek hull. He rubbed his hand over the smooth carving and felt a strange sensation as if he somehow had done this before. He lay back on the bed, he was happy, it was siesta time now.

He was dreaming he sailed on this wonderful ship. Now he was ashore where the sandy beach was sugary white, and the palms rustled. He was lying under the shaded trees and the beautiful girl was caressing his face with sweet scented fingers and soft hands. He reluctantly opened his eyes he didn't want to leave this place, or the girl.

She was kneeling by the bed and she pulled away her hand and stood up. "You are a sound sleeper I had a job to wake you, I have something to eat, come on sleepy get up."

He shook himself to make sure this was real. The meal of grilled chicken and fried pan cakes with savoury rice was delicious and he wondered how he could pay this generous girl without offending her. Well he thought he'd get to that later he had a bit of shopping to do now for some paints and canvases. They ate in a contented silence, an aura of comfortableness as they glanced from food to face with soft eye contact approval. Cormack sipped from a glass of water then spoke in a matter of fact gentle tone. "I want to go to an artist's shop to get some canvases and a few paints."

She picked a grain of rice from her lip, "yes I will take you to a shop where you can get all the art supplies, and we can go now it will be open for another hour."

He helped her put the plates in the sink and tidied off the table.

She looked at him with a smile of approval, "we'll leave the wash up until we come back, oh yes I nearly forgot you will have to change your International pesos into Cuban pesos otherwise they'll charge you too much."

He took out a fist of notes and held them out to her, "how much will I need to change?"

She took a fifty note, "this much should do." She went to her bedroom and returned with the exchange of money and handed it to him, "you seem to have a lot more now but what you want are not too expensive. You can use what's left over to buy in the market, you know you are not supposed to have it, but never mind nobody will refuse to take it."

He separated the two currencies one in each pocket so as not to get it mixed up; it actually looked very similar at a glance.

The little shop had a vast array of artist's paints and canvas frames, he enjoyed choosing the oil colours and all he needed, medium brush cleaner and some new brushes. He worried then if he had enough to pay for it all. Kathie placed all the purchases on the counter and the grey haired man smiled pearly toothed, his dark eyes animated his handsome sienna coloured face.

"This is everything?" As he put the small items into a bag, he calculated and smiled at Kathie speaking in Spanish.

She turned to Cormack, "sixty two pesos please."

He counted out the money and handed it to her. They left the shop he carrying the five canvas frames, and she the bag of paints and brushes. He turned to her and stopped, "Kathie you sure he didn't make a mistake and charged us not enough? Sixty two pesos is only less than three Euros."

"No he charged the right price that type of commodity is very cheap, as all the artists in Cuba are very poor and couldn't afford to pay anymore."

He looked astonished, "is there any other shopping you would like to do?"

"No we'll take this lot home and go out for a good night I'll take you somewhere special."

He side stepped to let a woman with two small children pass who smiled at him and said "gracias" so wonderfully polite and homely.

"But Kathie?" he stopped half afraid to broach the subject of her work.

"Yes" she turned to him, "what are you trying to ask me?"

"When we go out tonight what about your work?"

She walked ahead of him and looking at some youths playing she spoke without turning round. "Mother nature plays a part in women's lives and gives compulsory holidays to girls in my profession."

He felt himself blush, "I'm sorry for being so inquisitive, I never thought."

She walked on and he had to quicken to keep pace with her, "where are you taking me is it somewhere special?"

She turned to face him walking backwards, "I can't say, then it wouldn't be a surprise, and I like surprises don't you?"

He made a little childish smirk to her, "pleasant surprises are little joys never to be forgotten."

"I will remember that, it is also a sweet way of telling someone you like them."

CHAPTER 8

She called into him as he'd finished changing, and was liberally splashing after shave on, "are you ready?"

"Coming now," he stopped short when he saw how stunning she looked, a pale green blouse tied across her midriff, and a short skirt with wavy patterns, he smiled to himself 'forty shades of green.' "Tis you're the real colleen tonight."

She fastened a bright coloured scarf around her palomino mane tied under her ear from which hung a large gold band. "What is a colleen?"

"A colleen is the name given to a true beautiful Irish girl, and they usually wear green with a red shawl, a shawl is a kind of cloak draped over their shoulders."

"I will be your colleen tonight"

The evening was still holding the heat of the day as she led him along the dimly lit streets. They walked for ten minutes before she halted at a narrow alleyway, with only light from windows casting shadowy amber patterns on the worn pathway. She caught his hand, "come on it's just down here."

More people came into the alleyway behind them, and as they moved on he heard the music reverberating all around. It seemed to bounce from the stone buildings and envelope you as a sea mist conceals your earthly existence.

"Kathie" he asked pensively, "where are we going?"

She smiled a mischievous grin, "trust me and stay close, don't engage in conversation with any sex mad girls. You'll see it's just here."

He put his arm around her, "yes Mama."

The Santero's door was open and the interior was flooded by the light of forty or fifty candles, they went through an archway into a type of courtyard. Kathie walked over to the Santero and handed him some pesos, she introduced Cormack and the Santero welcomed him with a double hand shake and an embrace. He was old and wrinkled with a mop of close cropped white hair and adorned in a loose scarlet and blue robe. He had silver and metal chains hanging from around his neck, with medallions pendulum like across his bare frosty chest. Looking around Cormack could reckon there were about forty or fifty people sitting or standing around, like ethereal figures floating in a mantle of shadow from the light of the candles, and a fire in the centre of the yard. There was a large pot hanging over the fire on a black iron tripod, an old crone was bending over stirring the contents. Her wiry frame had bare thin arms and grey hair tied back with coloured ribbons, large dangling disc earrings reflecting the firelight. A scene from Macbeth was conjured up in Cormack's mind. Her sharp animated eyes were scanning the gathering, and Cormack noticed they rested on Kathie for an uncomfortable pause. The drums beat out a rhythm and people danced gyrating in the flickering light, and as more joined in the drummers seated together, increased the tempo. There was one beating narrow drums, and another with a gourd draped in seashells, one shook bells on sticks and had rattles round his ankles. They were dressed in pleated white shirts called a guayabera.

"Come on let's dance." She took his hand and led him in among the moving figures. They were swaying and moving with the dancers to a hypnotic mixture of Spanish Bolero, and French Quadrille, both colliding with the continent of Africa. As he got to the side where the drummers were he saw the frenzied beating of the tall Tumba, the smooth almost invisible massaging of the hour glass Beta and the rapid beating of the twin Congo's. One with staring eyes and shiny skin had a metal blade he struck in unison, with the ringing of the bronze bells. Kathie was attracting the attention of an amber coloured girl dressed in spandex pants, moving in fluid motion with a young handsome fellow.

After the dance he got two drinks, they stood sipping the cool fresh taste of mint and lime mixed into the rum. "This is delicious is it some secret recipe?" He asked Kathie.

She held the glass up to the light of the fire and looked through, "no it is laced with lime and mint, but if you want something strong I'll get you one of the Santero's specials."

He could feel the strong spirit coursing through his body, he felt lively and the music was beginning to invade his brain, he was swaying to the beat. "What are its special ingredients?"

"You see the old crone at the pot?"

He saw her ladling out some soup and meat from the big pot into bowls, he could smell the aroma and it made him hungry. "The soup smells good could we have some?"

"Yes of course will I go and get some bowls?" She finished her drink and turned to face him her eyes smiling as she leaned into his chest. "Boiling in that black pot is a mixture of pig's heads and offal like belly, shin bones and maybe some other special additives only that old crone knows about. She is the local C.D.R. for this block and do you notice how she observes everyone coming and going. She is a dangerous bitch. If you fancy some of her stew I'll get you a bowl?"

He finished his drink and took her glass, "thank you my dear" he put his face close to hers, "I'll pass on this one."

"I thought so but the drink you asked about the Santero's special that's made up of rum generally, home distilled, chillies, garlic, and turtle testicles, I've never ventured to taste it but now is the time if you feel like being adventurous?"

He almost gagged at the thought, "Jesus no thanks it sounds disgusting."

The girl with the white spandex pants passed close and looked at Kathie.

"It also makes you aggressive and causes people to fight, excuse me I must go to the ladies. You can refill our drinks while I'm gone, if you want to go I think the gents place is inside that door," looking to a door behind them leading into a house.

She left and he went to get their drinks, and as he turned from the make shift bar he saw a man standing in the shadow, and thought he recognised the face. He took a swift sharp look of his eyes as he turned his head away, as though he didn't want to be recognised. The disfigurement of his left eye was something he couldn't hide. Cormack felt a little uncomfortable why he was not sure, and then he knew it was the detective he'd seen at the airport. When he looked again he was gone. He stood back into the shade to wait for Kathie and smiled to himself at the thoughts of dining on the stew. Curiosity got the better of him and he went over to the old crone and she smiled a toothless grin.

"Would you like some delicious food?" Spittle flew like tiny flies from a toothless mouth. She picked up a bowl and poured a ladle of stew into it.

"What's in it?" he inquired of her.

She laughed an echoey cackle. "It's very good for you, and it'll make you very good tonight in bed with your pretty blonde girl, she likes very strong man between her legs."

He handed her some pesos and took the bowl. She picked up a pigs ear and put it into her mouth slobbering it between her gums with saliva dribbling down her chin. "You see good meat make strong man."

"Thank you." He turned and went back and stood in the shadows to wait for Kathie. Looking around he couldn't see her, she hadn't come out of the loo yet, he laid the bowl on a table maybe someone might eat it.

He sipped the cool drink and admired the young women twirling and dancing like swirling Dervish.

"Are you enjoying the splendour of sexual carousel?" She rubbed against him her warm breath on his face was luxuriously sweetly flavoured with rum.

Her rueful smile showed him this was only half meant, foolish though it was every time he looked at her like this he couldn't stop admiring afresh. The beautiful fair sensitive face that would defy time, the long pale neck against the silk blonde hair, the emerald eyes as clear as a child's but not as innocent.

"It's a truly amazing spectacle will we grace the dance area again?" he invited.

"Yes" she chortled as she caught his hand and led him to the fringe of the swaying couples. Dancing close she moved her body against his in her effervescent teasing. Feeling his arousal she moved away a space, a knowing smile mocking and teasing. Cormack felt like a teenager dancing close and embarrassingly shy. When the music stopped, he caught her and held her to him whispering in her ear. "You're a tease."

She boldly retorted. "You enjoy being teased and you savour the chase, until your cunning quarry allows to be caught."

"Yes you little vixen you are a special prize."

The music stopped and as they left the dance area he noticed Kathie looking at the girl with the white spandex pants. She was standing as if being confronted by the detective, who seemed to be blocking her way out through the archway.

"That man you're looking at who's talking to the young girl, he's a detective, special branch."

She turned alarmed, "how do you know him?"

"He stopped me coming out of the airport and questioned me as to where I was staying. I wasn't too pleasant as I didn't realise who he was until the taxi driver told me. The last person I was expecting to meet when I arrived here was a special branch detective questioning me."

"He is one to steer clear of, his name is Amadeo Montes and he was in charge of the search party who came to my house after my father died, and they found the stolen passport, I told you."

"Yes I know what happened, and does he ever bother you now?"

"No he never actually confronts me but he lets me know by his unseemly presence from time to time that he still watches me. Don't let him see us looking his way." She stood in close to Cormack and sipped her drink with her back to Amadeo who was now questioning the young girl.

Cormack observed over the head of Kathie as the young girl's boyfriend possessively put his arm around her, and then cheekily walked her out through the archway.

Amadeo went to the Santero, they shook hands. The Santero then turned to his drinks table and poured a small glass for his guest. Amadeo eyed the drink through the candlelight but could not offend his host; he threw his head back and swallowed in one gulp. He coughed and handed the glass to his host graciously refusing another. Cormack thought; 'that must be the dreadful Santero's special concoction that Kathie told him about.'

He whispered in her ear, "your girl friend is gone rescued by her boyfriend, and Amadeo is now talking to the old C.D.R. crone, she's giving him a bowl of her delicious soup."

She put down her glass and turning around she could see Amadeo's eyes glinting in the firelight gazing at her. She squeezed Cormack's hand. "You see when he looks at you with his staring good eye; the other one with its half closed lid is hideous. He had an accident when he was a child he was hit by a car when out playing on the street, the car never stopped. It was later found out that the car belonged to a wealthy American businessman's son, who was drunk at the wheel. There were never any charges brought as Bastista was in these people's pockets. He got as good treatment as possible in hospital but the scar will always be there and his vision is only fifty percent. He has no movement in that eye it just stares out of the socket. He was one of three children living with his father and mother in a two room apartment. His mother worked as a housemaid in some wealthy American household, and his father was a chauffeur for some German industrialist. They lived in relative comfort but could not afford the expense of an operation to correct his eye. I suppose at that time a poor Cuban kid was of little importance and dispensable. Growing up he was teased as the kids called a black eye 'An Amadeo', or would say if they were going to beat one another I'll give you 'An Amadeo'. He joined the police after the revolution and rose in the ranks to one of their top secret police detectives. Can you believe he hates all Westerners especially Americans, I'm not sure about Irish." She laughed. "You could be lucky." She caught Cormack and throwing her arms around his neck she kissed him full on the lips. Her tongue probed and wallowed sucking his mouth in an urgency of lust.

'This is not for real' he thought as he responded shamelessly.

Then she moved her lips back and murmured. "When I stop seducing you we're leaving." As quickly as she kissed him she stopped, and they both turned and walked slowly out through the archway along the dark narrow alleyway and onto the street.

They walked in silence listening to the loud salsa music coming from radios in the high rooms and open balconies all along the street. This blaring music fascinated Cormack and it created an atmosphere so unique lending these carefree people a sense of joyful release from lives where the basic necessities were often luxuries.

When they reached the Malecon Kathie jumped up and sat on the wall looking out over the sea. A three quarter moon hung suspended in the tropical sky, it cast a rippling path of orange and silver over the calm water. Cormack leaned his elbows on the wall gazing out towards the west pondering the celestial splendour. She sat in silence the soft moon beams reflecting on the gold banded earring, and throwing highlights through her ripe wheaten hair.

When she spoke there was a silvery ghost of lisping in her voice. "If I could walk on that moonlight path I'd go now, and not stop until I'd reached the shores of the U.S. where I'd be a free woman to mould my destiny in this world."

He reached out and held her hand. "It's a wonderful dream but like all fairytales there is an evil twist. Before you'd reach the shore the moon would sink below the horizon, and the pathway would disappear, and you'd sink in the deep ocean."

"Yes she whispered you're right all my dreams fade away with the coming of dawn, and another cruel bright day coaxes me into her bosom only to disappoint my hopes." She leaned over and put her arms around him, kissing his lips sweet and soft like her first nervous and gentle encounter with a boy. A languorously warm fragrant taste from her mouth permeated his being like an opiate. A little breathless they stared into one another's eyes; he saw the hopelessness concealed behind the beauty, like peering into a deep green tropical pool where danger swims deep.

"Do you think Amadeo will bother you again if he knows I'm staying at your apartment?"

She looked a little pensive. "He may use it as an excuse but he's not interested in that, you remember the girl I met tonight well he might bother her."

"Did you go especially to see her?"

"Cormack I shouldn't be implicating you in any of this but I thrust you, she, Maria, is my contact to get a passport, she knows a person in the passport office and she is the courier."

He was a little shocked being introduced into this intrigue. "How much does it cost to get a passport?"

She looked around and waited until a couple who were strolling past were out of earshot. "Fifteen hundred of your Euros or seventeen hundred and fifty Cuban International Pesos pay half now and the rest when the passport is handed over."

"How much did you give your friend tonight?"

"I gave her seven hundred and fifty Euros."

"If Amadeo had searched her, especially if he was suspicious you would have a serious loss."

"Not only a serious loss but she would have been arrested and interrogated, but there was no chance he'd find the money if he did search her, she had it well hidden."

"With her tight clothing she couldn't have had it in her pocket, and her bag was a dead giveaway."

"Yes you're so right but where she had it he couldn't look, you see I rolled it up tight and put it into a condom, and she deposited it in the only place it's supposed to go." She laughed. "I hope it made her evening that little bit more enjoyable."

They both laughed then he kissed her on the lips.

"You know you're a serious young lady."

"Come on" she said as they jumped down off the wall and walked hand in hand home.

CHAPTER 9

His resting naked body luxuriated on the comfortable bed, under a single sheet the warm air was like a balm. He listened to music coming from different houses echoing and vibrating through deserted streets, being mixed and blended into a paean of this Cuban life. A dog barked and was answered by another's howl, he felt at peace and secure as he slipped into the world of Morpheus, he slept a dreamless sleep.

He opened his eyes and thought where am I, a bright sunbeam like a golden rod came through a slit in the curtains and lit the room in a pale amber glow. He heard Kathie out in the kitchen, her firm steps and the clink of delft. He stood out and pulled back the curtains looking out through the generous window, it was a glorious day. He realised he was naked but thought who could see over the overgrown gardens and through the dusty glass. It wasn't like being in his Dublin apartment with windows looking into one another.

The knock on the door was slight, and when he turned she was standing an amused look on her face. "Oh didn't expect to find you up," she giggled looking at his flaccid manhood, "and ready for the day, breakfast is being served and the shower is vacant."

He looked down at the nub of her mirth and shaking the limp fellow spoke to him in an admonishing tone. "At least you could have enough pride to stand up for yourself." He was still enjoying his own joke when he sat down to breakfast.

"I'll take you to the beach today and you can take some photographs, there'll be plenty of nice scenery especially the young female type, good material for painting."

"Great, and do you think we should hire a car?"

She made pretence of cutting her fried eggs and without looking at him she said. "Not unless you expect to do a bit of travelling around, and a hire car can be expensive."

"Well maybe we'll just get a taxi, how far is it to the beach?"

She spread a liberal portion of homemade marmalade on her toast, biting off a large mouthful she looked at him and made a grimace. "Excuse me but I just adore this tangy spread and home baked bread it's the perfect start to the day, it's a recipe handed down from my grandmother who was a superb cook."

Cormack sampled the orangey green preserve and smacked his lips. "It's absolutely delicious, such a unique flavour of oranges and I'd venture a guess, a twist of limes."

"You're so correct but it's getting the mix right is the secret, now; the nearest beach is about five kilometres, so a taxi will be the best way." She stood up and took the dishes to the sink. "Have you a large towel?"

"Actually I never brought a towel I'll have to let the sun dry me."

"Yes but how will you cover yourself when you're getting dressed? You don't want to show off your more than adequate masculinity to the young girls, who no doubt will be watching you closely."

"I'll take a loan of your towel and not embarrass you, so I can maintain my dignity and decency among your fellow bathers."

She took a large white fluffy towel out of a drawer and threw it to him. "There'll be families more likely where we're going so a lily white bum might cause more curiosity than embarrassment, and don't forget your sun lotion, I don't want to be nursing a lobster like creature later tonight".

He caught the towel and went to his room gathering up what he needed for the day.

She hailed a taxi, and seating themselves on the leather back seat the big old red Buick reminiscent of the days of grandeur and Mafia gangsters, drove off the Malecon and into the tunnel under the harbour. Emerging out of the tunnel into bright sunlight they left Casablanca behind as they sedately drove the dual carriageway. The driver was nursing his sturdy comfortable but mechanically tenuous old girl at twenty miles an hour. Kathie pointed out places of interest along the highway until they turned off onto a slip road. The Cuban verdure of cultivated fields glistened in wonderful shades of green that dazzled and held your eyes in wonderment. The small amount of traffic they met on their journey consisted of old lorries with people crowded onto them, also numerous horse drawn carts, taxies, and buses, the amount of people hitching lifts was more than reminiscent of Ireland in the fifties.

The beach was stunningly beautiful, a walk through a palm grove onto white sugary sand blending into a sparkling sea that was streaked with amethyst to viridian, and milky jade where the sandy bottom neared the surface. Surprisingly there were very few people on this stretch of beach. Kathie selected a nice shady spot under some palms. She threw her bag down and sat cross legged looking out at the frail little waves lapping the white sand.

Cormack undressed and stood in his bathing suit ready to broach the inviting sea. His muscular six foot one torso was hard and fit and he sported a shock of salt and pepper hair that was beginning to lighten from the Caribbean sun.

Kathie stripped and stood in her bikini looking into his honest blue eyes, and with an admonishing tone she asked him. "Where do you think you're going just yet?"

"Out for a swim are you coming?"

She spread a large towel on the sand. "Just lie down there on your tummy and I'll put some cream on your lily white skin, you'd roast in half an hour in that sun." Her soft hands were firm and gentle as she spread the lotion across his back and down to the top of his swim trunks playfully she put her hand inside and rubbed his bottom.

"That's lovely but I'll hardly get burned there."

"Just being extra careful, now turn over and close your eyes."

He lay on his back with his eyes closed and felt her spreading the cool cream on his face, this he thought is what heaven should be like. She moved down his chest and he looked to see her smiling face just above him with her hair hanging down touching his neck. "You're so beautiful." He whispered.

"Close your eyes." She retorted laughingly. "Nearly finished now" as her hands moved down close to his waist line.

He felt a thigh on his either side as she straddled him and then the gentle weight of her as she sat on his lower body continuing to massage his upper torso, moving herself slowly down until she sat on his now aroused manhood.

"You're a naughty young man behaving so at this time of day."

"You're a temptress any time of day." He reached up to her shoulders pulling her down, but she resisted and kissing him on the lips she jumped up.

"You have to behave in public, now wait until that business goes back to normal" tipping his noticeable erection, "and we'll go swimming". She picked up her basket and putting her sandy foot on his chest as he lay looking up at her she left a slight imprint of silver on his sun lotion. "I must take this food to the shop we passed back near the road and ask if they'll put it in their fridge until later, be good until I get back." Laughing as she skipped away.

Cormack lay in the shade his eyes closed trying to fit into this wonderful picture, he felt like a piece of jig saw that he moved around but couldn't find its proper place. The reality of this girl and the peculiar circumstances of her life were so bitter sweet like finding an angel among devils.

"What country are you from?"

He sat up and blinking the sunspots away, his face was about level with the upper thighs of a beautiful girl in a sky blue bikini. "Hello" he stammered and when he went to stand up the girl put her hand gently on his shoulder and motioned him to stay sitting.

She sat down beside him squatting on her bended knees. "What country you come from?"

"Ireland" he almost stammered.

"Cold in Ireland now so you come to the hot sunshine?"

"Yes I suppose you could say that, but also I wanted to see your lovely country."

"Yes Cuba is a beautiful country but the people are very poor, now we have very few job opportunities."

"You speak very good English."

The revealing top of her bikini left little to the imagination as she leaned over towards him, her soft smooth coffee coloured skin brushing his arm. "I have a lot of education but cannot work, I have qualified as a doctor three years now and only worked for about ten months on and off in the hospital when they are short. But I hope to get a post overseas maybe soon. I have applied to go to Venezuela where there is a shortage of doctors." She smiled her pearly teeth framed between parting ruby lips and a mischievous twinkle in her gold speckled obsidian eyes. "If you have a little ailment I could maybe cure it, although you look healthy but pale. What's your name?" She proffered a firm but delicate hand and she held his grip. "I'm Mercedes I think you have a car called after me in Europe?"

"Yes and it's a very expensive one too, my name is Cormack and I'm very pleased to meet Mercedes."

A shy expression flitted beneath her fluttering lashes, "are you here alone with no friend?"

He loosed her hand and shifting himself he sat on his knees, and picking up two fistfuls of sand he watched it pour like a timer over his legs. His thoughts raced as he felt like a child in a shop full of sweets with no supervision. "I'm here in Cuba on my own but I have met a friend and she is just gone to the shop, her name is Kathie."

"Is she your girlfriend now or a friend for a day, because I can be your girl while you stay in Cuba?"

He bit his lip looking at her loosening her mane of dark hair to rearrange it into its red ribbon behind her head. They both turned their heads to the sound of a sweet whistling melody, and Kathie with lips pursed appeared silently on the soft sand with a bottle of cold drink in each hand. Mercedes went to stand but Kathie bade her stay sitting, she handed a bottle one to each, "It's probably not as good as your coca cola but it's the best around." Looking at the beautiful girl she said, "I'm Kathie."

Mercedes proffered her hand, "Mercedes pleased to meet you, but you have no drink here take this one." as she offered the bottle back to Kathie.

"No you drink it I'm not a lover of our Tu-kola, what do you think of it Cormack?"

"Actually there's very little difference in taste it's like Pepsi if anything."

As the two supped from their bottles a little silence reigned broken when Cormack stood up and declared he was going swimming.

Mercedes gave a little tug on her bikini bottom, "I must be going now and maybe we will meet again." Her limbs moved in synchronised beauty as she glided beyond the little grove of palms and was gone.

The silence between them was loud as thunder as the foot prints in the sand sat like a marker in history of a visitor leaving an untold chapter.

"She is very beautiful and would make you a sweet companion for your holiday."

He handed her the cool drink, "here take a swig you were generous to give Mercedes your one."

She drank and licked her lips. "You didn't answer me if you'd prefer to go with Mercedes."

He stepped against her and threw his two arms around her, feeling her smooth warm body wriggle against him; he whispered in her ear and felt her give a little shudder. "You know I want to be with you, you're enough of a woman for any man, and I don't believe I am man enough to keep you the way you deserve."

She ran her finger down his spine and the tingle sent shivers to his toes. "And what exactly do I deserve that you think you can't give?"

He stood back from her and held her at arm's length; his eyes swam with a confusion of feelings and emotions. "You deserve a dashing debonair wealthy young man who would worship at your altar of beauty and sensuality."

She put her finger to his lips and her mouth the colour of a ripe pomegranate opened in silent laughter, "when I find such a rare creature of this cosmos I'll certainly let you know."

He kissed her, and her open mouth played truant with her tongue as she gently pushed him from her. "No we cannot get too involved here it's not accepted on a public beach. Even girls like Mercedes only tease while in public, you would have to be in private to taste her love."

"Would you believe she told me she is a qualified doctor, it's hard to comprehend her trying to pick up tourists on a beach."

Kathie began tying up her hair; it's not hard to comprehend if you lived in Cuba for any length of time. You'd see there are literally hundreds or maybe thousands of girls like Mercedes, highly qualified with university degrees that simply can't get work. They are like me prostitutes, victims of circumstance because we want to live a little, and have some of the normal things young women take for granted in other countries, like yours and most developed nations. I want to have nice negligee, and maybe some cosmetics, nice clothes, not just cast down dresses made over into skirts and blouses with the worn parts taken out. I like shoes but I have only four pair and two are white runners. I like a fragrant shampoo, and a spray of perfume, but these things like most else here are impossible to get, unless you have the International Peso and the only way to get that is by selling the only commodity left to a young woman, her body."

He held her two hands in his and felt the sad gaze of her pale emerald eyes wash over entrapping him in a veil of despair. "Kathie I'm so sorry your young life is reduced to this, but maybe I believe, just maybe I will be able to help you."

Her face became animated and her eyes sparkled, she tightened her grip on his hand. "I must tell you a story I read in an American crime book, this very wealthy woman who was also very beautiful was one day attacked in her home by a man, who not only was going to rob her but he also held a knife to her throat and began sexually molesting her. She knew he was going to rape her and also kill her, she offered him money but he didn't want that because he was going to take it anyway, and all her jewellery, so she bravely told him he could have her anyway he wanted. This shocked him and when he loosed his grip on her she began to strip, he was so surprised he slapped her and told her not to undress. You see he was after losing control, he became confused. She stood and challenged him to, as the book said, 'fuck her' so he swiped at her with the knife and she thought he was going to kill her. When she screamed he had control again and this time he did as the book said 'fuck her' he left with her chastity, jewellery, and money, but she was alive. You see she traded the only thing she had for her life, she was then a prostitute of circumstance, you see this helps me at times to hope that I will not always be like this."

He wiped a little tear from her cheek, "no Kathie you will not always be like this."

She sniffled and wiped her nose with a tissue, her expression changed and the soft eyes took on a steely stare. "You're right Cormack my Irish Knight in shiny armour; I will get out of this country and take the things in life that I'm entitled to."

"Yes Kathie I know you will you're a determined young lady and you have your whole life ahead of you. But what of Mercedes and girls like her she seems so happy and content or is that just a show for tourists?"

"She wants more out of life like me and thousands of young people like us, but how far they are willing to go to achieve that is another thing. You must understand there are a lot of mixed people in Cuba. The Spanish blood is mixed with the native Cuban, and the Negro slave is still prominent but there is also a mixed race there too. We have a small amount of Chinese but they are mostly insignificant as population goes. The pure European people are still dominant like the pure Spanish, and other European people like me who still hold pure blood lines. My people are German Jews and the line is still pure, except now for my white Russian mother. The mixed Negro is very beautiful like Mercedes who probably has a Negro ancestor back a few generations. Now she will not marry only into a light coloured man, because believe it or not there is still a silent discrimination towards the Negro. You might ask why am I telling you this, well the people of the Caribbean are happy easy going. They like to enjoy life and are not demanding of their governments, and if they have the basics they will go on doing their manual work and chores. They enjoy cheap alcohol, and tobacco and a bit of marijuana with their singing and music, and in the most wonderful country in the world it seems it's easy to control the whole population. Yes it looks like that from the outside looking in, but it's not really so, only for such a heavy police presence and large army things could be a lot different. You see how many revolutions we've had over the last hundred years, the latest as you know still in control. Havana was more prosperous in the fifties than it is now, admittedly the peasant people were not being treated fairly but that could have been changed without the complete disruption of the whole governing system. Like all countries with a large Negro population the European can generally hold control because of the patient subservient nature of these people. Generally they are not as well educated or adaptable to education as their white counterparts, and that's not being racist I am being pragmatic."

"Kathie" he held her hand, "I don't want to seem rude but could we continue this later as I'd like to contribute and I think this is not the place." He nodded his head and a middle aged man and woman were standing behind Kathie seemingly interested in either their conversation or their relationship.

She turned her head and the pair walked away, she pulled on his hand, "come on for that swim."

They ran across the soft sugary white sand and out waist deep into the warm crystal water. Cormack took off with a strong overhand stroke and after about twenty yards he turned to see where Kathie was. At first he couldn't see her but then he heard her shout, she was twenty yards farther out than he. "Come on you're too slow you'll never make the team." She taunted him.

He tried hard to catch up with her but she was like an otter she glided away from him and he struggled in her slip stream. 'My god' he thought 'what a mover, she was as good as any swimmer he'd ever seen at the pools in Blackrock, and some of the Irish team trained there from time to time.'

She turned and came to him lying on her back she kicked without using her arms, and swam back to low water. Standing up she smiled her sensuous teasing as she tugged the top of her bikini up causing the firm nipples beneath the wet cloth to protrude.

He stared but quickly sought eye contact, "where did you learn to swim like that you could swim for Ireland in the Olympics?"

"Come on" she caught his hand, "more reason for you to get me to Ireland."

"Yes I agree, but at the end of the day would you miss this part of your life, we get a lot of rain and cold in Ireland."

She ran on ahead and threw herself onto the warm sand, "yes I know all about your climate silly, I've been imagining myself in warm jumpers and fur boots and hat, braving snow and blizzards under the Christmas lights, and slippery streets. I've seen it all in the movies and I think I'd get used to it."

He lay down alongside her brushing his thigh against hers, "of course we could always go to the warm countries for holidays."

"Yes we could." She rubbed her leg against his, "Your hairy leg tickles, no you needn't move it I like it.

CHAPTER 10

Back at the apartment the pink and rose shade of the setting sun tinted the silvery dishes and crockery on the table, "this coffee is so delicious, we never get anything like it at home and also your omelette is something special."

She tried to smile as she chewed, her blonde hair was strawberry roan and a large earring reflected a sparkle. She drank some coffee and baring pearly teeth she smiled, "thank you very much for the compliment but it's not easy to get the ingredients here for gourmet food but we make do. The omelette is a recipe from my grandmother I think I told you a bit about her she was a wonderful cook."

He broke some bread and wiped the juices from the plate savouring every last morsel. He blinked to reassure himself he was in a real world. "It's the tastiest dish I can remember eating, and certainly beats all the fast food and convenient restaurants I've been frequenting lately. Could we go out on to the Malecon Kathie and see the setting sun?"

"Yes come on its well on the way now, we'll leave the washing up until later."

Standing at the sea wall were three teenage boys, two strumming guitars and one beating a small drum, the song they were singing was sad and coaxed you to dance to its lively rhythm. They walked in silence and Kathie sought his hand and held it as they faced the setting sun. The music drifted back from the mirrored crimson sea and had a strange effect as if you were in an open air disco.

"I disrupted you on the beach as you were telling me about Cuba its people and her problems."

"Yes I can't exactly remember where I left off but forgive me if I repeat myself. I think I was telling you about the patient Negro people who still make up a large proportion of our population. The diverse mixture of bloods and the hot tempered Spanish, all these with the so called white Europeans are fused into what could be a powder keg, if the right circumstances just pushed them too far. There have been whispers of revolution in the past ten years especially coming from the exiles in Miami, and other parts of the world. The police and army are very strong and of course our famous C.D.R. 'Committee of Defence of the Revolution' I've told you about them. They could possibly be more dangerous to an uprising than even the army, as they nip the slightest sign they notice in the bud, by informing. The biggest threat will come from the internet and technology which the government are trying to control. But it will eventually have to be given its freedom, and then we might see another lever to push this Marxist crowd out of office."

They stopped to gaze at the sun's upper limb sliding beneath the fiery horizon, and felt the soft cool breeze brush their skin like velvet.

He turned to face Kathie and with a serious expression as though she was being wronged, and he being deprived of her. "Yes it will have to change but how long will it take maybe years? In the meantime you're a prisoner here, it's just not right."

"You'll be back in Ireland in a couple of weeks and you'll think of Cuba and Kathie, with memories like the closing of the cover of a good book after reading the final chapter."

Her words stunned him into a reality and his thoughts raced, in just a few days his world had turned upside down, and should he let go now and leave Havana, and spend the rest of his holiday touring the country. His gaze was out over the sea looking at the light purple shades appearing like stage lighting in the sky. He turned to Kathie and she had her back to him standing motionless and silent, he put his two hands on her shoulders and turned her round facing him. "Kathie I won't make any kind of promise I can't keep, but I will try to get you out of this country. Just how I can go about it I don't know, but you tell me what I should do and we could maybe succeed."

Her emerald eyes sparkled in the evening light, and pursing her lips in thought. "Cormack don't decide to help me with anything just take a few days to think about it. You could get into serious trouble if we were caught, we'd both end up in jail, and I'm serious."

A couple of young girls passed eyeing them both, especially Cormack, giggling as they shyly turned away their pretty faces.

"You see those two little 'jineteras' they're hardly sixteen and their little 'bombas' are as hot as charcoal. They'll have to have a man tonight whether for money or love, believe it most young Cuban girls are sexy hot at that age."

He smiled, "maybe it's the weather that makes them sexy."

She caught him by the hand, "come on we must go back to the flat I have something to do and I can't let you around here on your own. You'd be picked up in less than ten minutes."

He squeezed her hand, "you're the only one I want to be picked up by, and what's so urgent?"

She quickened her step "come on I'll tell you when we get there."

They entered the house and one single bulb gave a weak light around the bare floor and concrete stairs, she went in under the stairs and wheeled out a bicycle.

Cormack laughed, "are we going for a cycle, where's my one?"

"Sorry I've only this one and privileged at that, it's the contribution from the party to my father when he was a good loyal citizen, to get him to and from work. Our Comandante imported one million from China to replace public transport during the special period from August 1990. Now you're going to go up and wash the dishes after the tea remember."

"Yes I remember and will you be gone long, or may I ask where you are going?"

She leaned over and held his face close to her; he felt her lips brush against his ear lobe as she spoke in a low whisper. "I'm going to meet that same girl who was at the party, Maria, don't answer me just go upstairs, you know where the key is."

He was lying on his bed listening to the night sounds coming in the open window. A weak yellow glow came through the half open door from the single bulb in the living room, the large window captured sound but only a faint light from the star studded sky. The loud music filtered through from numerous radios from off balconies, and open windows where shadows flitted in a half light of low watt bulbs. He felt intoxicated with the vision of the beauty that Kathie conjured up in his mind. Dublin and his colleagues seemed so far away and Monica and her warm smooth body a distant memory. He gave a slight little jump when he heard the door open. Before he could get out of bed she was standing in the room. Her silhouette from the soft light lent her a surreal form as a forest nymph silent and graceful she glided to his bedside.

She knelt down and bade him stay lying as she sought and found his mouth, her lips were soft and sweet and her probing tongue played with his sensuality like a violin concerto. She lifted her face and whispered. "Goodnight Cormack I will continue the act tomorrow night to final curtain, sleep well." She moved her hand down his body lingering a soft touch on his aroused manhood, "he will be a welcome guest to my warm sweet pouch then."

"Goodnight Kathie." He noticed his voice was hoarse like a frog, she closed the door and darkness fell as a curtain on his longing senses. He lay with eyes closed his being exalted as the effect from some secret elixir; he seemed to soar above the sleeping city, a silver cord trailing to earth. He floated as a cloud wandering aimlessly till time and place merged, then stealing phantom like, sleep prevailed.

He was dreaming he was back at work and all the lights were out. He was trying to contact someone on his computer but it just kept talking back to him, they're here, they're here. He heard them knocking and was now fearful of opening the door to let them in. The loud banging woke him, the loud voices as the door was pushed in, he heard Kathie speaking in a distressed tone, then a male voice loud stern and dull.

Cormack looked at his watch, it was seven thirty, and he stood out and pulled on his trousers and slipped into a shirt. The daylight was just appearing over the tops of the neighbouring buildings. He ran his fingers through his hair, the loud male voice was commanding and bullying now. He went to the door, but as he went to put his hand on the knob the door was pushed open and Amadeo stood there leering. His backup a darker coloured fellow with the build of a heavy weight boxer stood behind him.

"Ah I see you have decided to move in with your prostitute friend, you know this is illegal under Cuban law, she is not a registered Casas and should not keep paid guests."

"I would like to remind you I have not had any paid or unpaid sexual relations with Kathie, and I am not paying her for staying here last night."

Amadeo smiled and waving his arm to include the whole room said to his backup "Trios search here."

Cormack went and picked up his suitcase and put it on the bed, he zipped it up then took it in his hand. As he walked out past Amadeo holding it high he said "this is not part of your remit and if you want to search it you may take me to the police station."

Kathie was visibly shaken as she stood in a dressing gown she had hastily pulled on when she heard the loud knocking. "I'm sorry Cormack about this if only I'd had any thought this would happen I wouldn't have let you stay."

Cormack threw his bag on the floor, Kathie he whispered "don't worry about it, I just hope I haven't gotten you into any trouble."

They could hear the room being ransacked, it sounded as if the bed was upturned and furniture being pulled about. Amadeo stood in the doorway supervising the search and watching Cormack and Kathie.

Trios came out of the bedroom empty handed and spoke to Amadeo in a barely audible whisper; neither Kathie nor Cormack could discern any word of it.

"We are leaving now" came the curt command from Amadeo, "and you" looking at Kathie, "present yourself at the police station in one hour."

They left and a visibly shaken couple stood facing one another, Kathie was first to speak. "Don't worry Cormack it will be just routine questioning they have nothing to charge me with." Walking into the bedroom she gasped as the furniture was upturned and the bed lying on its side.

"My god" exclaimed Cormack as he righted the bed and replaced the mattress and sheets.

Kathie threw the pillows on and began examining the carving of the ship at the headboard.

He stood beside her. "Hope they didn't damage that wonderful carving?"

She caught his hand and moved it to the back of the headboard, searching with her fingers on his until she found a small vertical slit barely the width of a finger nail. "Feel that?"

"Yes"

"Now watch." She put her thumb nail into the slit and pulled gently, a small section of the timber moved leaving a space a couple of inches square. She smiled at him "Glad they didn't find here."

A noise in the front room alerted them.

"Quick Cormack, just sit on the bed I'll go see."

He heard her talking to someone and hearing a woman's voice knew it was a neighbour. He heard her closing the front door and sighed with relief.

"You look like you're still in shock," she stroked his hair as a mother would a child. That was my next neighbour from downstairs, she heard the noise and came to see what was happening she's a bit nosey but okay wouldn't do you any wrong. Look Cormack this needs to be turned." She inserted a small knife blade into the slit and turned. The front part shaped as a ship fell off the headboard. Two rolls of notes fell out; "There" she said as she picked them up, "that's what they were looking for."

"That's a great hiding place, and why were they looking for money?"

"You see they know I work with the tourists and I get Canadian Dollars and Euros, and I can use it for bribery with the government staff. You know the girl we met last night well they're plenty like her but only do favours for Dollars or Euros."

"Why are you showing me your secret hiding place, why do you think you can trust me?"

"Well maybe I'm presuming too much but I thought if they kept me for longer than I expect on some trumped up charge, I might want to use some of that money to get myself out. So I thought I could ask you to do courier for me as I have no one else I could trust."

"I intend to leave Cuba as soon as I get a flight, I couldn't really enjoy myself looking over my shoulder for that detective fellow, probably imagining I was seeing him everywhere I go. But don't worry your secret is safe with me."

She turned away and replaced the money closing the secret panel. "I am sorry Cormack I did presume too much and I must go now. I'll say our goodbyes and I apologise for ruining your holiday, I seem to have a way of spoiling things for other people." She kissed him full on the lips and pressing her body against him she whispered in his ear. "Don't think too badly of me and the girl who left you is very foolish, she will be sorry and will make up to you again. Goodbye Cormack."

As she turned away he saw the tear drops on her cheek. She went into her bedroom and Cormack picked up his bag and left.

Back at the hotel he asked to see the manager. He told him what had happened and asked could he phone the Air France office and arrange a return flight as soon as possible. The manager was disappointed and tried to persuade Cormack to change his mind, but he decided he'd had enough of Cuba. The manager seated him in the lounge and sent the breakfast waitress to him. He ordered a full meal and enjoyed the delicious coffee, and the same seductive girl gave him her full attention. His thoughts were full of Kathie and how he just walked out on her, she was in custody now and no one to turn to for help. Ah to hell it wasn't his problem he had to be careful or he might end up there himself. He admonished himself, what a disaster of a holiday, and what a laugh the lads would have when he arrived back after six days. Monica would surely read something else into it, like you couldn't live without me ha ha.

The manager came to his table. "Could you come into my office Mister O' Gara please?"

Cormack followed him and there sitting was a middle aged woman who stood up and introduced herself as Cristina Garcia. She was slim and attractive fifty looking thirty, her dark eyes smiled as her firm hand shake introduced authority.

"I am sorry to hear you are leaving after so short a stay, Ernesto our manager here has told me what happened in the house you were a guest in. May I call you Cormack?"

"But yes of course."

"Well Cormack I am from the department of tourism and as you can understand I have to look into any complaints from tourists, we are trying very hard to develop a good tourist trade especially with Europe. Ireland is especially dear to us as a country and we have special relations with your government. Now what happened is completely out of character for any visitor to Cuba to be treated to this type of behaviour. I will say in defence of those detectives they did not know you were staying in that particular apartment, and if they did they would not have went there to investigate the occupant. Now it's not for me to comment on the person living there, but seemingly she has been known to the police and also some of her family, so it was very unfortunate that you befriended that girl. I would like firstly to apologise to you for what happened and also to offer you a two week stay in any hotel in Cuba free, you may take up this offer now or anytime in the future."

"Before you decide Cormack" Ernesto nervously sitting with his hands between his knees. "I tried the Airline and they can't get you a return flight for five days, all out bound flights until then are full. So I wanted to offer you to stay with us here until then."

Cormack felt humbled that he should be treated so well and didn't really know how to respond to this generous offer. "I will certainly stay here until the flight is ready, and Ms Cristina I want to thank you for your kind offer."

She stood up and put out her hand to Cormack," I hope you do forgive our misplaced treatment and don't speak too harshly of us when you get home. Please stay and enjoy the real hospitality that is Cuba." She shook his hand and walked out.

CHAPTER 11

Cormack went to an internet booth in the hotel lobby; he decided it was time to check up on belated e-mails. His miserable day was compounded more when he saw no mail from Monica. He opened one from his company partner Derek hoping for some good news on the business front. The first salvo came jumping out at him. Monica had left the job and as far as he knew the latest news from her friends was, she had gone to New York with her new boyfriend Uriah Cashel.

He closed the site and went to his room, his thoughts were a jumble. This news was so final and no word from her, he thought, 'should he e-mail her, but she would maybe have changed her address. New York, Havana, Uriah Cashel, his apartment in Dublin, what a maze of confusion, he felt his life was on a merry-go round.' He sat on the bed and suddenly realised he hadn't phoned Air France, he wouldn't get a flight for a few days so he had better make the best of what he had. He began talking to himself, holiday, painting, dusky beauties on white sandy palm fringed beaches, swimming, drinking rum in the moonlight, making love. He stopped; Cormack you don't deserve any of this because you are a miserable selfish wretch, no wonder Monica left you. Now Kathie, you just walked out on her as if she was a leper. He felt sorry for himself but ashamed at his selfish behaviour. There she was now through no fault of her own in a police interrogation room, and maybe he was partly to blame, sleeping in her apartment. It struck him suddenly, if Kathie was in Dublin she wouldn't even look at him, she'd have the pick of the most eligible men in the City. 'God' he thought 'what a presumptuous old bollocks I am, just because of her circumstances you treat her so badly.'

Full of remorse and good intentions he made his way back to the apartment. He timidly knocked, then harder but no reply. He tried the door and found it open, the lock had been damaged. He went inside and to his horror he saw the place was in a mess, cupboards opened and contents scattered, drawers emptied onto the floor. He went to his bedroom and everything was thrown around, the little hiding place was intact. 'You dirty bastards you didn't find it.' He began to put the furniture back in order, he felt like crying at the hopelessness of Kathie's situation. 'Jesus' he thought 'she would want to be made of steel to cope with this kind of harassment, and no one to turn to for help.' Then he saw the bed linen on the floor, with all his tubes of paints trodden on, and what a mess of colour plastered onto the white linen bed sheet. The canvases were also trodden on and smashed, this looked so deliberate. He realised they had come back again to do a thorough search when he and Kathie left.He began cleaning up this mess realising it was his fault, as these were his paints. He knew the linen sheet was too marked so he used it to wipe the floor and put all the mess into it. He carried it out to the kitchen and looked around for a rubbish bin, as he was stuffing the lot into the small bin he heard a voice from behind. "Cormack."

He turned to see her face ghastly pale and shock in her beautiful eyes. "I'm so sorry Kathie this was my doing, the paints they walked on them and messed up the bed linen and the room floor."

"Cormack that's okay I'll clean up." She ran into the bedroom and examined the secret hiding place. "Good at least they didn't find it." She looked around at the mess and broken furniture, "they knew there was money here and got frustrated when they couldn't find it."

Cormack went and held her. She laid her head onto his shoulder. "Kathie I'm so sorry about all this and walking out this morning, what happened at the police station?" He could hear her little sobs and he stroked her silk hair, "it'll be okay I'll stay with you, and we'll work out something to get you out of this horrible country."

Between sobs she relayed the scene as she was asked to account for Cormack staying at her flat. "I had to make a statement and promise not to take in people to stay unless I had a licence as a Casa, you know guest house."

"I'm sorry for getting you into this mess."

"It's okay you were only an excuse to search this place, they also asked me how much money I earned from prostitution and did I pay any of it to the government."

"What did you tell them?"

"I told them I had to use whatever money I earned to keep myself, they may cut back on my free rations and food coupons now. You see the old crone who is a member of the C.D.R. well she might take more interest in the number of clients I take here from now on, so I will have to go to the hotels or apartments to do business." She looked at the broken crockery and some china belonging to her grandmother that was in the family since they first came to Cuba. Picking it up she held it in the palms of her hands, she was crying and big soft tears fell on the beautiful shards of china. "This is the last thread of our family history here and it's been trodden into the ground," she threw it into the dustbin and looked at Cormack. "I have no place in this country; our family has been stripped of all dignity and personal wealth, even our meagre possessions." She walked into her bedroom and the disarray was huge, bed overturned and furniture broken, even some floor boards lifted. Her clothes were strewn around and some were deliberately torn.

Cormack stood aghast, "my god they must have thought you had a lot of money hidden to do that, but also shear spite."

"Yes! There is no future here for me, not that I really ever had one, but how to throw off these shackles and get free?"

He noticed the desperation in her usually calm voice, "I'll make a cup of coffee." He left her to sort her room and he began tidying the kitchen and boiled the kettle for coffee, at least there were a few cups unbroken and the fridge was still intact. Funny how they never tried the fridge or the top little freezer, it was a favourite hiding place for some people. He remembered one of the lads he went to college with often hid his money rolled up and pushed into the frozen peas. He put some biscuits on a plate and made the table look normal, "come on your coffee is ready."

She sat with a kind of resignation, and sipped the refreshing liquid. Cormack picked up a biscuit and handed the plate to her. "Come on eat one, look Kathie we'll think of something to get you out of this, and this time I'm not making false promises."

She smiled and put her hand over his. "Cormack you have your life to live and my situation is just too complicated for you to get involved."

"Right I see your point but we'll play it by ear and see how the next few weeks evolve, I'm going to hire a car and get away for a while." He held her hand and looking into her sad eyes, "would you come with me and we could plan your escape from Cuba?"

"Are you sure you want to do this? I'll come with you it would be great to get away from here, 'hope breeds eternal' "misery" but what else is left?"

"Kathie you're young and beautiful, they can't take that away, and you are a vibrant young lady with your whole life ahead, but we're going to have to fight for your chance to live that life."

She threw her arms around him and kissed him on the lips, "you are a romantic Irishman with a wild sense of adventure, '*nothing ventured nothing gained*' so I hope you don't end up in a Cuban prison cell."

CHAPTER 12

The Lada was just about roadworthy as he drove back to the hotel to collect his bags.

Kathie was waiting at the apartment when he arrived she was paying Manola for fixing the lock on the door, he threw her bag in the booth (trunk) and away they drove, first stop Matanzas.

Two young men hitching were put into the back seat, and Kathie explained to Cormack that picking up people who were hitching home from the city was normal, and not to pick them up would actually be insulting to them.

The two young men were heading home from their day at university, they lived near Matanzas. Surprisingly they had good English and questioned Cormack about life in Ireland. They didn't hide their ambition of hoping to emigrate to work so they could send home much needed monies to their parents. Dropping off the two lads and reluctantly turning down an invitation to visit their home, they drove on, and checked into a small hotel overlooking a beautiful beach.

Evening sneaks closely behind the setting sun and brings the velvety dusk. The beach was deserted as they strolled casual and carefree listening to the lapping wavelets on the sand, and the slight rustling of the giant palms. Cormack was reluctant to speak as if he broke the spell this might all disappear. A large orange moon slowly rose behind the beach and it cast dark shadows through the palm trees onto the sand. They stopped to look at the twisted shapes like gnarled old people in silent repose on the washed sand.

"Those shadows are weird don't you think Cormack?"

"Yes they remind me of old people that are lost and wandering."

She held his hand, "they could be all the displaced people looking for peace, the tortured souls of those murdered during our revolution."

"God Kathie every country has its hidden history, my country is no exception we have a heavy legacy of death and execution. Look now the moon is rising and the shadows are disappearing like ghouls creeping beneath the trees. Let us put the past behind and be happy."

"Yes you are right." She ran to the tree line and beneath a small palm she kicked off her shoes, her skirt dropped and when Cormack came close she was naked except for her panties. "Get undressed and come on."

Undressed he stood before her a little embarrassed, naked and awkward.

She pulled down her little pants and then kissed him full on the lips. "Come on." She ran to the water and he could hear her splashing.

He ran behind her and dived into the warm refreshing sea, he stood up and looked around and could see no sight of her, then he saw the ripples of gold and the blonde mane as she swam silently like an otter. She came close to him and disappeared beneath the glittering surface. He felt a grip on his ankles and he was pulled back and down to the bottom, he could just see her face as she kissed him. He swam observing the sparkling sea creatures like fireflies on the sea bed, he was mesmerised by this wondrous marine world. He surfaced and he saw her standing knee deep in a moon river, her laughing taunting gesture as she ran up the beach. He followed but lost her as she faded through the shadowy trees. He was somewhat startled when he heard the singing voice, he tried to discern from where it was coming, but as he walked towards it he heard it from a different direction. The sad notes were a lilting lullaby so soothing and loving, the thought of someone lost like a child, struck him. He couldn't understand the language but the words were soft and beautiful. Her clear voice and perfect diction lent a haunting to the wandering melody, as it echoed off the sea and played truant through the rustling palms. It stopped and he felt he had lost someone he loved.

She stood before him her nakedness like beaten silver in the broken moonlight. She held him and kissed him full on the mouth, he gently laid her on the soft sand. His desire to love this woman was more than he thought a man could bear. She gently eased him between her legs and moved her lower body as she found his strong manhood and hungrily took it inside her. She threw her legs over him and held him to slow rhythmic movements as she cooed into his ear and stroked his back with strong firm fingers. Her hands clutched his buttocks and she pulled him hard into her, she moaned and whimpered, then like a birthing cry she shuddered and scraped her nails across his buttocks. She lay quivering as he released a flood of his life fluid in a ritual that seemed to be a primitive sacrifice to humanity.

Exhausted they lay together and she spoke first, "that was the most intense orgasm I think I've ever experienced; just hold me a little longer while I recover."

"Kathie I felt our bodies were conjugated and I could feel your orgasm vibrating through me. It was the most wonderful experience of my life, thank you."

He rolled off her and they lay looking up at the starry sky with a moon peeping over the tree tops. She caught his hand and standing up she pulled him to his feet. "I'm so hungry I could eat you, get dressed and we'll be back in time for dinner."

As they walked back he asked her about the haunting melody?

"It's a very old Hebrew lullaby and my grandmother used to sing it to us at bedtime, I don't really know it's translation as the words are from some ancient dialect, long lost in the deserts of the Middle East. It tells the story from what she told me of a mother looking for a lost child, and calling out to the vast dessert and the lonely winds to help her find her child, it's sad but beautiful."

They walked in silence holding hands, a permeation of love like an aura.

There were four cars in the hotel car park, and as they got close Cormack felt Kathie's hand gripping his in a fierce hold. She stopped staring at the licence plate on an old American car.

"What is it?"

"That car, you see the licence plate it's coloured light brown," she whispered "they're the licence plates of a government official like as not an undercover policeman."

Cormack looked at their car and saw the licence plates were dark red with a T.

"I'll explain later" she said "but don't say anything when we're in the hotel."

When they entered their room she rushed immediately to her bag, she put her fingers to her lips motioning to Cormack not to speak.

"We'll go down to dinner."

"Yes it is just time" Cormack put his arm around her and they walked out of the room.

The dining room was largely empty with only two tables occupied. Kathie walked to a table away from the ones occupied and sat down.

"I couldn't talk to you in the room I'm sure we're being followed and my bag was searched."

"Are you sure we're being followed, and why do you think your bag was searched?"

"Firstly I put a small piece of soap on the zip of the bag, and it was spread when the zip was opened. I knew my clothes were disturbed and some small bottles of lotion."

"Who do you believe is following us the same man who searched your apartment?"

"It may not be him but when I saw the licence plate in the car park I knew there was some undercover agent around. You see you can tell who is driving a car in Cuba by the licence plate; even the foreign diplomatic corps have different colour plates to denote their rank. It's a real Russian style police strategy."

The waiter came and took their order.

"Don't say too much in his presence you can't trust anyone here just now. We'll walk outside for a few minutes when we finish our meal and I can tell you more, for now just trivial talk about just how much you love me, and desire my beautiful body."

Cormack smiled brushing her leg under the table, "that will be my pleasure madam."

Later out in the car park Kathie examined their car to see was it opened and was satisfied it hadn't been tampered with, she placed small fronds of grass in the door rubbers.

"What are you doing now? Cormack asked.

"If anyone opens the doors these little fellows will fall out and they won't see it, but tomorrow we will if it happens."

"You are like a secret agent where did you learn all this stuff?"

"I had a bit of military training as most young Cuban people do, but I being a nosy young girl I read a lot of that stuff during the boring off duty time. Now I will explain more tomorrow when we are on the road, it's time for a couple of drinks before bed, just something to make you sleep and be a good boy."

"If I be a good boy just how disappointed will you be?

She tugged his arm, "come on and I'll show you."

CHAPTER 13

Next morning when they arrived at the car park with their bags they were surprised to see the agent's car was gone. Kathie examined her security grass and saw the doors hadn't been opened. "It looks like our little baby hasn't been tampered with, would you mind if I drove for a while?"

"Of course not, I never thought you might like to take her for a spell, she's all yours here are the keys."

"The only thing is I haven't driven for a while and I might be a bit jumpy, but give me some time and a little patience, I should be okay." She started her up and the take off was especially bumpy, but she wasn't long before they were smoothly doing thirty miles an hour on the quiet but rough roads. The scenery was beautiful, and Cormack sat back admiring this wonderful new world and thinking life couldn't get any better than this. But the thought of last night and fear that they might be followed took him back to a reality. He glanced at Kathie and her concentration betrayed a look of maybe not fear but anxiety.

She turned to him, "well how am I doing?"

"Absolutely great but where are we going? Not that I care very much as I am in your capable hands."

"We have a stop in a town where we'll lunch, and then a drive into the country. I have someplace to show you so sit back and relax."

They stopped in Varadero for a snack and coffee, the morning was moving towards noon and the heat in the car with all windows open was still a bit stifling.

She gave him a peck on the cheek when they got back into the car, "we haven't far to go now and we'll have a nice siesta for a few hours; how does that strike you?"

"Just being with you strikes me as wonderful, what is the name of the town we are going to?"

"It's a very old colonial city not too big about ninety thousand population, but you'll love it, it's not far from my home."

Later as she drove into Cardenas and parked outside the Hotel Dominica, she looked around, "not much has changed here since I was a young girl, not the most palatial but the best around here."

Their hotel room was airy and bright with a great big double bed, onto which Cormack threw himself and bounced on the creaky springs."Just what the doctor ordered, come here and try this." He pulled her onto the bed and they kissed and rolled around until she sat up, and straightening her skirt she whispered in his ear.

"Now you sexy young man behave we can talk freely here I was a little apprehensive about the car, as they may have had time to put something into it while we were on the beach. So to be safe we can just make small talk while driving."

"Yes madam I'll remember, do you think that fellow Amadeo is following us?"

"Not us as such! But me, and you just happen to be my unfortunate companion."

"You have a nice way of putting that, companion how are you, I'm a little more than that. Would you not like lover?"

She put her arms around him and held him very tight, they kissed passionately and he could feel her longing to make love as strong as when on the beach."I have a lot to tell you and could we sit here," she sat on the bed and bade him sit beside her, holding his hand. "Would you like to come and visit my old home place this afternoon? I haven't been back there for years, and you can see the wonderful old world colonial house, where I spent some of my youth." She turned away and her voice was shaky.

He turned her face to him and saw she was crying, her golden lashes wet and big salt tears shining on her cheeks. "Come here" he pulled her to him.

She sobbed, "I'm sorry I haven't cried in years but remembering the happy times I spent here with my family is just breaking my heart. This is the hotel we came to when we were in the city for shopping." She stood up and wiped her eyes, sniffling into a tissue. "I'll be alright in a minute, go and have a shower and I'll join you in a minute, and then well go for lunch."

He stripped off his perspiration damp clothes and stood into the shower. The tepid water was soothing as he rubbed shower gel round his body, shampooing his hairy crotch, and half heartedly chastising himself for an involuntarily erection.

She stepped in sliding her smooth body against his and turning her face up to the shower, she smoothed back her long blonde hair with both hands. Cormack squeezed the gel on her chest and rubbed the foamy suds around her perfect breasts. She leaned back against the tiles pushing her lower body against him. As the water washed the suds from her breasts he could feel and see the hard nipples protruding like ripe berries as he rubbed them between his fingers. She put her hand between his legs and held his stiff standard pulling it down to her wet bush. She was too low to enter even as she stood on her toes. She threw back the shower curtain and holding his hard staff she led him to the bed. She fell backwards onto the white linen. "Come and do what you will to me." She held up both hands and drew him alongside her, their wet bodies glistening with little droplets. He found her open mouth and she kissed him hungrily her tongue deep into his mouth. His hands moved up her wet body from her lower belly to her left breast, he fondled her and tweaked her nipple between his fingers, and felt her shudder as he nibbled her neck.

She caught his manhood and massaged it, her breath coming fast as she sighed and moaned. "Now lie over I want to be on top," she straddled him and held the old iron bed stead in her two hands, moving her lower body as she arched and fed him into her. Her movements were slow as she pulled on the old iron bedstead feveriously taking all was on offer. Cormack held her two shapely bottom cheeks squeezing and massaging them as he held her onto him. He felt her hot breath on his neck as she began to sob and squeal, she rattled the old iron bedstead as she moved her lower body in frenzy. "Slap me Cormack."

He slapped her soft bottom slow and easy.

"Harder! Slap me hard."

He slapped her hard and she cried out, her body shuddering as she pushed herself onto him hard.

"Again" she cried.

He slapped her again, and she moaned as he filled her with nature's precious homogenises. He held her onto him until she collapsed onto the bed and they lay entangled exhausted and damp with shower water and perspiration.

At lunch Kathie rejoiced renewing some old acquaintances with the hotel staff, and then they were on their way. Outside they noticed the car with the official number plates parked at the end of the car park.

Cormack nodded towards the car. "Our friend is still with us."

"Yes, and he's determined to stay with us, if we go now we may get off before he notices we're gone."

Cormack thought he recognised a slight hint of fear in her voice. She drove, but stopped about half a mile out the road to wait and see if they were being followed. After about five minutes she drove on. Glancing in the rear view mirror a few times she shook back her hair and turned to Cormack. "I'd say we're clear for a while anyway."

"What the hell do they want with you anyway, is it because I'm with you?"

"I can't explain all to you now but you are not in danger. He; that is Amadeo, wants to see where I'm going, he has an ulterior motive and it's about my family. Anyway he's gone for now so relax and we'll soon be at my old home, it's not far from here."

The afternoon sun was hot and the car was stifling even with the windows down. Silence is golden ran through Cormack's mind as they wove the bumpy road meeting an odd horse and cart or stray bullock. The few people they met waved to them in friendly greeting and reminded Cormack of rural Ireland, and the friendliness of the people. They came to a stretch of road where the huge hardwoods leaned with their ancient gnarled leafy branches touching from both sides to form a green speckled canopy. The air cooled under these gentle monsters.

"Nearly there now," she glanced in the rear view mirror and shifting on the warm seat she turned to Cormack licking her lips and pursing her mouth, anxiety making her green hazel eyes staring. "No sign of our pursuers," she paused and frowned, "yet."

"God Kathie this is real 007 stuff, only I don't feel or look like Sean Connery and I'm getting worried for you."

"Don't worry for me where we're going is only a visit to our old home, and here it is."

She turned into a tree lined small road bumpy with potholes so she drove slowly. Cormack could see a large house up ahead and when they entered the courtyard it was very impressive.

"This you're old home?"

"Yes do you like it?"

"It's absolutely magnificent it reminds me of the beautiful old houses you'd see in the U.S. films of the South, like 'Gone with the Wind'."

"I've never seen that film we don't get to see too many American films." Glancing around she observed, "It's quite now, siesta time."

She stopped the car and they sat looking at the big house, she pointed out the windows of the different rooms. "That one on the left wing was my bedroom. I lived here until I was six years old we were allowed the top floor. Then when there were only father and myself we moved to Havana to be near his work."

Cormack could detect a quiver in her voice and he turned to hold her hand, her lower lip was trembling and her eyes clouded.

"This is very traumatic for you."

She threw her arms around his neck with her face on his shoulder. "Hold me Cormack; I'm sorry I'll be alright in a few minutes."

He could feel her wet tears as she sobbed. "Kathie he whispered it's going to be alright, you're young and beautiful and have all your life ahead of you."

A man walked around the side of the house and stood looking at them, he was dressed in a ragged shirt and white canvas trousers, and an old straw hat shadowed his moustachioed face.

"Kathie look" he nodded towards the man, "we have company."

She sat back and looked out to see would she recognise the man, yes she thought 'its Juan, he looks so much older.'

Cormack handed her a handkerchief, "dry your tears with that."

"Thanks, do I look a mess?"

"No you're fine."

She blew her nose and dabbed her wet eyes, she stood out and threw back her hair in her familiar way, standing now a very imposing young lady.

Juan stood, his dark eyes taking in the recognition, he lifted his tattered hat and his grey hair fell in locks over his ears. He walked to Kathie holding out his arms, and she ran into his fatherly embrace. Cormack heard him call her some endearment in Spanish, and could make out the 'bambino' so he knew this man was one old servant from her childhood.

She was breathless with excitement as she beckoned. "Cormack this is Juan."

He shook the strong gnarled old hand and saw the truth and joy in the smiling brown eyes.

"You Kathie's new man friend, she like my baby girl so you make her very happy."

Kathie blushed as she watched these two men being her proud guardian angels.

"Yes Juan I will make her happy if I can get her back to my home in Ireland."

"Oh you from Irelando, I know your country, Cuba's friend."

"Yes Ireland is a good friend of Cuba."

"Now Kathie my bambino what brings you back to your old home?"

"I came to visit my old home and meet some friends, I also want to visit the grave and see how it is."

"I look after your family grave and keep the tomb stone clean, all your family are like my family."

"Thank you Juan I will go and say a prayer for them."

"Come back and Margarita will make you a nice coffee, she will want to see you."

"Thank you Juan I will, which part of the house do you live in?"

"We have two rooms on the first floor, all the house now is divided up for four families, come in the back door and our living room was your old bedroom."

"Come Cormack it's hot here in the sun."

They walked through the yard past the big open slatted barns where the tobacco was hanging up in shaggy bunches drying. A small overgrown lane leading away from the yard took them to a small rise of high ground which was cleared but surrounded by giant hardwoods. It was a quiet and peaceful place with only the sound of insects and a lone bird chirruping high up in the leafy trees.

"This is our family grave." She walked over to a large tomb standing about a meter high and about three meters by one and a half. It was cut from a pink colour stone, and the top slab was about fifteen centimetres thick with a

Beautiful rounded finish. The names of the people interned were written in deep black lettering.

Cormack stood back a little to give her privacy as she rubbed her hand over the names and then knelt down to say some prayers. When she rose he walked over to her and made the sign of the cross in respect for her deceased family.

"Will you take some photos for me as I may not be back here for a long time again?"

"Of course," he got the camera ready and snapped a few with her standing at the head of the tomb. She stood with her back to the stone and her hands placed so her fingers were under the thick flat top slab.

"Now you Cormack stand there and I'll take a few of you." She placed him in the same position as she had been in, with his hands on the stone slab, she clicked four shots. She stood on her toes and kissed him on the lips. "Remember this place, now look around and make sure you can find it again."

He was a little apprehensive, but quickly realised this place held some very important secret, and he was involved now. Before he could ask her why he should remember they both turned at the sound of footsteps cracking the dry sticks on the pathway. Kathie pulled him into the cover of the leafy trees her arm held tight in his.

Juan stepped into the clearing and walked to the tomb rubbing his hand along the smooth surface of the stone slab, he glanced around and pursing his lips made a thin shrill bird like sound.

"Come on" she pulled on Cormack's arm "it's only Juan, I know that whistle."

They came out and he called to them, "here Kathie" there was a sense of urgency in his voice. "We have a visitor at the house asking about you, he is one of those special detectives I know the car plate."

"Thanks Juan for coming to tell us, he has followed us here. They searched my apartment a few days ago; I don't know how he knew we were coming here."

"If you are in some kind of trouble with them I will try and help, are they looking for your families," he stopped, "don't go back and let him see you were here at the grave, so go around and come in the back of the drying sheds."

"Thank you Juan."She walked through the dense undergrowth and then out into a tobacco field.

"My god" Cormack stopped to gaze, "this must be the biggest field I've ever seen, it grows tobacco?"

"Yes it's about three hundred acres of the best soil for tobacco growing, a small part of our once family farm and farther over there are thousands of hectares of sugar cane."

Cormack was silent as they made their way to the large tobacco drying sheds. "Here we are now" she said "look at all the tobacco hanging up to dry it looks like they had a good harvest." She stopped when she saw Amadeo walking through the hanging tobacco leaves. "Come on" she tugged Cormack by his arm, she walked with him to a corner of the shed and started to scrape the floor with her shoe. She looked to see had Amadeo seen them, and when she saw him looking through the hanging bunches she knew he had seen them. She pretended she hadn't seen him and pulled Cormack between her and Amadeo, "stand there." She bent down and brushed away the loose dirt on the stone slab floor, and when Amadeo came on them she stood up pretending to be surprised.

He smiled at her a cynical grin, "Did you lose something?"

"Yes as a matter I did but it was a long time ago now, just can't remember what it was." She walked away Cormack holding her hand.

He snarlingly said, "It might be good for you to remember, save us a lot of precious time."

Juan was waiting for them at the front of the house; he walked to Kathie and held her hand looking around to see he wasn't being observed by the detective. "Goodbye my dear and if I can be of any help to you let me know."

"Come to the car with us, I'm sorry we better not stay for that cup of coffee but give my love to Margarita. Juan if Cormack ever comes back here again could you make it easy for him to go to the tomb."

He looked at Cormack who looked surprised when he said "why should I come back again."

Kathie put her arm around him. "I'll explain all later on, and don't talk when we get into the car."

Juan shook his hand and said, "goodbye now and don't look around we are being observed, come back and I will look after you for Kathie."

They got into the car and Cormack drove, Amadeo walked over to Juan as they drove away.

CHAPTER 14

"How did you like my old home? it's not in as good repair as when we lived in it."

"Absolutely beautiful, will you give me directions we are nearly onto the road?"

"Turn right we will head for Cienfuegos a beautiful city you should see."

"I've been so impressed with your beautiful country so far, I would love to get to a beach for a swim but we are too far in land for that."

She smiled, "yes we will have to wait a few days until we get back onto the coast again, could you stop soon as I need to go to the ladies."

"Yes Mam nature is also calling me." He pulled into an entrance to a wooded area, "this okay?"

"Yes will do fine." She nodded to him to follow her. When they were away from the car she turned him around away from her. "Do your wee and don't look around until I say."

He heard her make wee as he peed against a tree, buttoning up his fly he asked "can I turn around now?"

"Just a minute, okay I'm decent."

He went and held her giving a light kiss on the lips, "can you tell me anything of this covert plan of yours."

"Cormack I'm so sorry to be treating you like this but I was suspicious of the car and I'm sure it's bugged, he may follow us on I'm not sure as yet."

"But how does he know we came this way, we could easily have gone back to Cardenas."

"He would have had a man at the end of the lane into the house watching to see which way we went. That's why I said to you where we were going, so he will believe we are not aware of a bug in the car."

"Jesus Kathie this is for real, this Amadeo really means business, just what! Or am I allowed ask, what does he want from you?"

"At least you've deduced that he is looking for something that only I know where it is. Cormack I will tell you all tonight as it is going to take time and you can decide then to just go as this could get nasty."

"Okay until tonight."

"Now we will not make Cienfuegos tonight so we will stay in a small town called Colon, and tomorrow we will go to Cienfuegos and I think we should change the car, the same hire company will be there so we can make an excuse to get a different car."

"Great thinking" he said as he sat in and started the car. "We can talk in comfort and stop if we need to do the bold thing."

"The bold thing, just what might that be?"

"It's our Irish way of talking about sex without actually saying the word itself."

"How strange a people you are, but I like you all the same."

Colon was a small town, and he drove slowly observing the dilapidated houses with occupants sitting around, and children playing. He turned off the main street and she put her hand on his arm. "Stop here," she spoke slowly as if she was being overheard, "this looks like a nice place, I'll go and ask have they a room for two."

He had the bags ready when she beckoned him to come into the neat two story house. He followed her to a room on the first floor it was clean and bright with a veranda and a nice view, there was a light breeze coming through the open doors.

"This is very homely" he put down the bags and took off his shirt to cool off.

"Yes and we can talk safely now." She kicked off her sandals and sat into a soft lounge chair. "Do you want me to tell you all about your dangerous mission?"

"Yes I'd like to know what my role is going to be, especially about going back to your old home."

"Will you pull over that chair and sit close to me so I can hold your hand if need be" and when she smiled that heart melting expression with those green hazel eyes, squeezed his heart and he knew he would do anything for her.

She became serious, "now remember Cormack you can say I'm out at anytime and I will understand."

He stared into those sad eyes. "Yes I know that."

"To begin, my family were very wealthy and my grandfather had shares in some big U.S.A. oil company going back to the very early founding of this company. I'm not sure of the name as he never spoke much about this part of his wealth. There is also some numbered Swiss Bank accounts, and also the title deeds to our home here in Cuba. There is an estate in Eastern Czechoslovakia that was taken over by the Russians but can now be reclaimed by our family. This estate is some five thousand hectares with a great family home and from the stories the old people told it has about forty rooms. Now to reclaim this property is not going to be too easy as you can imagine, but the deeds are in the Swiss Bank. Also with these deeds and shares documents, there are some precious stones, a small amount of gold and jewellery in this sealed safety box that's hidden on the estate near where I brought you today. Now the box came from my grandfather's sister who left Germany with her son David to escape the round up of Jews. They sailed on the cruise ship S.S. St Louis, to a new life here in Cuba. They left Hamburg May thirteenth, nineteen thirty nine and arrived in Havana on May twenty seventh, the ship was anchored in the harbour and all passengers were refused to land. The diplomatic wrangling went on with C. Hyman the executive director of the Joint Distribution Committee in New York, and Milton Goldsmith in Havana but they were unsuccessful in getting all passengers to land, a few were let ashore. On the second of June the St Louis departed Havana and eventually arrived back in Antwerp on June seventeenth. Before the ship sailed my grandfather's sister and her son David sadly knew their fate, so she heroically passed this security box over the side to my father, knowing neither she nor her son could enjoy its wealth. I knew about this famous box but never knew what it contained or where it was hidden. When they arrived in Antwerp they were sent to a work camp 'Westerbork' and then on to Belsen, we never heard about them again."

She paused and a strained look on her face told Cormack that the reliving of the events was taking its toll. "Amadeo knows this wealth is hidden so when I was scratching on the flag stone in the tobacco house, I knew he was watching me so I'm sure he'll dig up that stone slab. There is a big space underneath there that was used to hide guns for Castro's rebels. I'd say there could still be some there; it's not what he'll be expecting so he'll be thoroughly disappointed. There are some oil paintings by the old masters that we must get out of the country as well as the safety box. These old paintings are very valuable and have been in our family for a hundred years or more. The Cuban authorities or as they are better known Committee for the Defence of the Revolution; C.D.R. for short, and they will confiscate any valuables or the shares to the oil company which I own. They would have to torture me to sign all these documents over to them; otherwise the U.S. authorities would not entertain their claim to them. Some of this stuff can be complicated, and the likes of Amadeo would keep for himself valuables and jewellery which he could sell off on the black market. He could have them sent to Florida to some of his friends there. This whole system is corrupt to the core, and my life would be worth nothing if I gave them the safety box and the paintings. You see Cormack these are the only things keeping me from being ignominiously killed, and my body disposed of never to be found. This is the way of these people."

Cormack's look of incredulity had him speechless as he held her two hands in his. "Kathie I can hardly believe what you've told me, it's like something out of a 007 book. Would you not be better to try and get out of the country and leave that stuff behind? If you're caught with the stuff you'll be put behind bars for life, do you think it's worth that?"

"Maybe you're right Cormack, but the number for the Swiss Bank accounts is in that box and I cannot reclaim any of the family estate or monies or valuables without those numbers."

He was biting his lip and words didn't come easy. "We could go back there or maybe I could go back and retrieve the safety box. I could get the bank numbers write them down and put the box back again."

"Yes you could but it's not as easy as that, that box is there over fifty years and there's a combination lock that only I know the number, and even with that it might prove very hard to open. It would be quicker to take the box and just go, I don't know how big it is but it can't be very heavy. Juan will help you and make sure you are not being followed or watched."

"You make it sound quite easy, but how will I let Juan know when I'm coming, so he can meet me."

"I'll make the arrangements with Juan and he'll tell me the best time for you to go there." She smiled a strained tightness to her mouth. "You will be a wealthy man Cormack I can assure you that, and you must take my word on it. You will never have to work a day for the rest of your life."

Cormack sat back and closed his eyes, his mind was in turmoil. 'Yes, yes,' he thought 'I can pull this off,' but then it struck him. "How are we going to get out of the country? I couldn't bring this stuff on a plane."

"I agree there is no way we could get out with this stuff by plane, so we would have to make other arrangements. Would you prefer to leave it at that for now, and in a few days when you have given the whole thing your best consideration we can discuss the remainder of the plan?"

Cormack let out a big sigh, "okay I'll go along with that but the suspense is getting to me. I wonder is there any place around here we could get a nice bottle of wine I could do with a drink."

Katie stood up and shamelessly pulled up her skirt and sat astride him. She whispered in his ear nibbling and probing with her tongue, "I'll go and ask the lady of the house if she might make us some dinner and include a bottle of wine." She felt him aroused so she stood up and taking off her small damp briefs she threw them at him. "Too warm to be wearing these, throw them in the bath I have a wash to do later."

He felt like putty in her hands she was capable of getting him to do anything she wanted.

A delicious meal, a bottle of crisp cool wine and awesome sex, concluded a day with a night shade of blissful slumber.

They were gently disturbed when awakened by the chirruping of elegant tropical birds.

He looked at her peaceful angelic face as she slept a slow rhythmic breathing betrayed her as a masterpiece. He stepped out of the bed, and as she threw her arm over to the empty space she woke, and a fear crossed her sleepy eyes.

"Ah there you are," when she saw him standing gazing at her from the foot of the bed.

He realised she was a little startled when she missed him. "Did you think I had gone and left you?"

"Cormack don't even joke about it. Maybe there will be time enough for that when it happens; I don't want to think about it now."

He sat on the bed and held her, "Kathie I never thought I could be as happy as I have for the last few days. There is no way I'm ever going to leave you and if this plan doesn't work out I'll leave no stone unturned to get you out of Cuba."

They stopped for refreshments in some of the small and wonderful sleepy picturesque towns on the near hundred kilometre drive to Cienfiegos. The conversation in the car was strained and consisted of small talk, so to be in their hotel room was a relief as they could converse freely.

Showered and refreshed she stood naked brushing her hair when Cormack slapped her bare bottom. She raised the hair brush and pouting her rose petal lips she said, "first things first, we will change the car and tomorrow our life on the road will be free and easy. I can freely say what I like to you then I might even talk about your bold thing."

He brushed his hand down her back and over her round buttocks, "I'll keep you to that."

The car hire company were very helpful but couldn't find any fault with the old car when the mechanic drove it. But Cormack insisted he didn't like the steering as it had a wobble, and persisted in having another car. They drove away with a nice old fiat that had seen better days but they were happy and felt a sense of freedom.

As Cormack drove back to their hotel Kathie showed how relaxed she felt. She threw her head back and looked around the car, "I can say what I like now and first I think Amadeo you are a treacherous and dangerous man. I hope someday to repay you for all the trouble you have caused my family." She sat upright and swept her hair back with a flick of her head. "I hope you don't mind me saying that Cormack but I do hate him so much."

"I can only imagine the terror and fear he has put into your life, I am only here a short time and he has taken a certain control of my movements. You will need to get away from here and this Amadeo before he destroys your life. If as you say he trumps up some charge to get you into police custody, god knows what could become of you."

"Yes Cormack he has become much more insistent of late, it seems to me he has gotten some information about the contents of the safe box, and that is why he's so determined to get his hands on it."

"But I thought you were the only one who knew what the contents of the box were?"

"I could be wrong there are some on the fringes of the family who are supposed to be confidential people. They may have picked up some small snippet going back to my parent's time. When propositioned now with some reward they would become informers. This Amadeo will leave no stone unturned to get his hands on this wealth, and he feels he's close to it now."

Cormack parked in the hotel car park and they looked at all the cars and saw none with the hated govt. number plates.

"Well Kathie my dear what should we do now?"

"There's still a little daylight so I think we should go and explore this beautiful city."

He locked the car and took her by the hand, "let's go, your wish is my command."

They spent a wonderful evening in this unique city even taking in some dancing at a late night club. Cormack couldn't believe how friendly the people were and their sense of fun and laughter was amazing, it was a carefree life he could only wish for.

He swirled her round in reckless abandon and she was like a floating Ballerina as the dance floor filled with gyrating hot and sweating bodies. Mixed with the smell of tobacco and alcohol, the dim lighting and hazy atmosphere together seemed to blur the vision. The beating drums pumping through the veins made lithe of naked flesh, numbing the senses, in this gyrating scene of colourful cotton, flowing black hair and smiling white mouths

Sitting down with clothes stuck to their hot flesh Cormack gulped a pint of cold beer, and Kathie sipped her cool mojito.

"Tell me how are all these people so happy and able to be out enjoying themselves, when this is supposed to be a suppressive regime with little employment,"

"Don't believe all you hear about life in Cuba, there are very many happy and well off people with good govt. jobs, and the remainder get subsistence to buy their everyday needs with food coupons. There are no hungry people or badly off people here, the state looks after everyone and we have a great health system. The education is first class and if you work hard you can achieve any heights at your chosen subject. The only drawback is, there are very few jobs and the ones that are, pay very little even for professional people. So when Cubans look abroad and see the living standards especially coming from Florida, they want a bit of that. But if you can't have that you settle for what you've got and most people do so and are happy."

Next morning when they left the hotel Kathie refrained from driving in case she might be pulled over; she had not the legal right to drive this car. Any excuse could land her in a police station for questioning. They were glad to be back on the road again, as they drove on out of the city, and on towards the coast.

Cormack felt like singing even though he had the remnants of a hangover, and Kathie was cheerful and full of the joys of life, the strain of being followed seemed to be lifted from them.

"Kathie I feel like we are free and if I could sing I'd sing you a sweet song"

She laughed a sweet treble, "I have a few notes in my head but I can't remember when I last sung a sweet song, only the night on the beach and that was a type of lament, but what a wonderful experience of love."

"I can't sing, he admitted, as a matter of fact if I was hanged for being a singer I'd be hanged innocently. Well my pet if you can bear with me I'll recite you a poem here goes."

He gave a little cough, and Katie sat back and closed her eyes.

'It is good to be out on the road, and going one knows not where,
Going through meadow and village, one knows not whither or why;
Through the grey light drift of the dust, in the keen cool rush of air,
Under the flying white clouds, and the broad blue lift of the sky.

And to halt at the chattering brook, in a tall green fern at the brink
Where the harebell grows and the gorse the foxgloves purple and white;
Where the shy-eyed delicate deer troop down to the brook to drink
When the stars are mellow and large at the coming of the night.

O, to feel the beat of the rain, and the homely smell of the earth,
Is a tune for the blood to jig to, and joy past power of words;
And the blessed green comely meadows are all a-ripple with mirth
At the noise of the lambs at play and the dear wild cry of the birds.'

Kathie sat silent and Cormack slowed the car a little to look at her and see how he must have bored her.

"Stop the car a minute please." She put her hand on his arm, closed her eyes and squeezed out glistening little tear drops. "That was the most romantic little poem I ever heard and no man has ever taken time to recite something so beautiful. It sounded as if you wrote it especially for me you Irish men are truly romantics."

He leaned over and gently kissed her on the lips, "it's a beautiful little poem for a beautiful lady."

A horse drawn car came towards them on the road, they looked at one another and spoke together, "we better keep moving" and they laughed, their souls overflowing with mirth.

They drove until the middle of the day when they had to pull over into some shade and they both dozed for an hour. They made it to a small village on the coast just at dusk and were too tired to go to the beach for a swim. Their little room was comfortable and before they settled down for a night's sleep

Cormack couldn't contain his curiosity any longer. He went to the little fridge and took out two bottled beers "would you like one just a little nightcap?"

"Yes please."

They sat sipping the cool refreshment when Cormack twisted on the soft cushioned chair. "Kathie, could you tell me more about how we are going to get you and the safety box out of the country?"

She moved a little uncomfortable and took a sip from the bottle. "To tell you the truth I haven't settled on a plan as yet, as I will have to have help."

"By help would I be enough, maybe to take some of the paper stuff in my luggage? Or as I was saying earlier just leave the safety box and get out yourself. You could maybe come back some years later when things have cooled down a bit, and retrieve the box. "

"That sounds very feasible but you don't realise that these people have connections abroad. I could be picked up anywhere and held captive, and tortured until I told them where the safety box was hidden. I would have to sign over all the wealth including the oil shares which are U.S. A. and would be useless to them without my signature, and also all the monies in the Swiss Bank accounts. My life abroad would be worth little when they got their hands on the family wealth. You see its only lately they've got some information about all this, and it's from a family member, who's out of the country at the present on Govt. business. Any more I can't tell you Cormack as I have you involved enough. The only way I can see to get me and all our future wealth out is by yacht, and I believe I haven't got a lot of time before I'm arrested and questioned seriously about this whole business. I'll put it to you straight, you will have to go to the Cayman Islands and hire a yacht and come back to the Havana yacht club. I will be ready and organised to sail with you. The only problem is they will be watching me, so I can have no contact with you when you get back with the yacht."

"How will I retrieve the security box and also let Juan know when I'm coming to get it?"

When we get back to Havana, you will not stay in my apartment but go to a hotel and book a flight to the Cayman Islands. I will meet you to arrange places where we will leave signs for one another. I will have my passport waiting when I get back, you will take it with you and hold it in safe keeping for me. When Amadeo realises you are booking a one way flight to the Caymans he'll think you are not coming back to Cuba again."

"How long will it take for me to get to the Caymans, hire a yacht, and get back to Havana?"

"I'd say about a couple days should do to hire a yacht, and then a few days sailing back again."

"Will I have to tell the yacht owner what our intentions are, just in case he decides not to take you when he knows you're getting out illegally?"

"Yes you will have to be straight with him and he'll charge accordingly, but I should be able to reimburse you for all the expense."

Cormack drank the last of his beer and stretched his arms over his head, "Maybe we'll just leave it at that for now and we can both sleep on it."

"Yes I think that is a good idea, and if you are still wanting to go along we can make plans tomorrow on the drive back to Havana.

CHAPTER 15

Next day they spent on a small beach far from the world, they only saw one person as they frolicked and swam in the warm crystal sea. The sand soft and fine as sugar caressed their feet as they ran from the water's edge to the shade of the rustling palms. They picnicked on crisp sandwiches and a mellow ruby wine sitting naked on large beach towels. Cormack thought could this be paradise as he struggled to comprehend the beauty of this perfect woman, so picturesque against the tropical master's mosaic.

She stood to put the bottle and paper napkins into the basket, and leaning over to take his wine glass he held her hand. She knelt down and sat astride, her soft thighs moving along his sides. He held her as she kissed him hungrily and he pulled her buttocks onto his hard manhood. She moved her lower body in slow rhythmic movements rubbing her open rose petals against his staff. Her warm breath against his neck was like a lisping whisper; she nibbled his ear and put her tongue around the lobe. He held her firm bottom massaging slowly as he drew her to him. Her breath came in gasps and she stopped her movement, she pressed her breasts against him and lifted her lower body, he felt her hand guide his staff into the soft warmth of her erogenous blooming rose. She took his hard rod with a shuddering sigh and moaned as though her whole body was impaled. Her climax was fierce and slow as Cormack felt her taking his whole being into her he stifled his moaning against her neck. They stayed coupled for some minutes as if reluctant to be realised from this world of ecstasy. Slowly she slid off him and lay on her back pulling a towel across her modesty.

Cormack lay beside her and held her hand. "That was so wonderful, if someone told me making love could be as great as that, I would never have believed them."

She turned to him smiling, "I have never enjoyed anything as wonderful as our love making, is it too good to last Cormack? You know such happiness is rare and so tenuous, to be frightening."

The sun was casting long shadows of tall palm trees like sentinels on the white sand as they left the beach to drive on to their small hotel.

Kathie looked around and could see no sigh of anyone having come to the beach but themselves. "I'd say we are clear of our spy for now, it might take him time to find us and start tailing again. Would you mind if we drove back to Havana tomorrow? I can't help feeling I haven't much time before I'm going to be arrested again and questioned seriously this time."

Cormack was amazed as he drove on that they hadn't seen one person all day and the road was clear and deserted. "It's uncanny how alone we are here Kathie, if only we could stay for a few more days. I understand how serious your situation is and we'll be back in Havana tomorrow, we'll leave early in the morning it's a long drive."

They started out at seven in the morning and watched the sun creep above a lemon streaked horizon. The day was cool until midmorning as the golden furnace climbed to its zenith. They went off the main road and stopped for lunch and some cool refreshment in a small sleepy town with only one restaurant, a main street, and a few stray dogs curled up in the shade of a lemon tree. Sipping cold beers and while waiting for their lunch order Kathie stood and excused herself to go to the loo. Brushing down her skirt she turned back with a provocative smile. "I think both men and women share the same loo."

He followed her after a minute and when he pushed open the door he could hear the flush of the toilet. She stood there her pants around her ankles and her skirt pulled up around her waist. She dried her perfect blonde bush with a fistful of tissue and stepped out of her pants. "Don't just stand there when you see a girl in distress." She caught his hand and pulled him inside the small loo and bolted the door. "This is better than your bold thing in the car."

He left a gasp, "Didn't expect starters to be as good as this."

She put her finger to his lips "you will have to be very quiet, can't have the lady who's getting our lunch catching us behaving like teenagers. Sit on the loo."

He dropped his trousers and sat on the toilet seat she stood into him and put her hot pussy up to his lips. He licked her rose petals and held her buttocks pulling her to him.

"Oh god she cried, she put her fist into her mouth and moaned, she pulled his hair and then slowly pulled away. "Cormack that was great, I will return the same to you on next bed we get onto." She sat down on his hard rod and moved in a circular motion until she felt the rush of ecstasy. She then sat motionless and enjoyed the fullness of her womb.

They both grinned as they sat at the table, just in time as the portly lady came with two large platters of food. They ate ravenously, and spoke little, made eye contact, and grinned like the two cats that had got the cream.

"Cormack when we get to Havana we will only be able to see one another for short periods of time, I will have to make it look like I have finished with you and not make any of our C.D.R. people suspicious. He will be looking out for my return and the old crone I told you about who is our C.D.R. will inform him the minute I arrive back."

"I'll book into the Inglaterra Hotel again, and how will I arrange to meet you."

"I will have to see my contact tonight and I'll see you at the 'Church of Angel Custodio' tomorrow at two o clock. You will easily get there it's only walking distance from your hotel. Walk down the Prado towards the Malecon, and at the Hotel Caribbean turn right, and a couple of blocks you will come to

Ave De Las Misiones and you are right there. Think you can remember those names?"

"Yes turn at Caribbean I know that and a couple of blocks over Las Misiones, I'll find it okay."

"When you see me follow me into the church and kneel in the pew in front of me, I can talk to you from there. I will be wearing a black lace mantilla covering my head and some of my face."

"Right I have all that and we should be in Havana shortly, I will book a flight to the Caymans for the next day, shouldn't be any bother as there are a few flights a day. Now when I get back on the yacht how will I let you know I've arrived? We will be berthed at the Marina Hemingway with all the other tourists I presume."

"Yes that's the place for all visiting yachts and when you arrive you can't visit me, you will have to leave messages at the church I'll show you tomorrow, and you will have to hire a car to go to Juan to collect the box. Now get the photos developed the ones of the grave, bring them with you tomorrow you can get quick development at the hotel. I will arrange for a contact with Juan and the time will probably be seven in the evening when things should be quite there. I'll confirm that with you when you get back, we will be able to exchange notes at the Church; I hope"

"Where will I drop you, we are coming to the Malecon?"

"Sorry I'm not looking at the road, just pass the Prado and pull in I'll walk the short distance from there, better not have anyone see you with me when I get to my apartment."

Cormack pulled into the curb and Kathie jumped out with her bag. She put her head back in the window. "Don't forget to give this car back in the morning."

He blew her a kiss, "yes darling I'll not forget, see you tomorrow."

Kathie was apprehensive as she opened the door to her apartment, but after looking round she was happy there hadn't been a search while she was away. She tidied up and showered then went to her safe hiding place and took out a fist full of notes, she counted out what she needed and put the rest back. She kissed the ship on the polished bed stead and whispered "thank you my secret friend, and also for you being Cormack's, 'An auld Bed in Havana' this would never have happened." She rolled the money tightly and placed it in a small plastic bag, then made her way down to the basement and took out her bicycle. She pushed the bag of money up the open end of the handle bar and put the rubber handgrip back over it. Satisfied she was on her way. Her contact lived about fifteen minute's cycle away and she hoped she'd be at home.

She climbed the dark stairway to the apartment she shared with her mother and young son, and tentatively knocked on the door. After a little wait her mother opened just enough to show her face. She had never met Kathie and she was immediately suspicious. "What do you want?"

"Is Maria home I want to speak to her?"

She shouted "Maria someone for you."

Kathie was not invited in as the door was shut in her face. Maria came and apprehensively opened the door. "Ah Kathie I'm sorry about this but I will explain, come we can go out."

Down in the dimly lit basement Kathie took the roll of money out and asked Maria "have you got the business done?"

"Yes I have it but I cannot get it tonight, why mother was so afraid was we had a visit from that Amadeo and his men yesterday. They searched all in the apartment and my mother was very upset. I don't know what they expected to find but they are onto something so I have to be very careful."

Kathie took out the roll from the handlebar of the bicycle. "Here's the rest of the money can you hide it at home?"

"Not really safe." She opened a small money purse and took out a condom opening it she put the money roll into it. "Yes I have someplace to put it, you know where, until I can get it to a secure place tomorrow."

Kathie laughed, "that 'bomba' is not only good for fun it has its uses. Can you meet me tomorrow at the Church of Angel Custodio at one forty five and bring the business with you? I will be inside the Church wearing a black mantilla."

"Yes I will be there." Maria bent down and pushed the money bag into her vagina, "now that's safe do you want to come for a walk?"

"No Maria I think it would be better if we weren't seen together, especially until we get the business done tomorrow."

"Okay Kathie goodnight see you tomorrow, yes you are right, it's just I need a night out so badly, that money thing has made me randy."

Kathie laughed," there's plenty of the real ones around and you've lots of time."

When she arrived back at her apartment she could see the old crone standing on her first floor balcony surveying all that was coming and going in the street. 'Damn' she thought 'I hope all goes okay tomorrow.'

Cormack was welcomed at his hotel but the manager showed disappointment when he said he was only staying one day. He had a fitful sleep and was at breakfast early, he wondered about getting the photos developed and decided to give the car back first. He went to the reception and asked to book a flight to the Cayman Islands. There was one at eleven and another at three that afternoon.

"Please book the afternoon one for me." He paid for the flight and his stay in the hotel, now he thought he was on his way. He returned the car and went looking around for a shop to get the photos developed. He walked over towards the Church of Angel and found a photo cum pharmacist shop. The development took about five minutes, and he walked towards the Church with his packet of photos. The interior of the Church was cool and people were coming in for mass, he waited and the priest came onto the altar. It brought back teenage memories as he hadn't attended mass for some years since he left home. After the mass he went outside and sat on a stone seat. It was hot through his light flannel trousers, and he wondered in the very hot season could you really cook an egg on it, I'd say probably a little slow but possible. He took out the photos and went through them. Kathie looked stunning especially on the beach in her bikini. The tombstone ones were okay and he wondered what significance they could have with this safety box. The one she took of him sitting on the slab stone was the one she was most concerned about. Well he'd know shortly it was noon and he decided to go for a light lunch before coming back here again.

After a cup of black coffee and some stale biscuits Kathie went shopping. Her mind was in a turmoil hoping Maria could get the passport to her safely, and Cormack would turn up and hadn't changed his mind. She must remember to ask Maria would she go to her home when she wanted her to, and arrange with Juan the day when Cormack was arriving and confirm the time. If she couldn't do it she would have to go herself, and if she was being watched it would be too dangerous, it could ruin all her plans. She wandered around the market and kept glancing over her shoulder, she was getting nervous. She realized she would have to pull herself together or this plan would go nowhere. Looking at the time it was one o clock so she decided to go to the Church and not go home. Having her purchases in her basket lent her a feeling of normal housewife. She walked the long way round and stopped to buy an ice cream. There were lots of foreign tourists around and looking at them with their carefree and affluent life style she envied them, and thought 'could she someday have a life like that. To be able to travel to any country you choose and never having to look over your shoulder, just to be free.'

She arrived outside the Church at one thirty five and stood watching tourists taking photos. She walked round to the side of the Church and there was the tomb to one of the old Spanish founders, a small path around had small black and white stones scattered on it. That'll do she thought as she picked up two stones one black the other white and put them in her basket. She went up the steps and stood in the porch, taking her mantilla out of the basket she arranged it over her head partly covering her eyes. I feel like some kind of bandit she thought as she tied it under her chin. She took notice of the two small holy water font's one at each side of the porch and went to dip her fingers in one. She dropped the white stone in, yes she thought it was dark and it was nearly full of water it wouldn't be seen. Taking out the stone she blessed herself and went inside. She could see there were only four people kneeling scattered around at different altars, so she went to a side altar on the right side and knelt.

She observed the small slips of paper that people had written asking petitions from the saint, and dropped inside the rail to the foot of the altar. She observed at the corner where she knelt where a small roll of paper could be concealed.

She heard a cough and looked around Maria was kneeling a little down in the main pews. Kathie went and knelt behind her and Maria sat back and passed the passport to her. She placed it in the basket. "Thanks Maria is everything okay?"

"Yes I will not delay if you need me come here tomorrow at the same time." She stood up and left.

After a few minutes Kathie looked at her watch and saw it was a couple of minutes to two, she walked to the porch and stood looking out over the sun kissed square with its movement of people. He came round into the square and took his camera out of its case and started taking pictures. She stood out at the entrance and for a few moments she could see him anxiously looking around and not seeing her. She went to the top step and he saw her, turning around she went back inside to the same little altar and knelt, she hoped the few people who were praying didn't take notice of her.

He came in and knelt beside her, "you look so pious with that mantilla."

She smiled her face full of tension, "I don't feel so pious, you see this little space here," pointing to a split at the side where they knelt. "Will you leave a message there for me, the name of the yacht spelled backwards?" She took the two stones out of her basket and showed them to him, "these you can get outside at the old tomb, take these two. Now the white one is to be placed in the water font in the porch if everything is okay, if there is something gone wrong place the black one in. Now as you come into the porch the right water font is yours and the left one is mine. I will do the same white for okay black for not okay. When you come back you will have to hire a car to go to Juan, I will have arrangements for the time and day. If I place a black stone in the font I will also place a note here, and you do the same. Also look at the times of opening for the Church it's written on a board outside."

He looked straight ahead and spoke as if to the saint in front on the altar. "I am leaving today and hope to be back in five days, so look out for my stone and message."

"Did you get the photos developed?"

"Yes I have them here."

"When you come back to meet me bring the photo of you sitting on the tomb stone." She took out her passport from under some fruit in her basket and handed it to him, "take good care of this my life depends on this little booklet, go now Cormack, and." She turned to look at him, "I love you and nobody tells a lie inside a Church."

"I love you Kathie, I'll be back."

CHAPTER 16

Cormack arrived in Georgetown and booked into a guest house. He walked the dock and went into the Hard Rock Cafe where he noticed a lot of yachting people mingling with tourists. When his order arrived two young blonde men came and asked him could they share his table as the place was full. They sat down and were speaking in some of the Norse languages, and he presumed they were yachts people. He ventured to engage them in conversation.

"Do you speak English?"

"Yes we speak English, but because we are both from Finland and seldom meet fellow countrymen, we are enjoying a chat in our native language. Now that you are a guest with us at the table we will speak your language, which I presume is English."

"Thank you that is very gentlemanly of you, I am Irish and I appreciate your courtesy."

"Ah! I have known one Irishman who sailed with me on a chartered yacht, nice man good sailor. I am Jorgen, stretching out his hand, and my friend Anselm."

Cormack shook both their hands, "My name is Cormack."

"Pleased to meet you Cormack and what are you doing on Cayman, you on holidays?"

"No not exactly I'm looking to charter a yacht to go to Havana."

"How many people are with you to go on this charter, and where will you go when you reach Havana?"

"I will probably come back here again."

Their food arrived and they ate with relish, both big strapping young men in their mid twenties, with huge appetites. With mouths full they just nodded to Cormack's reply eating was a serious distraction. Jorgen sipped his drink and asked. "Will you not cruise around the coast of Cuba it's so beautiful with some fantastic beaches?"

Cormack didn't want to tell him his true mission to Havana, "Yes I mean I would come back here after a cruise around Cuba."

Anselm spoke with a very serious tone. "You realise Cormack it is very expensive for one to go cruising, normally a cruise consists of a party of maybe four or more, sometimes more depending on the size of the yacht."

He felt out of his depth now as he knew nothing about yacht hire, he spent some time sailing with his friends out of Dun Laoghaire but this was beyond him. "I've never hired a yacht before, so how expensive would it be for one person, say for a week's hire?

They both looked at him and Anselm clearing his mouth spoke first. "Again it all depends on the size of boat with us we have four crew and we take six people. But what you want is a small yacht with just one crew, and the passenger would have to share the crewing. As you said you have sailed before so that is what you are looking for."

"Do you know of any yacht that would suit me?"

They both looked at one another and forking more food into their mouths, they chewed for what seemed a terminally long time before Jorgen spoke. He turned to Anselm, "would you say Allen might be his man?"

Anselm looked at Cormack and back to Jorgen; taking a drink he wiped his mouth with a napkin, laid his two hands palm down on the table then spoke. "Jorgen I'm afraid I will not recommend Allen and his Sea Gypsy, not that the yacht is not a good boat and he is not a good sailor. But you know he has a shady side that is never spoken of."

Jorgen looked at Cormack and back to Anselm, "Yes I agree we have heard stories but you can say the same about half the yacht skippers in the harbour. For Cormack he just about fits the bill, I don't know of any other small yacht he could hire."

Cormack ate his food half choking when he heard this recommendation, 'God' he thought 'he's just the man I need.' "I suppose I could go and see him, and maybe you could recommend some other ones if he is not available."

"Yes" Jorgen cut in "there's the Dansey Blue a fellow from England owns her, he doesn't do much charter work but he'd be worth a try. He's a straight laced fellow, probably prefer if you were gay, how does that strike you?"

Cormack shifted himself around on his chair and looked at them both, "I'm afraid it doesn't strike me at all," quick thinking he said, "not that I have anything against gay people, some of my work colleagues are that leaning and great friends."

"Well" smiled Anselm "that's out so you had better try Allen."

Cormack stood up to go to the loo his appetite had waned, "thanks Jorgen and you Anselm" he shook hands with them both.

They spoke together, "hope you get fixed up okay."

He left the Cafe and strolled along the docks and in the fading light he saw the Sea Gypsy. 'Well' he thought 'here goes I'll have to broach the situation, time is the essence and Kathie is waiting.' He walked alongside and saw a light on in the cabin. He chanced going on board and shouted, "hello anyone below?"

A hatch door opened and a young man appeared, "good evening welcome on board, I'm Allen Trotman skipper of Sea Gypsy."

Cormack stretched out his hand, "I'm Cormack O'Gara pleased to meet you."

"Come below your just in time for a cup of tea." He seated Cormack in the cramped little dining cum galley, handing him a mug of tea, "milk and sugar here. Now what can I do for you?"

"I want to charter a yacht for a trip to Havana and back again, just me on the trip over, pick up a girl for the trip back."

He handed a plate of biscuits to Cormack and seated himself down, holding the mug of tea in both hands he leaned closer to Cormack. "My dear man do you know what you are asking, is this young girl trying to get out of Cuba illegally?"

"Yes I suppose you could say that, but to gain entry here she has a valid passport."

"No she hasn't a valid passport she has one of those illegal ones, if she had a valid one she could leave whenever she wanted. You are asking me to smuggle a girl out of Cuba." He smiled, "not the first time but if we're caught they could hold the yacht there for a long time and you would have to pay for each day I was held, could work out expensive. There's also a chance we could get a stretch in jail there, and that's not a nice prospect."

Cormack sipped the tepid tea and began to realise the enormity of this undertaking. Allen sat grinning, and Cormack thought 'he is painting the worst picture to extract as much money out of me as possible.' "Well I suppose I better forget it and maybe try some other way I don't relish a stint in a Cuban prison."

"Maybe I went a bit too far there, but I do know if we are caught we could get away with a warning, and a not to come back again, but your friend this girl it would go much more severe for her."

"Okay" Allen said. "If we do decide to go how much is it going to cost?"

He rubbed his chin, "let me see now three days and a half each way if weather conditions are right and two days there. Will two days there be enough?"

"Yes I'd imagine two days should be enough, and Allen if you do decide to take this on what would the chances be, of her being caught?"

"Well to be honest a lot depends on luck, is this girl known to the authorities, in other words the police, if she is it's another ball game."

Cormack lied, "she has no police record, and do they search the yacht before sailing?"

"Not necessarily unless they're suspicious of something like we're talking about. Also we will have to lie about out next port of call when we're sailing. If we said we were going back to the Cayman Islands they'd become suspicious. We'd have to say we were sailing to another port in Cuba, that wouldn't be a problem. Just I'd have to stay away from Cuba for a long time."

"Well what would the cost be?"

"I'd have to get seven hundred and fifty Euros before leaving and the same on our safe return. That's not too much considering the risk involved."

"If I was to agree when could we sail?"

"As soon as I get supplies on board, ten hundred hours tomorrow would that suit?"

"Yes that would be suitable."

Allen stood up and put out his hand "let's shake on it, be here with your kit at nine hundred hours, and I hope you can do a trick at the wheel?"

"Yes I've done a bit of sailing that won't be a problem."

"Good Cormack and anymore we have to discuss we can get straightened out on the trip over. Well I'll let you get on with it, and see you in the morning."

Cormack stood to go, "I'll have your money in the morning good night Allen."

When he went back to the hotel he drew out as much cash as he could and he'd get the rest in the morning. He decided to go to the bar and have a few to settle his nerves, 'God almighty what am I after getting myself into' he thought, 'I do really love her.'

He was on board promptly and handed over the money to Allen, they were out of the harbour and sailing with a fair breeze at ten hundred hours.

Kathie went to the Church at the arranged time and as she knelt she heard a cough in the pew behind her. She sat up and leaned back so Maria could hear her, there were no one only tourists in the Church so she felt safe. "Maria I want you to go to my home place you know where I grew up."

"Yes Kathie it's a long way but I was there with you before, I know how to get there."

"Here is a slip of paper and it will tell you who to meet and he will give you instructions for me. Can you go today? and I'll see you here same time tomorrow. I have given you some money in that folded paper note if you need taxies, and I'll give you more when you get back, its important Maria."

"I will have to go immediately or I might not get back until tomorrow."

"Thanks Maria I will remember this for you and I promise we will have good days." She heard Maria get up and leave, Kathie stayed and prayed to who she knew not. As her religious beliefs were so diverse, but God was the same for all, merciful and kind, she begged Him to help her. On her way home she called into the shop selling the art material and bought a tube for the paintings, it was so important to get these out with the security box.

Back in her own street she saw the old crone standing on her balcony, she had the distinct feeling she was being deliberately watched and also being reported back to Amadeo. She approached the apartment door always apprehensive that they may have been back and searched again, no everything was okay for the present. She took down the paintings and examined the back of the frames. She needed a sharp knife to cut the tape to release the pictures from the frames. She carefully cut round the first one and it came out easily, now to take off the top picture and see what the old masterpiece underneath looked like. These pictures had been disguised like this as long as she remembered and she didn't know who the artists were. She peeled off the front picture and revealed the real picture. It was a basket of potatoes and not very colourful, she had to look close to see the artist's name and she could barely make out Van Gogh. 'My goodness' she thought 'it's probably worth a good deal of money if I can get it out of Cuba.' The next one was a portrait of a young woman and the artist was Josef Israels, never heard of him she thought but then again she wasn't well versed in the names of artists. Probably Jewish and that would fit with her early European family, "support your own", she giggled. The third and last was a painting of the well known Japanese Mt. Fuji and the artist Hokusai.' Another unknown to me' she thought 'but maybe it's worth enough for me to risk taking it out.' She rolled the three together and put them neatly into the tube, "hope I can get you onto that yacht, even if only for my family's sake." She spoke to herself.

She pushed the frames and other canvases under the auld bed and smiled at the memory of how Cormack pronounced it. She now went to a drawer and took out all the family photos, the ones in frames she took out and when she had them all together she could fit them into an A sized envelope. She collected some small trinkets and family papers she thought she might need, including her birth certificate and other documents of use. When she had all these plus the paintings packed into a back pack she hoped she would get out of the street unnoticed on her bicycle. She looked at the time and thought 'it will never be tomorrow until I hear from Maria, and hopefully from Cormack in a few days.' I must go for a walk now to get my mind off things, and the old crone will think I am back at my old job.

At noon Allen called Cormack to take the wheel while he went to the galley to drum up some lunch. "We are making good headway the wind is very favourable and at this rate we could be in Hemingway Marina in three days."

"That would be great, just show me the ropes here before you go below."

Allen stood behind him and leaned over to grip the spokes of the wheel. "You won't be long getting her measure she's taking about half a wheel to starboard and we're steering 310." He put a bit more starboard wheel on her as she was falling off to port, "there Cormack you think you can manage?"

"Yes Allen I have the hang of it now, she's nice and easy."

"Yes she's a great little sea boat."

They sailed before the wind on a course to the North West tip of Cuba. Cormack did the next four hours and then he went below to his little cabin for a bit of shut eye. He stopped to study the chart and familiarise himself with the

G.P.S. yes it was all familiar after a short time and he felt confident about sailing again. He went to his little bunk and stretched out as far as was possible. 'If Monica could only see me now sailing like a Sir Galahad to the rescue of a fair maiden, she'd surely become jealous like women are and want me back again.' He felt his life had taken on a purpose even if it was a dangerous one, and he could likely end up in a Cuban prison. He dozed off to sleep thinking about Kathie and what life would be like when they were together, her freedom like an elixir to her well being.

Kathie was up early next morning and decided to go to the Church to meet Maria. She had a full morning to get through so she decided to cycle out to the Hemingway Marina to get some idea of the mooring of the yachts and the site of the harbour offices. She also wanted to see were there many police around keeping an eye on the girls doing business with the sailors. She was surprised to see how big this place was and the number of yachts tied up was more than she expected. It was a buzz of activity and as she strolled around she didn't see any police or harbour officials, everything seemed to be low key. This would be in keeping with a tourist area. She felt a little more confident about getting on board the yacht without being stopped or questioned. If she was questioned by some harbour official she could say like all the girls around here, she was working. She envied the people coming and going from their beautiful sleek yachts, and couldn't help but notice some young Cuban girls sitting on the decks under sun shades sipping cool drinks. She didn't want to be propositioned so she moved on quickly. She knew if she delayed standing around pretending to be admiring the scenery she could be invited on board very quickly. She moved on and looking at her watch saw how the morning had flown. She decided to cycle back to the Church and she'd be there a little before Maria would arrive.

She parked her bicycle at the side of the Church and took out her mantilla. She strolled around listening to tourists talking, recognising Canadian accents and others, she thought, 'a mixture of European.' French she knew but the Norse words sounded all the same. Some of the middle aged men were eyeing her up behind their wives backs. One fellow had the audacity to wink and smile at her. A few easy Euros she thought if she was still in the business, Cormack is my only lover from now. She went into the porch and put on her mantilla, she decided to go to the side about halfway down, and she could see if anyone she thought, 'suspicious came in behind her.' She knelt down and could see most of the area with a slight turn of her head. She looked down on the seat in front of her and saw a beautiful rosary beads, 'someone has left it behind' she thought' she picked it up and felt the smooth worn beads between her fingers. She automatically started praying, Jewish prayers on a Catholic rosary, she felt calm and at peace.

The cough was soft, Maria was kneeling right behind. She sat on the seat and leaned back. "Maria how did it go had you any bother?"

"Kathie Juan is gone he was sent to a farm fifty miles away, I will not stay long as I have a feeling I'm being followed, don't come to my house it's too dangerous. Goodbye Kathie and good luck."

She stood up and left, Kathie was devastated, 'why did they shift Juan? He'd been there years; it must be that bastard Amadeo.' She stayed and prayed on the rosary beads and felt despair creeping slowly over her like a cold hand. She wanted to cry when she looked up at the weeping face of the Blessed Mother as she tried to comfort her son as he carried the Cross to Calvary. 'Suffering' she thought 'is part of human existence since the beginning of time. I won't let him beat me, I won't.'

Sea Gypsy was making good headway before a fair wind and Cormack was a good and confidant crewmember now. When he went to relieve Allen at fourteen hundred hours he asked him "what time do you reckon we'll be picking up the coast of Cuba?"

Allen made a little grimace as he looked at the horizon. "We should be rounding Cape San Antonio about midnight, and depending on the wind we should be in Hemingway Marina around midnight tomorrow night. I hope everything will go smoothly when we get there, do you intend staying long?"

"I'd imagine two days should be enough time to get this girl organised and on board safely."

"She must be a beauty for a fellow to risk so much, it couldn't be money as these Cubans are as poor as church mice."

Cormack smiled. "You're right there it's purely for love, when you see her you'll understand."

"Don't get me wrong Cormack but this love business is not part of my curriculum vitae, my little Sea Gypsy is all the love I need, and she never gives me a back answer."

Cormack laughed "you have a well organised life happy and easy going."

"And I hope to keep it that way any trouble around these islands can ruin a fellow and his business, even one as small as this."

A shoal of flying fish broke the surface and skimmed over the sparkling sea like silver coins being flung from the hand of a giant. Cormack watched the beautiful scene, and looking farther out he could see a yacht with full sail cruising through the water with a bone in her teeth. He turned to Allen, "are you long in this business of chartered sailing?"

"I was born to British parents in Jamaica, we had a sugar plantation there but things didn't work out. My parents divorced when my mother caught my father in bed with a coffee coloured housemaid. He sold up and went back to England, I was sixteen and when I finished my education I came back to the islands, and I've been here since. I enjoy this carefree life with no other responsibilities but to earn a living. How about you what brought you here, and a love affair hanging over you like the Sword of Damocles?"

"I came on holiday, met this beautiful girl and the rest you can guess."

"I can guess and keep guessing but I still can't make sense out of it, with so many beauties around all these islands you can change them as often as the wind, and they don't think any the worse of you, it's a way of life here."

"I am beginning to realise that now, but anyway it's steady as she goes, and I hope all will go okay in Havana. Tell me can I use my laptop here is there any signal? I couldn't get a signal in Cuba I could only use the hotel computers."

"Yes we're just about on the edge of the signal from Cayman, but we'll lose it soon. Here put her on automatic for a while and come below."

Allen gave him the dongle and he went to try his laptop. It powered up and he got a signal and as he was into his e mails the signal got weak and he had to leave it. He went back on deck to relieve Allen and do his trick at wheel duty.

"Thanks Allen I was reading some in mail when it went weak but I can use it on our return trip, and catch up with my work colleagues and see what's happening at home."

"Yes we're on the edge around here, she's steering okay I'll go below for a few hours shut eye, call me if you need me."

He felt invigorated with the primitive feel of the deck planks beneath his bare feet, as he leaned to the pitch of an easy sea swell. This is a life I could very easily get to like, carefree like Allen said, and everyday like a holiday. 'But' he thought, 'was the great man Shakespeare right when he said, *If every day was playing holiday to play would be as tedious as to work'*. 'I can put some credence in that quote. He wondered what was Kathie doing now and had she been harassed by Amadeo. It was so frustrating not being able to communicate but one more day and he'd see her.'

Kathie was upset with the news from Maria, her thoughts were running wild. She hoped if she had been questioned by Amadeo she hadn't told him anything. When she got to the apartment she put the cheap paintings back into the frames and hung them up, 'god' she thought 'how stupid of me if he saw the frames with the pictures out he'd surely suspect something. I'm getting careless now that I'm so close and it's now I should be most careful. How are we going to get to my home to retrieve the security box, god I hope Cormack comes back I'm beginning to despair. I should hear from him in a few days if he got a yacht, how can I get to home for the box.' She put the tube of paintings into the closet and covered them with old clothes. She realised her hands were shaking. 'I am letting this get to me. I suppose Cormack will have to hire a car and I will have to go myself. I know the paths through the trees best and I can get to my old hiding places if I need to. I'm sure I will be able to open the secret vault in the tomb.' She lay on her bed and tried to rest even just to pass the time but sleep evaded her. As evening came and the light faded she decided to go back to her old job lest the old crone get suspicious. She showered and put on a revealing blouse and short skirt, she could see the old crone was sitting on her balcony, 'does she ever leave there' she thought.

The Malecon was busy with tourists and young hustlers selling their wares cheap. Well I can compete, they had youth and exuberance but the older guys prefer more mature girls like me. Some of the darker skinned girls were shabbily dressed and were not much in demand so they usually went to the bars and side streets. She spotted two middle aged guys walking towards her they slowed as they came to her. "What country are you from?" She asked.

They stopped, one sporting a pleasantly lecherous smile. "You speak good English."

"Yes I do, are you English?"

"I'm Canadian and my friend is Italian he speaks some English. We're both going for a drink can you take us someplace lively?"

"Okay come with me and we can enjoy ourselves, how long are you staying in Cuba?"

"We arrived yesterday and we're staying two weeks, but we're leaving for Varadero tomorrow."

"Yes that's generally the way these package holidays work."

The bar was crowded and smoky, and they gave Kathie the money to buy the drinks, she was sure the Canadian was showing enough interest to come back to the apartment.

After two drinks the Italian went to the loo and the Canadian asked her.

"Do you take men back to your house?"

"Yes would you like to accompany me for to stay overnight?"

"Yes I would very much like that; will we go after this drink? I'm sure my friend will understand."

They parted company with the Italian outside the pub but he was talking to a dark coloured girl who had hold of his hand.

"Do you think that girl will go with my friend?"

"I'm sure she will she seems very interested."

They turned around together and saw the other two were walking back the street, they laughed at how sudden it came together.

She arrived at the end of her street and the lighting was poor but she looked up at the balcony to see was the old crone insitu, she was. Good that's just what I need now. She turned to the Canadian when they entered the house "I see my husband's bicycle is here" pulling at the handlebars of her bicycle. "I better go and see has he come home a day early, wait here."

"I didn't know you were married."

"Yes, but we do this business when our husbands are away, he is free to sleep around its part of life here, but I cannot take you to bed if he's in it."

She went up to the apartment and opened and closed the door, she waited a few minutes and came back down. The frustrated man was standing in the dim light under the stairs. She went to him and gave him a sad look. "I'm sorry he is back and in bed waiting for me, I was so looking forward to making love to you," she moved in close to him and put her hand down between his legs. "Oh you are big she cooed, what a pity."

"Could we have a quickie here he gasped."

"No I'm afraid not, some of the residents could walk in." She went and looked out into the street and saw the old crone had gone inside, 'good' she thought. "Come on you better go." She closed the door behind him, 'Kathie she admonished herself, and you are a bitch.' Walking up the stairs she rubbed her crotch, 'now you are feeling horny yourself, serves you right.'

She slept fitfully thinking 'if they are watching her she is back to her old self and Cormack is gone. How long before Amadeo will wait before he decides to take her in and get rough with his interrogation, maybe not very long more. The information he's gotten from the person she suspects, is eating away at him, and he is consumed with avarice. This could make him a very dangerous man and I have no defence while I am living here.' She took her breakfast to the window and looked out on the bright day as she ate and planned. No she would not go to the Church today, there would be no message. She smiled as she thought of last night and the look of disappointment on the guys face. She never believed she would ever do something like that, she enjoyed thinking about it.

The time rounding Cape San Antonia was a little earlier than expected, and they should be in Hemingway Marina at twenty two hundred hours next day. Cormack was relieving Allen at midnight as the lighthouse was flashing astern.

"There's one alteration of course Cormack in about two hours, she should keep this course okay until then. Just call me if you are concerned but you can check the chart yourself."

"Yes I'll be okay I can check the G.P.S. and make the alteration, will we have any bother docking at night when we arrive?"

"No problem it's well lighted, at least it was when I was here two years ago, so no worries there. Will you be going to meet the girl when we arrive?"

"I don't know maybe I might wait until next day but we should be ready to sail in two days."

Allen turned to go below. "I'm off for a bit of shut eye."

Cormack liked the night watch as he never got tired of watching the phosphorous glowing in the water swishing along the yacht's side as she glided through the calm sea. If only Kathie was here to enjoy this, well he thought 'another day.'

A fair wind pushed them through a sun kissed turquoise sea with their sails puffed and full. Cormack during his off duty was getting ready for his visit to the church, he had a small square of paper and he wrote 'YESPYG AES' it looked so strange. He went over the colour stone drill, yes a white one in the right hand font. He felt everything was going to be okay.

Kathie wrote a small note to place for Cormack, and the black stone would tell him something was not right. Hire a car she knew he would do, so she wrote for him to meet her at the railway station at fourteen hundred hours. It would not be unusual for cars to be around there and it was on route to her old home. She was not sure when he would arrive but she had to be ready in case.

There was a change in the weather as they were docking at twenty three hundred hours. Safely tied up Allen went to the harbour masters office to report their arrival. The rain was heavy as Cormack went to his bunk and the heat was oppressive as he twisted and turned. He had a restless sleep listening to the heavy rain beating on the deck and port window.

CHAPTER 17

He sat up when he saw the first rays of sun peeping through the light curtain. He jumped out and dressed, and looking out he could see it was a bright day with the sun low on the horizon. He had plenty of time so he fried some bacon and eggs and brewed a pot of coffee. He decided not to call Allen. Well fortified he set off for town and went to the car hire first, they were just opening when he arrived so he had no trouble as they knew him. He was a bit apprehensive when they asked him how long he would want the car for. He lied and said five days; he thought 'little things could be tricky.' He took the car and went to the Church and parked a few streets away. It was after ten now so the Church would have been open since nine o clock. He went up the steps having gotten his little white stone and placed it in the right font. He crossed over to the left font and when he saw the black stone he took it out. 'My god what could be gone wrong,' he thought 'this whole episode was going to be over soon as Kathie has been arrested, and maybe sent to jail.'

He walked into the interior and looking around he saw there were only two women kneeling up close to the Altar. He went to the little side altar and knelt down, he fished the slip of paper out of his pocket and decided to place it in the tiny slot anyway. Then he saw the end of a bit sticking out, he pulled it out and put it in his pocket. He stayed a while and prayed, 'please God she hasn't been arrested, and asked the saint to protect her.' He walked back to the car before taking the bit of paper out, it read. 'Meet me at the railway station at fourteen hundred hours.' His heart gave a flip; if she came back to the Church she would know he'd been there, when she saw the white stone and her black one gone. He'd have to hope she would as it was too dangerous to go to her apartment.

Kathie was restless as she got out her back pack and put the tube of paintings into it, yes she thought 'they fitted snugly.' She wondered how big the security box would be; also she needed a small torch. She went to purchase a torch and asked the man in the shop for a light for a bicycle, these were common and cheap but would do what she wanted. It was near noon so she decided to walk back to the Church, she was not too optimistic about Cormack being back yet, but she wanted to check her black stone was still there. She dipped her hand in the font and felt no stone, she looked in it was gone. She went to Cormack's font and when she saw the white stone she almost cried with joy. 'I better check to see has he got my note,' she went to the side altar and looking down, she saw he'd taken the little slip of paper. Great he'll be there, she bent down to feel around the slit to be sure it was gone, and found the one left by Cormack, yes great; her heart was beating like a bird in flight.

Back in her apartment she decided to take the pictures and all her money from their hiding places. She had a nice new pair of dark sun glasses and a blue floppy sun hat and thought 'she could easily be taken for a tourist'. She looked around the apartment and felt a bit sad, and wanted to take some small things but had to control herself. She put the A sized envelope and tube of pictures into the back pack and a couple of bits of underwear and a favourite blouse, 'that's it' she thought. She went to the secret place on the bed stead and took out all her money, 'An auld bed in Havana is all I want' he said. She looked at the antique bed which had been in the family for generations, "thank you lovely bed you have been a great friend."

She was still so fearful of Amadeo and his henchmen she took one hundred Euros out of her cache and placed it in her purse with her Cuban Pesos. She had to use the old condom trick with the rest, 'too much to lose to him if he caught me and searched,' she thought. She looked at her watch it was time to go, she looked around the apartment for one last time and whispered goodbye. One last look up at the old crone who was standing in her faded green smock and who didn't see her as she was preoccupied with something at the other end of the street. She felt free already as she walked to the station, but to get the security box, she hadn't decided yet how to go about it.

She was standing among a group of tourists when she saw him pull up just a few meters from her, he didn't recognise her until she walked over and asked for a lift to Matanzas.

"God Kathie I didn't recognise you, get in quick," she was only in when a couple of people came to ask for a lift. "I'm sorry I'm not going far he said."

They didn't speak until he was out on the road.

"Where to Kathie, God you look beautiful, what happened for you to put the black stone in the font"

"Keep going Cormack, you are the most wonderful man in the world, we will have to go to my home today so you are on the right road."

"I thought I was to go on my own and meet Juan."

"Yes that was the plan but when I sent Maria to make arrangements she found Juan had been shifted to another tobacco farm fifty miles away."

He put his hand across to touch her, "I really missed you."

"I missed you very much Cormack, at times I thought I might never see you again that you might not be able to charter a yacht. What is the yacht captain like; does he know what we're doing?"

"Yes he knows we are picking you up and going back to the Caymans, and I'd say he has it reckoned into the price. He'd strike me as this type of having done this type of work before. But they're the only kind you would get to do this so we should be grateful, and it's only another few days. How do you intend to get the box will we do it tonight or will we have to sleep over and do it tomorrow?"

Cormack," she leaned over and kissed him on the cheek, "as much as I'd like to sleep over I think we should do it tonight and try and sail tomorrow."

"It's okay with me so we better keep driving and see can we get there sometime after dark, but not too late as it might cause suspicion seeing a car around there late at night. Will I go to the place to get it?"

"No Cormack you will drop me off at the bottom of the small road and drive away, then delay for twenty minutes. When you come back I should be ready to meet you on the road."

"You think you can do it yourself or should I go with you and leave the car?"

"There's no place to park the car without arousing suspicion so you will have to drive away and come back."

"Where is the box do you have to dig it up is it buried."

"No Cormack the reason I asked you to bring the photo of the grave the one of you sitting on it, is because there's a secret vault at that end and the key to it is under the top slab. To open it you have to press a small area and a section opens. You can put your hand in and press a lever to drop down a front part which opens to the vault. I'm only hoping this will all work as it has been years since it was closed up."

"I don't know if you can do that on your own, maybe you should drive the car and I'll get the box."

"No Cormack because if anyone comes I know some hiding places, and I know every inch of the woods back to the road, you could get lost."

He looked at her and saw the steely determination in her eyes. "Hopefully Kathie you can do it."

It was mid afternoon when they arrived in Matanzas. Cormack slowed down in the quite streets and turned to Kathie. "What do you think, should we stop for some refreshment?"

Looking around she pointed to a small restaurant with parking at the front. "Stop here outside that Cafe Velazco."

She took her back pack with her into the Cafe and placed it on a chair alongside where she sat. "Cormack I'm going to the ladies you order for us both, we have plenty of time we don't want to be at the place until after eight o clock, when it'll be dark. If you want to go to the gents don't go until I come back because I can't leave that back pack out of my sight. She leaned over to whisper as the lady serving the tables was walking to their table. "I've got the pictures and other valuables in there." She pursed her lips in a mock kiss and smiled.

The three course meal took them an hour and a half to eat as they talked and made plans. She kept a sharp eye through the big window to the car parked just outside. Kathie decided she would go back to the yacht tonight as she couldn't take a chance on going to her own apartment. They refrained from drinking beer or anything alcoholic as the task in hand would demand all their best resources.

"Cormack I think we should go over our plan for tonight again."

"Yes we have to get this right first time, what will you use to carry the security box do you want to take the back pack?"

"Yes to be safe I can carry it in that on my back, although it can't be too heavy and it should have a handle on it. When you drop me off I should be about twenty minutes so you will have to drive away and put in the time. Do you remember where we pulled in off the road to go to the toilet last time?"

"Yes about a couple of miles from the entrance to your house, and with the lights off it shan't be seen from the road, an ideal place."

"Be careful before you drive in and make sure it's not too soft, we've had a good lot of rain and the last thing we'd want is the car to get stuck in the soft ground."

"Kathie you sure think of everything, I'll walk in first and be sure it's okay. I think we should go we can stop for a bit of touristy sightseeing to kill an hour, and then at my sedate driving speed we should be there at around eight o clock."

"Yes that will do nicely, a pity we can't stop for a bit of the bold thing, even with all the tension I feel a bit horny how about you, have you been missing me at all?"

He put his hand on her thigh under the table, and he could feel her tremble, of course I am missing everything about you, that especially."

She pushed his hand away, "better stop or I'll have to bring you to the ladies with me, come on we better go."

Cormack was paying the bill as she walked out, looking up and down the street watching for anyone suspicious. She was sure no one had tampered with the car. She put her back pack in the rear seat and got into the front, she thought 'my goodness petrol we better fill up.'

Cormack seemed more relaxed when he got in to drive "well everything to your satisfaction madam."

"Yes but I don't like that madam title it makes me sound old."

"Okay my pretty, beautiful cherub how does that sound?"

"Like as if you are making fun of me."

He leaned over and kissed her "you know that could never be, you're too beautiful and wonderful for that."

She smiled and pushed out her tongue at him, "accepted, but now we must get petrol."

Cormack turned on the ignition and looked at the petrol gauge, "you're right we're half full, will we look around for a petrol station here?"

"There's one on the road out I remember passing it on our last trip here," she looked at her watch, "let's go to the beach and have a little walk to pass the time, we've got about an hour to waste."

They parked under some tall leafy palms and looked out at the beautiful pale blue sparkling sea. Families were relaxing on the soft sugary white sand, and children were playing in the small white waves as they tumbled and gently lapped the wet sand. They got out and walked under the rustling shady trees, he slipped his hand around her waist.

"I'm going to take you to a beautiful hotel when we get to Georgetown, it's called Treasure Island Resort and we'll have a week of relaxing or longer if you wish?"

"Cormack that would be wonderful, do you think it'll come true? I despair sometimes that it's too good to be true, something is going to go wrong."

"If all goes to plan tonight we should be at sea this time tomorrow, how do you feel about what you're about to do?"

"I feel confident if the vault opens without too much trouble, I can't see anybody snooping around after dark."

"Have you anything to help you prise the stone open? Look here" he took a pocket knife out and handed it to her. "This might help" and he showed her how to open it and the different size blades on it "put it in your back pack just in case."

"Yes you're right Cormack I might need it if the stone is difficult to shift." She looked at her watch "we must go back and get some petrol I'm not sure if these petrol places close early."

It was near six o clock when they pulled in for petrol. The pumps were of the old type and it looked like business was very slow. The old man sitting in a basket chair under a faded old canopy waved to them to help themselves. Cormack filled her up and handed Kathie the money to pay. The old man shuffled down to read the dial and accepted the round figure she gave him, a few pesos for himself. He asked did they want air or water so she said "no" and thanked him.

When they reached Cardenas the sun was setting in a bowl of crimson, a mist of scarlet and pink filtered up to meet the dark fading blue of the eastern sky. The streets were quite with all shops closed, and too early for bars to be busy. There was an odd straggler slow walking, like shadowy phantoms to a gathering of ancients. He drove slowly through the streets and out towards Kathie's home and destiny. Darkness comes quickly and when they reached the small road entrance he stopped. Kathie had everything ready she'd emptied the back pack and put in the knife and torch.

"Good luck he whispered" looking at their watches it was eight thirty, "ten minutes to nine," he said, allowing for the agreed twenty minutes.

"Ten minutes to nine" she repeated.

He had a knot in his stomach as he slowly drove to his pull in spot.

She got into the cover of the high trees, and a small path through the low thorny brush gave her a feel of confidence. She had the torch and didn't want to use it unless she had to.

He drove slow and didn't want to miss the turn in, he felt it was a couple of miles but he was so confused he couldn't calculate distance; he'd just have to watch out for it. A pair of headlights came towards him and he pulled in close to let a small truck pass. Then he saw it, he stopped and turned the lights to parking, got out and walked in to see how soft it was. He was happy it was okay so he drove in and switched off the lights. He then checked his watch it had taken him five minutes. He'd drive back faster so he reckoned three minutes. His hand was trembling as he leaned over the steering wheel and closed his eyes, 'where am I, and what am I doing, is this for real?'

Kathie's path took her close to the house and she saw lights on in all the windows, she just thought 'there are people living on all floors.' She walked into a fallen tree and had to climb over it, 'must remember this on the way back.' She got into the little grave compound and put her back pack on the tomb and took out the small knife. She knelt down on the wet damp grass and felt under the top slab, she knew it was in the centre of the tomb. She pushed with her fingers and felt the slight movement of a section moving up, she pushed harder and it seemed to stop. 'Dear God help me' she turned on the torch and looked up under, good God it was a bit too bright, but she saw the section of stone had moved about half an inch upwards. She got out the knife and used it to push the stone and heard it fall into the interior. She sat down with her back to the cold slab and listened. She thought 'she heard a voice, maybe someone from the house going out.' She got down on her knees and put her fingers into the open slit, she found her hand would fit in. She felt around and her fingers caught a cold round bar. She stopped she thought 'she heard a foot step,' her heart was beating faster than she'd ever thought it could. She pulled the bar and felt the front of the large slab move outward, she pulled at it and it was hinged and came right to the ground. She put in her hand and felt around she was afraid there might be rats in there, she caught the side of it and pulled it out. Thank goodness it's not too big, it was about two foot by one and about ten inches high, it wasn't too heavy as she put it into the back pack. She stopped she heard footsteps and someone talking like to a dog. She flashed the torch into the vault to be sure there was nothing left in there. She turned and saw a small white dog sniffing at the rail around the grave. She hadn't time to put the slab back she ran down the path and she fell, the dog started barking and the man shone a torch round the tomb. She clutched the back pack and ran, she remembered the fallen tree and when she got to it the dog was at her heels. She put her hand into the pack and took out the knife opened the blade and waited. She crouched along the fallen tree and got in under a large branch. The torch was searching now and the dog was sniffing her out, he loomed large upon her and caught her in the beam. She managed to turn her face away and she lurched at the big figure and drove the blade into his thigh. He let out a roar and fell clutching the bleeding wound. She was gone and as she passed the dog she kicked him sending him squealing backwards. When she reached the road she ran towards where Cormack was coming from. She was frantic and ready to jump into the side of the road if a car came from the other direction. 'He's here', she stopped and he pulled up, she opened the door and fell into the back seat. "Oh drive fast, I was seen and we could be followed."

She related to Cormack what happened, and she was sure that Amadeo would be informed before long.

It was before midnight when they got to the Marina, and people were coming and going from yachts. Cormack parked away from the Sea Gypsy and walked with Kathie to the yacht. Allen was ashore but he knew where the key to the cabin was and they went in.

"Kathie in here is our bunk and put on the kettle outside there in the galley and we'll make a cup of tea. Now I'm going to shift the car and park it away from here and let the keys in it.

When he got back she had some tea and a sandwich ready, they both were too stunned to talk and they looked at one another as they munched their sandwich.

Kathie composed herself and poured more tea. "Cormack we can't leave this box and the paintings here in the cabin, is there someplace better you can hide them? We couldn't thrust this man or captain whatever."

He got up and took the back pack with the paintings and box and went to the sail locker, he hid them under a bundle of old canvas sails.

The footsteps on deck told them Allen was back. He breezed into the cabin a glow of beer and Cuban rum on his enquiring face.

Cormack was first to speak, "Kathie this is our captain Allen."

The British gentleman was to the fore as he shook her hand and welcomed her on board. "Now I see you've had a bite to eat, so what about sailing arrangements?"

Cormack was anxious so he faced Allen and said, "we'd like to sail first thing in the morning or sooner if that's possible."

"I'll go to the harbour office now and tell them we want to sail at first light, now I'm going to tell them that we're sailing to Matanzas. If I said we were going straight back to Georgetown in the Cayman's they'd be suspicious. But if they think we're staying on the coast it'll pass off okay."

Allen went to the harbour office and Kathie lay down on the small bunk, Cormack made himself comfy on the settee.

Allen came back and announced, "okay first light, so I'll call you at 0700, sleep well."

Amadeo's phone rang a little before midnight it was his C.D.R. man at the farm. He related to Amadeo what had happened and was berated for not phoning sooner. He tried to explain he had to go to a doctor to have his leg dressed and he had to cycle the five miles. Amadeo was so sure that this was Kathie his anger was palpable and distressing. He couldn't sleep and at five hundred hours he left for his office. He ordered two men to keep watch at Kathie's apartment and if she appeared arrest her. He ordered a car and drove to the farm where he arrived before the workmen had begun their daily labour. He took his man out of bed and they went to the grave, he was fuming with rage when he saw the vault open. "You incompetent fool you let her get away with the security box." He struck the cowering peasant worker and knocked him to the ground, whence he kicked him.

He arrived back in Havana and went straight to Kathie's apartment, and on questioning his men, she had not appeared. So he decided to go and search the apartment. The door gave way easily with the surround around the lock having been sparsely repaired. He kicked the furniture with temper when he saw she was gone. He couldn't be sure if she had made a long distance get away as there were a lot of her possessions still here. He thought;' he hoped she would be back.' He'd have her now after attacking and wounding a man, she would get jail, and interrogation would be easy.

Allen called them both at six hundred hours, "right let's have ye on deck we're sailing it's a bright morning we better be underway. Cormack go ashore and let go the mooring ropes, Kathie go forward and take in the mooring rope."

He started up the diesel engine and she sounded loud on the still morning air. He went aft and took in the mooring rope and saw Cormack jump on board. "Kathie you can drum up some breakfast, Cormack coil up the ropes and stand by the fenders in case we touch the quayside on our way out."

The open sea was a delight to behold as they sailed northwest into the fading night; as the rays from the golden orb chased the stars to a new night.

"Cormack" he called, "we can heap on as much canvas as she'll take the wind is fresh and fair. By the way we're sailing northwest and not south west along the coast, as the sooner we get out of Cuban territorial waters the better. They raised all the canvas she could take and like a true greyhound of the sea she took to her task lying over racing across the light busy little seas.

Kathie called "breakfast up."

Allen told Cormack, "go and get fed, I'll wait as the stomach is still a little unsettled after last night's session."

Cormack had an air of purpose about him as he put his arms around Kathie and kissed her on the cheek. "Well we're over the worst of it now we should be well away from Cuban waters in twelve hours."

Her face was flushed from the heat of the little galley, and she looked like a teenager on her first trip away from home and a little mischief the order of the day. "Sit down and relax as I can't, because I'm not able to believe I'm a free woman of the world." She placed a full plate of fry in front of him. "Eat up now you're a hard working man."

He looked searchingly at her. "Come on and eat, I'm so excited I have butterflies in my stomach. I hope they'll find the car in a couple of days, the deposit will cover the extra time so I didn't cheat them."

Kathie swallowed and drank from her coffee. "You know if Amadeo got me now after stabbing that man in the leg he could put me away for a long time. He's not going to give up too easily so we'll have to be careful even when we get to Georgetown."

"I'll feel safe when we're home in Ireland, no one can touch us there."

Kathie didn't say anything as she kept her eyes down and fiddled with the bacon and sausage on her plate.

Amadeo ordered Maria to be brought to his station for questioning. He also went and questioned the old crone and she told him Kathie was back at her old game, as she saw her bring a man back to her apartment. No she thought 'nothing strange was happening.'

Maria was visibly upset as her mother had begged the security men not to break up their little apartment. She knew it was possible as they threatened her if she didn't co-operate they could arrest her mother.

She was seated at a small table and Amadeo came into the sparse room, no window just a bare light bulb. He threw a half smoked cigarette to the floor and crushed it out with his boot. He stood with a clipboard in his hand. "Tell me what you know about your friend Kathie, and remember if you don't co-operate and tell the truth you could lose that apartment and your job and end up in the countryside."

"I don't know anything about her I haven't seen her for a long time."

"What is a long time and tell me does she have a passport, you work there and would know if someone was looking to buy one?"

"I never heard her talk about a passport, and I only heard her talk that she was working the yachts instead of the bars and the Malecon."

"The fucking yachts" he spoke to himself in a low tone. "You can wait here, and think of any other information you might have, and I'll let you home." He went to the outside office and called two of his men into his office. "You Rolando go to the Marina and check all the yachts that arrived in the last week and the names of crew, also check if any of them sailed lately. You Trios check the car hire companies they must have had a car to get to her old ranch."

Kathie and Cormack were enjoying a break from deck duty. Cormack took out his lap top, "I'll try and see can I get any joy from this we could pick up the signal from South Florida on my little stick. He pushed in the dongle and switched on, "did you do much work on computers?" He asked Kathie as she leaned in over him willing the little screen to come on.

"Yes I worked with them all the time when I was doing my research with the university, and after when I worked with the biology department. The only difference was we couldn't have a personal e mail address, and were forbidden to have social media contact like Face book or Twitter. The woman in charge of computers scrutinised our activity everyday to make sure we stayed inside the rules. Look Cormack you have a connection."

"Great I'll look through my e mail and see if there is anything interesting for me." He scanned down and opened a few from his work colleagues the rest were not important so he passed over them.

"Cormack I want to open an e mail address, it's something I wanted to do all my adult life since I was introduced to computers."

He pushed the lap top over to her, "it's all yours go ahead."

She moved her fingers over the keyboard with such accuracy that it astounded Cormack. He turned away to give her privacy to open her e mail and put in her password. After some minutes she turned to him with a smile like a child who has got what she wanted and more from Santa. "There now; my darling I've sent my first social e mail, go to your inbox and read it."

Cormack clicked into his inbox and his heart skipped a beat when he clicked to open her first sent mail. "To my darling Cormack I want to thank you for everything you've done and are doing for me, I love you so much, Kathie."

"That's the best e mail I've ever received." He threw his arms around her and held her tight, and I love you more than I can express right now."

The spell was broken when Allen shouted down, "come on deck we're running into some fog."

Visibility was reduced to about two hundred yards and the wind had dropped to a light breeze. Allen asked Kathie to take the wheel. He turned to Cormack, "go and tighten the forward sail and take in the slack on the others. I must turn on the radar, and also get our position."

Cormack went about his duties and came back to Kathie, "this is the best thing ever happened if Amadeo was trying a search he'd never find us in this. Have they many naval ships around here?"

"To be honest I don't know much about their ships, but they have fishery protection boats which are armed. But they think we're headed for Matanzas isn't that what Allen told the harbour authorities?"

"Of course but that Amadeo might not fall for that he's a wily old fox, don't be alarmed it's just me being over cautious."

Trios went into Amadeo's office with a list in his hand, "here are the cars that were hired out to foreign tourists in the last five days."

"Give it here to me, foreign tourists! Who else would hire cars here, our penniless Cuban tourists? "

Trios looked away his expression saying all, you cannot please this man.

"Here" he shouted and stood up, "that stupid Irishman Cormack O Gara hired a car two days ago, and according to this it has not been returned yet."

Trios smiled, "good what shall we do?"

Amadeo sat down again, "sit there" he commanded, "it looks like they may not have gone too far, has Rolando come back from the Marina yet?"

The door opened and in walked Rolando, "sir I have a list of the yachts that docked and left in the last five days." He handed the list to Amadeo who snapped it and banged it on the desktop. He scrutinised it, "Here" he shouted "a yacht Sea Gypsy docked three days ago and sailed early this morning, crew Cormack O Gara and skipper Allen Trotman, bound for Matanzas. That could explain it the Irishman is taking her to Matanzas and they are going to leave from there."

Trios looked at the list of cars," here sir is the number of the car O Gara hired."

"Good get a message to police from here to Matanzas to look out for this car and not to arrest anyone but just report back to me. Don't forget to give them the car plate number."

"Okay sir I'll get that done right away."

"Rolando, were there many yachts at the Marina?"

"No sir, it was about one third full why do you ask?"

"It's a place we don't have much control over, the customs and harbour authorities seem to keep it under their umbrella. If that was the airport I would have known about that stupid Irishman coming back into the country. What is it with these Irishmen wanting to be heroes; they seem to crop up in the most unusual places especially if there is some kind of trouble or conflict. Here is this fool trying to smuggle this woman out of our country, what is it Rolando love, or recklessness?"

Rolando pushed back his shoulders. "Maybe adventure or gallantry, who knows but my great grandmother, was Irish her name was O' Malley. I won't say anything against Irishmen, also Che Guevara's grandmother was Irish named Lynch. We also have O'Reilly Street named after one of our revolutionary heroes. So what can you expect from Irishmen when they decide to be gallant."

"You have a way of glorifying this O Gara's conduct but for me it's my duty to put them both behind bars. Rolando will you get yourself to Matanzas right away and look out for that Sea Gypsy, if she arrives contact me right away.

"Right sir I'll be on my way."

Sea Gypsy was becalmed in thick fog her sails hanging limp and damp as small drops of condensation trickled down in thin streaks. Allen had kept one on deck as lookout there was no need for wheel duty as there was no movement from the little craft. Cormack came on deck to relieve Kathie and walked silently up behind her. "Well" he said as he caught her from behind, "see anything?"

"You gave me a fright, yes a few busy porpoise hanging around, they are very curious creatures coming close to have a look at us, and making their strange high pitched clicking noise."

Cormack looked out at the calm sea. It's so quiet and peaceful, I hope this fog lifts soon and we get a bit of wind. The forecast is good, a fresh north westerly wind so that should suit when Allen decides to alter course for Georgetown. We are 'like a painted ship upon a painted ocean' a line from the poem *The Ancient Mariner* you know the one 'water water everywhere and not one drop to drink'."

"Yes I know the one, are you trying to educate me in English literature?"

"Far be it for me trying to educate a brilliant mind like yours."

"That's a strange sentence you know, I love some of the expressions you have for expressing difficult wording into a simple language."

"It's an Irish way I suppose of saying things that will not exactly commit one to a proper statement."

"Yes I suppose that's a good way of putting it. I better go below and drum up some grub are you hungry?"

"Yes I'd eat a bit, wish this fog would lift."

Allen came on deck, he walked up to Cormack. "I've just put a position on the chart its nineteen hundred hours and we're twelve hours out. We made seventy four miles, but I'd like to be about one hundred miles off the Cuban coast to be safe from their naval craft. That is if they are looking for us, which they are probably not. What do you think?"

"I don't know but it would be safer as you say, could we use the engine for a bit?"

Allen looked askance at him, "I generally only use diesel in emergencies and when docking."

"I'm sure we can compensate for a little diesel it may not be for too long, I heard the weather forecast and it gave fresh north westerly winds for later."

"Yes I heard it and hopefully it will be sooner than later. Right I'll start up the engine, so go to the wheel, steer same course and we'll make a bit of headway."

An off duty policeman came into the office and asked for the man who was in charge of the investigation relating to the car. He was sent into Amadeo.

"Sir there was a notice out about a car and I found it near the Marina in a side street. Here I have it written down." He handed him the slip of paper.

"Thank you I'll look after that now. He called out "Trios."

He came with a run, "yes sir."

"We've located the car so I want you to go and put surveillance on it, here is the street where it's parked. Get someone to relieve you I want twenty four hour until I tell you different."

"Right sir I'll be there, it's near the marina."

Amadeo sat and pondered! 'What if he left the car and they both went in the yacht. They are gone over twelve hours now, at best eight knots, ninety six miles at best. I'll alert the naval authorities, damn,' he thought 'they have little to do all I need is a look out for that blasted yacht.' He phoned the naval office and explained his predicament to them. They reluctantly said they would get the fishery protection vessels to look out for them, and some fishing boats that were in that area. "Are we to arrest the people on board and on what charges?"

Amadeo spoke with authority, "Arrest the Cuban girl she is a fugitive and wanted for a serious charge of attacking a man, and wounding him with a knife. The Irishman on board you can arrest as he is aiding and abetting, let the yacht go."

The word went out Sea Gypsy was a wanted yacht.

The Sea Gypsy's engine pushed her along at about four knots, Allen stood on her foredeck smoking and looking into the fog. Kathie stood with Cormack as he turned the wheel slightly to starboard to keep her course steady. She turned her face to look up into the fog, "look! Cormack a patch of blue it's clearing."

The sky began to open and the fog as if by the wave of a magician's wand dispersed, they could feel the first caress of a breeze.

Allen came quickly to them, "Kathie take the wheel we've got the breeze back again. Right Cormack let's get some sail back on her."

The wind freshened and Allen shut down his precious engine, he went below to get a position. On deck she leaned over to her speed position as the wind freshened and the sea and sky cleared.

Allen came back on deck and announced the welcome news. "We can change course in an hour to take us to Georgetown we'll be about a hundred miles off the coast of Cuba then."

Cormack relieved Kathie at the wheel. She went below and brewed up some coffee, the aroma drifted up from the little galley. Cormack inhaled the soothing aroma, that's a smell that will always remind me of this little yacht and our Caribbean cruise. He felt content now they were on the home run.

She arrived at his side. "Here's your coffee and biscuits."

"Thank you" her smile told it all, as she laid the mug and biscuits on the shelf at his side.

The sun was setting on their port side and the orange light was suffusing the rigging, slowly giving way to the purples and blues of a Caribbean sunset. A shoal of flying fish broke the surface scattering colours like a kaleidoscope. She stayed chatting as they watched the light spray lift across her decks and dampen their faces. He blinked the damp drops off his eye lashes. "I'd say we're doing nearly nine or ten knots what would you think?"

She threw her damp hair back off her face. "I don't know much about yachts or speed, I can read a G.P.S. and steer this little girl but other than that I'm learning."

Allen came on deck, "right we can alter course now bring her round to port easy."

Cormack put port helm on and Allen lowered the main sail, he shouted to Cormack "steer two hundred and twenty five" he repeated the course back to Allen. She came round onto her new course and Allen hoisted her main sail, she leaped like a greyhound with the wind on her starboard quarter throwing up spray across her foredeck. He stood at the main mast looking forward, "that's it my little beauty show us what you can do."

He came back to Cormack and Kathie and he was so proud of his Sea Gypsy. "Just look at her she's doing ten maybe eleven knots, we're going the long way round but at this speed another two days should see us close to home."

Kathie couldn't contain her joy as she hugged Cormack and gave Allen a light embrace. "I can't wait to see Georgetown and experience western life and all its glorious decadence." She laughed a little mirthful giggle, I'm sure I'll enjoy it."

CHAPTER 18

When Allen came on deck at four hundred hours to relieve Cormack at the wheel they were still making about ten knots before a fair wind. He handed over the wheel duty, "she's taking half a turn to starboard, beautiful night a full dome of stars."

Allen looked up at the stars. "Yes it inspires a line from John Mansfield's poem '*I must go down to the sea again- to the lonely sea and the sky- and all I ask is a tall ship- and a star to steer her by'* this night suits the mood. I put our position on the chart on my way up and we're making a bit of port leeway, so I'm altering ten degrees to starboard. We averaged nine knots since we altered course. We have to pass close to the Cuban coast tomorrow morning but I doubt if we will have any visit from their fishing patrol boats."

"I'm sure they won't bother us now, we are well clear" replied Cormack in a positive tone.

"Look at the chart we will pass fairly close, but we're probably being over anxious." Allen seemed reassuring.

"I'll get a bit of shut eye." He looked at the chart on the way down to his cabin yes they would be close to the Cuban coast sometime this morning. He decided not to say anything to Kathie he didn't want to alarm her. She was sleeping soundly in the small bunk so he quietly undressed and lay on the settee. He was dozing off to sleep when he heard Kathie turning and she spoke in an anguished low tone. He couldn't be sure, it sounded like Yackob and she seemed a little distressed as she turned her face to the bulkhead. He thought 'he heard her sob.' He fell into a dreamless sleep all the tension of the past week draining away, a slight draft of cool air wafted through the cabin making it soothingly comfortable.

It was the loud voices and running footsteps that woke him, he looked over to Kathie, and she had heard it too. They sat up; fear drained their faces as she jumped out of the bunk and ran to Cormack. "My god what is it are they after catching us."

"Stay here I'll go and see." He pulled on his jeans and before he could leave a big burly man came into the cabin.

"Right" looking at Kathie, "get dressed and out on deck."

Cormack stayed and stood in front of Kathie while she dressed, then he got a severe shove. "Out on deck, and one wrong move and you're a dead man, understand."

He thought, 'now we're heading back to Havana, how could this happen?'

Kathie looked at him, defeat written all over her face.

Allen had taken down all sail and they were lying still in the water, a big launch was alongside, Cormack looked to see was she flying the Cuban ensign. No she wasn't, and neither was she a Cuban patrol boat. Allen threw them a line and it held them together, a man on the launch handed bales over to Allen. This other big surly chestnut coloured fellow was also catching bales. He turned to Cormack, "here take these and put them below, hurry man."

He did what he was told and then he saw her name as her bow swung around, Cape Rondon, and she was registered in Santa Marta. That's not Cuba these are smugglers, my god Allen must be one of them. He decided to do what they told him and hopefully they'd get out of this without harm. He carried all the bales and stacked them below, when he came back on deck he heard Kathie's screams as this big fellow caught her arms and pushed her to the railing.

"Now get on board or I'll use this," he held a gun in his hand. She got onto the launch, and he jumped after her.

Allen pulled in the rope as it was let go on the launch, and the two craft were moving away. Cormack thought he heard the fellow say 'good Allen,' Kathie was manhandled below decks. That was all Cormack saw, his mind was a blur and he went to the rail and vomited over the side.

Allen spoke with authority. "Right get some sail back up we better get on with it."

Cormack watched the big launch speed away with a great white wash down her sides. "Allen what's going on, what's going to happen to Kathie?"

Allen stood his hands gripping the steering wheel so tight his knuckles were white. "Cormack those were Columbian drug runners and you don't argue with them, we will do what we have to or end up as shark food."

Cormack was angry as the full extent of the situation was beginning to register. "Allen I'm asking what's going to happen to Kathie?"

"Listen to me we have bales of drugs on board and the sooner we get rid of them the better. These people are doing this all the time picking up yachts and giving those drugs to drop off. They invariably take a hostage to be sure we drop the drugs where we're told to. They then let the hostage go dropping them off on some of the islands."

"Are you sure, can you guarantee me Kathie will be okay? Have you had this done to you before?"

"I can't guarantee you anything but if we don't do as we've been told it won't matter because we won't live to talk about it. These are Columbian drug runners and we are pawns in a huge operation, which, if it goes wrong you'll never see that green isle of yours again."

"I can look after myself but tell me what is going to happen to Kathie?"

"Do you really want to know?"

"Yes I do want to know, haven't you a radio you could report this."

"Yes I could and to whom and what would they do about a Cuban fugitive gone with some Columbian drug runners. There's no country around here would bother, only maybe the C.I.A. and do you know if they caught us with this cargo, you'd end up in Guantanamo prison. Nothing you could say would convince them you weren't involved with the drugs."

"You are telling me Kathie might be brought back to Columbia or some other foreign country?"

"Yes if she's lucky she might end up back in some brothel in Columbia."

Cormack almost hit Allen, he sensed a quirky 'see what you got now' about the way he spoke. He knew he could handle him in a fight, but he wasn't sure what it would achieve with getting Kathie back. He was convinced he was part of this smuggling. "Where have we to go with these drugs?"

"We have co-ordinates that they gave me and we have to drop the drugs there, they're weighted so they'll sink to the bottom. When their men collect the drugs they might let Kathie go, just hope."

"When have we to drop them off, sometime today?"

"No it'll be later tomorrow when we're near the coast of the Caymans."

Cormack went to go below and Allen shouted after him. "Make a pot of coffee and some breakfast, we have to eat."

He stood in the little galley and searched around he knew what he was looking for, but could he find something that would do the job.

Kathie was pushed down the stairway and bundled into a cabin then she heard the door lock. She looked around this luxurious space with its bathroom en suite, television and sound system. She didn't touch anything but went into the bathroom and poured cold water on her swollen arm, where she'd struck it off the bulkhead as she was pushed down the stairway. She began to collect her thoughts, there are two of them, big burly cruel Columbians. These are ruthless brutal men and her life meant nothing to them, they might decide to keep her until they tired of her sexually.

She looked out the small port and could see the new sun shimmering on the cerulean blue sea. She couldn't see any ships or yachts. She heard the engines slow down and their speed dropped away they were only barely moving through the water now.

The two Columbians were arguing who would have her first; they sniffed a few lines of coke and then tossed a coin. The fellow who had taken her off the Sea Gypsy won first turn with her. "Okay I go easy with her I won't rough her up too much I leave plenty of good fucking for you, maybe I only use one hole." She heard the key in the door and she braced herself, she threw off her shoes and flexed her sore arm. He was grinning and she could see the white powder under his nostril, 'he's very daring now' she thought.

"Come now you pretty little Cuban 'hucklebicho' I'll teach you how to fuck, for Cuban you are rare with your blonde hair." He sniffed, "ah 'chucha pig' I like that smell."

She moved back as he came towards her, "when will you let me off onto some island?"

He moved menacingly towards her and with a swipe he struck her across the face with his back hand. She screamed and fell back against the bunk bed. "You be good and if I enjoy you fucking I might keep you for some time, otherwise you go for shark supper pretty quick." He pulled her blouse and tore it from her, she was naked underneath. "Get your clothes off you Cuban 'fufurufa'."

She stripped and stood naked; he looked her up and down smiling, baring crooked bad teeth.

He opened his belt and let his trouser fall to the deck; he undid a holster around his waist and put this with its gun behind him. He fumbled with his underpants pushing it down his legs. "Now how big do you like em?" He began to shake his penis which was flopping around. He saw her looking at it, "don't fear you will get him hard, come here and bend down on your knees and suck him gently."

She sized up the distance between them, one half step should do. She smiled holding her hand under her left breast in a provocative gesture. "I'll get him hard and big so you can fuck me good."

"That's what I like to hear." He held his limp cock in his hand pointing it at her. "Here get him in your mouth."

She shuffled half a step forward her eyes on his scrotum, and with a swift motion her right instep struck straight and true between his legs. He gasped like a stuck pig throwing his head back in agony. Her next blow was swift and sure as she struck him in the throat with her side hand. He stood and she saw one testicle hanging down his thigh and the other pushing through the skin having been driven up into his stomach. He collapsed gasping for air the carotid artery was ruptured and his neck and face was turning blue, his two eyes protruded and he kicked in a dying spasm. She dressed quickly and picked the gun out of the holster, she had practised with this 'Glock' pistol and she checked it, yes full loaded and one in the breach, 'good' she thought. She looked at the dead man and spoke to herself "I can thank you Castro for one good thing my army training and martial art classes, never thought it would save my life. Not finished yet there's another one." She had to think quick as the other fellow could be down any minute. She sized up the space, where to stand when he came through the door. He won't be expecting to see his mate lying on the deck. Surprise will be my weapon. She sat behind the door and waited gun in both hands between her legs. It seemed an eternity before she heard the footsteps.

"Are you finished in there yet how many times have you fucked her?" The door opened and he walked in, he stood shocked when he saw his mate lying on the deck, he looked around and ran across to him.

She stood up and came out from behind the door pointing the pistol at him.

"He had a little accident." She sarcastically intoned.

He turned to face the pistol and scowled, "You fucking bitch I'll kill you for this."

She saw his right hand go behind his back. "Put that gun down and talk, I'll let you off in the Bahamas we're heading there."

She saw his hand come round and the pistol pointing down. "You murdering pig," He scowled.

The first shot hit him in the middle of the chest, he staggered back his gun rising pointing at her, next bullet in the middle of his forehead. 'Good shooting Kathie you were always accurate.' She smiled as she went to the controls, the engine was idling and the launch was lying still in the water. She went back below and thought, 'I better try all the cabins maybe there are more of them.'

She picked up the gun and made her way along the port side cabins carefully going in and searching. She moved to the starboard side and when she came to the third cabin it was locked. She tried the handle and had the gun ready as she prepared to kick it in. Then she decided to go and get the key from one of their pockets or in the wheel house where she saw a keyboard. As she turned to go she heard a whimpering from inside, she stopped and listened, yes it was like someone crying. She stood back and kicked the door just under the lock, it flew back in. She held the gun in both hands and slowly walked in, the whimpering came from the bunk, and she saw someone covered with a sheet sitting up on the bunk. "Come out she commanded or I'll shoot."

The sheet was pulled aside and a face peeped out, "don't shoot I'm sorry."

She ran over and pulled the sheet off the terrified young girl, "you're safe now I won't hurt you."

The terrified eyes were swollen and her face was bruised, "where are they?"

"Do you mean the two men who held you here?"

"Yes they will kill us," then she saw the gun in Kathie's hand. "I heard gunshots was that the men shooting at you?"

"No that was me shooting at them I killed them both, how many of them were there?"

"I only saw two who used to come here to rape and beat me." She started crying.

Kathie held her in her arms "it's okay now they're gone, I must search the rest of the cabins to be sure there is no one else. What's your name? I'm Kathie."

"I'm Chantal."

"Chantal get dressed and go up to the wheel house I'll be up in a few minutes."

It was then she saw the bruises on her body and an inflamed weeping wound under her left breast. "What caused that?" pointing at the wound.

"One of them put a lighting cigar there."

"We better look after that and those bruises."

Kathie searched the remainder of the cabins and the engine room, she went to the cabin where the dead men were and took the gun from his lifeless hand. She was happy now that they were the only ones on the launch.

Back in the wheelhouse Chantal was marking in their position on the chart. She turned to Kathie as she came in, "we are here" she pointed to a mark on the chart, "where should we go to, the Bahamas or maybe Cuba is not far?"

"We're definitely not going to Cuba," she told her story, and asked Chantal how she came to be on the Columbian's launch?"

Chantal related how she and her father and mother and her friend Emilie were sailing on their family yacht from the Bahamas to Bermuda, then onto their home in France, when this launch came alongside and one fellow with a gun boarded. "They put bales of drugs onto our yacht and ordered my father to take them to Bermuda and drop them off the coast at the co–ordinates he gave him. He took me and Emilie and told my parents when he dropped off the drugs he would release us on some island near the Bahamas. I heard Emilie crying two nights ago as they dragged her out on deck, she was in the cabin next to me but I never heard her again. He told me he threw her overboard and I would be next when he got some fresh whores to fuck. Excuse the language but that is what they said, my beautiful friend Emilie she was such a pretty girl only seventeen years old."

Cormack was cooking up something for them to eat. He was thinking about the co-ordinates given to Allen, they must be in shallow water near land, so they could retrieve the bales when thrown into the sea. Those bales of drugs were the only weapon he had to use to get Kathie back safely. He was looking in the freezer when he saw the large frozen fish, he lifted it and it weighed about four pounds, and the narrow tail end had a good grip. He wrapped it in a dish cloth and swung it round. Yes the grip was good and the weight and force should do the job, if not he was in big trouble. He searched around for some light rope and tape and found both in an oilskin locker. The clock on the bulkhead told him he had ten minutes before going on wheel duty to relieve Allen. He poured some coffee and ate a meagre meal of bread and cold meat, his appetite was gone since this episode of the drugs and

Kathie's kidnapping. Allen is more involved he believed than he liked to say. He picked up his fish and holding it behind his back he walked on deck to take wheel duty. Allen had his back to him as he said "how's she steering?"

"Great she's taking a few spokes to port we are making good speed and should be near Caymans tomorrow night."

"Good." He swung the fish and struck him behind the ear, he fell to the deck. He trussed him up with the rope as quickly as he could, ankles tight and hands behind his back well tied. He worried when he hadn't woken up after a few minutes so he checked his pulse, 'yes he was alive, didn't think I hit him that hard.'

Allen opened his eyes and with a glazed vision he looked at Cormack, "what happened did I fall or get a blackout?" Then he realised he was tied up. "What are you at man what's this all about?"

"Do you remember me asking you the same question about Kathie? Well unless she's returned safely those bales of drugs will not go where you want them to"

"Cormack don't do this they'll kill both of us."

"Stand up and get down to the galley." Cormack half lifted and dragged him to the galley and put him sitting down, he tied him to a chair and taped his mouth. He left him and went back to wheel duty he'd have twenty four straight hours wheel duty without any relief. He scanned the horizon and saw a couple of yachts and a freight ship, also coming towards him what looked like a cruise ship. I've got plenty of company now when I don't need it. He pondered where to drop these bales, in a quiet place also in shallow water where he won't be seen.

Trios reported to Amadeo there was no one came to the car in the two days. So he gave him the order to tell the car hire company where the car was and abandon the surveillance. Rolando reported from Matanzas that the yacht hadn't arrived there. So he was ordered to come back to Havana. Amadeo called them into his office, they were nervous having got no results, and feeling guilty as if they had somehow failed. Such was their fear of this ruthless man.

"They've given us the slip but they haven't got away they are surely headed for Georgetown in the Caymans. I want one of you to accompany me on a flight this evening to Georgetown." He looked at them both his good eye moving from one to the other and the other eye holding them in a fixed stare.

Showing fear was paramount to cowardice, so Rolando said. "I'll come with you sir, will we be there for long do I need to bring some changes of clothes?"

"We could be there depending on our success for a week so bring what you think necessary."

"I'll be at the airport."

Kathie asked Chantal to leave the wheel house and come below. She was confident and protective as she spoke. "Before we decide anything you better come and have that wound dressed, also I think there might be something to bathe those bruises to ease the soreness."

The first aid locker was well stocked and Kathie was well trained in combat field dressing. She dressed the nasty burn and put some ointment on the bruises. "Now Chantal that burn won't get septic I hope, we'll keep it looked at for the next couple of days until you can get proper medical attention."

"It feels better already the pain has gone from it."

Back in the chartroom they searched for a good place on the Cayman Islands to land, it would have to be night time and easy to get close inshore with this big launch.

Chantal was expert in reading charts, she picked out a spot on the North West of the main island. "There's Anchors point, and you see Spotters Bay, that's where I think we should land, it's a good sandy beach so we can get in close and won't have to swim too far."

"Yes that looks good and I presume you're a good swimmer?" Kathie volunteered with a smile.

"That I am and I love swimming, Emilie and I used to have great swimming races when we were at anchor in our lovely yacht."

"Now that we've decided where to get ashore we better set a course for the beach, and Chantal you work out at what speed we should do to get there in the dark. I'll leave you to it and I'm going below to do some more searching around and I'll cook up something to eat."

She went into the captain's saloon and took stock of the beautiful surroundings. The furniture was dark polished tropical hardwood, there was a large desk with green leather top, and carved leather cushioned arm chairs. She went to all the shelves and had a look at books and delicate ornaments, music C.D.s by the thousand, large music system and big flat television. She opened the mahogany doors revealing shelves with books, and one had some large carved cigar boxes full with her native Cuban cigars. The surprise was a safe and when she saw the door partly open she clucked her lips and thought sarcastically, 'how thrusting'. Opening the door the sight inside made her gasp, she pulled out one bundle and saw they were all one hundred U.S.A. Dollar notes. 'My god' she exclaimed as she took them out and placed them on the desk. They were marked twenty five thousand, and she counted thirty eight full bundles and one part one. Goodness nearly a million Dollars, she went to the desk and opened drawers. She took out books and papers, one book like a ledger had hand written entries. She scanned through it and on the last entry she saw Sea Gypsy and a sum of five thousand paid, and a small entry at the side, five on completion. 'The dirty bastard he was part of this whole set up, god I wonder how Cormack is faring? He could have orders to kill Cormack when the drugs were dropped off.' She opened the lap top on the desk, 'great' she thought 'I can email Cormack and tell him I'm safe.' To her disappointment she couldn't get into it as it had an encrypted password, she banged down the lid with frustration, 'blast'. She left the saloon and went through all the cabins, she found a good sized backpack and a lot of girls clothing. She pulled out what she thought herself and Chantal would need when they got ashore. She found some shoes, also girls, 'my god' she thought 'how many girls did these dirty bastards kill and abuse?' She packed all the clothes and shoes they'd need into some plastic bags she found in the store room. She also helped herself to the best of food. She packed all the dollars into plastic bags and put all into the backpack, now she was ready. She cooked up a sumptuous meal and opened a fine bottle of Chile wine. She called Chantal who put the craft on automatic steering, and they sat down to a delicious feast. After eating they walked the decks and looked around to see was there any craft nearby. It would be dark soon so what they had to do next would be better done as night fell.

Kathie looked at Chantal and thought she detected a little fear. "We must be sure what we are going to do is best for us both, and I hope you are fully in agreement."

Chantal's voice was timid. "Of course I am sure, it's just the thought of getting them up on deck and you know," she paused "throwing them into the sea."

"We have no choice and it's a fitting burial for them two brutal beasts."

"Of course you're right Kathie it's too good for them but we must be sure it's our secret and no one will ever know."

"Chantal, it will never go past our lips and we will have to stick to our story, that they let us off at the beach where we're going, and never tell even our own family."

"I am agreed to that, so on our lives, only we will ever know what happened to them." She took Kathie's hands and they shook on a pact and hugged.

"We better get them up on deck and have them ready to go when we decide the coast is clear." She caught Chantal by the hand and they walked to the door leading to the cabins. It took all their strength to pull and haul these two big stiff men onto the deck, and lay them by the door that opened for the gangway. They were both panting with the exertion. Kathie searched their pockets for anything that might identify them should their bodies be discovered. They had nothing on their person only tattoos that could identify them, "well nothing we can do about those things," she said as she pulled a shirt off one.

"I don't think we need worry unduly about anyone identifying them once there overboard." Said Chantal as she looked to the west and the sun's lower limb was sitting on the horizon, "I'll go to the wheel house and see are we all clear."

"Right" said Kathie leaning on the rail, "if we are clear stop the engines and shout down to me I'll do the rest."

Chantal shut down the engines and they came to stop on a low glassy swell. The crimson sphere spread a veil of purples into a cloudless sky and a gory river shone rippling on the calm sea.

"It's all clear." a shout from Chantal.

Kathie caught them feet first and tipped them over the side; she heard the splashes but didn't look. She closed the door and sat on the deck, her thoughts were in turmoil and the silence was eerie. How long she sat with her eyes closed, and her knees up to her chest with her arms around them, she couldn't be sure.

Chantal sat in the control room and said a prayer, her Catholic upbringing was in conflict with what she knew was justice.

A splash brought Kathie to reality and she stood up and looked over the side. The two bodies were a short distance from the launch, and then she saw the first fin circling and another coming up from underneath, a huge mouth catching a leg and pulling the body under. The body came back to the surface and another one grabbed at it with its huge jaws, then more and more fins and tails breaking the surface. It became a savage frenzy as they pulled them from limb to limb. One body disappeared under and then came back up, and an arm flailed upwards above the grotesque head as if waving to her. She turned away and hoped Chantal didn't see this, as it would show how her lovely friend Emilie may have suffered if she wasn't dead when she was thrown over.

She went to the controls and found Chantal sitting and murmuring to herself, she sat down alongside her and they both hugged and she tried to comfort Chantal. "It's all over now and we're lucky to be alive but we have a lot to do, what time will we be at the Cayman beach."

They stood up, "yes Kathie you're right we must get ourselves together. I worked out a course and at twenty knots we should be there just at sunset tomorrow." She put the throttle forward and set her back on course. "Now in about twenty four hours we'll be at our beach, and also there's a main road not far from where we land. It goes right round the island so we should be able to hitch a lift to Georgetown."

"Great stuff and I found some clothes and shoes and I have them in a back pack so we will look some bit respectable when we get ashore. I'll explain what I think we should do with this launch when we get off it.

Cormack scanned the chart looking for a likely place to dump the bales of drugs. He decided on Cayman Brac the small island, he picked out Goat Bay which he thought would suit as the water was shallow and it was easy to get in and out. He laid out a course and went back to the wheel and changed course, putting her on auto pilot he went below to feed himself and the captive Allen.

He put in the hours at the wheel and with a moderate breeze he made good time. It would be near midnight when they'd be off Goat Bay, he blind folded Allen so he couldn't see the lighthouse flash as he'd know exactly where they were. When he got into the bay he took G.P.S. readings and when he was happy with his position he threw the bales overboard. They sank straight down as they were weighted. He wrote down the co-ordinates in two separate places in the small chart room, as these would be his bargaining chip.

He set a course for Georgetown and arrived at seventeen hundred next day. He tied up at the same berth they had left from, he went below to Allen. "I'm going to untie you before I leave so you better co-operate for your own sake. I'll give you the co-ordinates of where I dropped the bales of drugs when Kathie is brought here safe and sound."

Allen was in shock, "please Cormack give me the co-ordinates now and I'll get Kathie back, you don't realise they will kill me and you'll never see Kathie again."

Cormack realised Allen was begging for his life but Kathie's life was all that concerned him now. He went to the locker and took out the paintings and security box. He packed all in a large back pack, as he was going to make a quick exit when he released Allen. He had rope ready and was practising his slip knot, he hoped it would work. "Come on up on deck" he caught him under the arms and helped him onto the deck. "Now you know what I'm going to do so for your own safety do as I say."

"Are you going to throw me into the dock with my hands tied behind my back?"

"Good guess, but I'll do my best to release you on your way in."

"What the fucks are you on about I'll drown tied like this."

"Shut up you miserable whining bastard only for Kathie's safety I would throw you in tied up." Cormack loosed the rope on his ankles so he could take them off easily. Then he made the slip knot on his wrists and took off the other rope. He opened the small door and dropped over the ladder, "right now are you ready Houdini, and I'll be in touch, I have your mobile phone number." He pushed him and as he went head first into the clear blue water he pulled the rope on his wrists and he was free. He could open the ankle ones now himself and climb back on board. Cormack was well gone when he climbed on board.

Chantal was at the controls as they approached Anchors Point, Kathie was down in the engine room preparing old cotton waste and rags used for cleaning down the engine. She inspected the diesel tank and tested its strength with a marlin spike; yes she knew she could easily puncture it. She went back up to Chantal and they were rounding Anchor Point into Spotters bay.

"We're nearly there" she excitedly said to Chantal.

Chantal eased back the throttle and they were cruising at five knots.

Kathie went over their plan again "you can bring her onto the beach; I have the ladder down so I'll get into the water and swim ashore with the back pack. Now when I come back you just turn her out to sea and put her on auto pilot. I'll do the business in the engine room and when I shout, ready, you push the throttle to half ahead and come down to the ladder."

Chantal was watching the depth sounder and they were now in very shallow water, it was important they didn't run aground as it would throw all their plans adrift.

Kathie was looking out into the clear night and could see the lights of passing cars on the highway not far from the beach.

"Kathie we've touched bottom" she stopped engines.

"I'm off" Kathie ran down to the main deck and with the back pack climbed down and into the water. She swam pulling the pack behind her and she was in the small breaking waves after a couple of minutes, then she touched bottom and walked up onto the sandy beach. She left the pack and looking out at the launch with all her lights out she was like a ghost ship silhouetted against a starry sky.

Back on board she went straight to the engine room and punctured five holes in the diesel tank with the marlin spike. She doused the rags and old cloths in the pouring liquid and set the fire. She watched from the door on deck for a few minutes and was happy with the blaze, the gas tanks weren't far away from the fire. She ran out to the ladder "right Chantal we're ready."

Chantal had the yacht facing out to sea. She put the throttle on half speed. She was down at the ladder in less than a minute and both jumped into the warm water. They were a little farther out now so they started swimming looking at one another in the glooming light, smiling and happy.

"Chantal look" they both turned to look at the fiery spectre sailing away, "she's burning well, oh look there a big flame now."

"God Kathie I hope she sinks." Chantal said with a wry smile.

"I'm sure she will, look she's burning really well now." Kathie's voice was animated, with a job well done.

As they both watched in awe at the bright flaming pyre there was an explosion, and a bright yellow crimson tinted flame lit up the sky. As quick as it happened it disappeared.

Kathie put her hand over to Chantal and they clasped hands, they spoke almost together, "she's gone."

As they swam slowly to the beach Chantal felt as though this fiery demise had somehow cleansed her soul and body of the dark evil she had endured.

Kathie was happy at the hope of a new beginning, if only she knew if Cormack was safe and they could find one another.

They lay on their backs on soft sand gazing up at the stars, each with their own thoughts. Kathie broke the spell "come on we must get off this beach someone could have seen that fire and come to explore if there are survivors around."

They changed clothes and with the back pack headed up onto the roadway.

Cormack got a taxi to the Treasure Island Resort and booked a room. He took out his lap top and tried his mail hoping against hope Kathie might have got access to a computer, no such luck he began to fear the worst. He didn't want to think about that, he still had the co-ordinates as a weapon for her safety. He needed sleep after almost twenty four hours on his feet. He lay on the bed and like a dark curtain sliding over his being he fell into a relaxed slumber. He woke sometime during the night and seeing it was dark, fell back into the world of Morpheus.

He felt refreshed after showering and enjoying a big breakfast, now to decide what to do. How was he going to go about contacting Allen without giving his own whereabouts away, and have these Columbian drug gangsters abduct and torture him. Knowing if he revealed the position of the drugs they'd surely kill him. He was thinking about the police but couldn't see that they could do much as Kathie could be hundreds of miles out to sea. He went and purchased a pair of dark glasses and a panama hat, not much of a disguise but maybe a help. He walked the harbour and looked out at Sea Gypsy silent at her mooring. He watched from a distance to see was there any activity of people coming or going on board. He sat on a bench reading a daily paper for over an hour and still no sign of anyone, not even Allen coming on deck. An English man and his wife came and sat on the bench and engaged him in frivolous conversation. This was the first day of their holiday and although they were late sixties he thought 'they acted like honeymooners.' He bade them enjoy their holiday and got up to leave, he saw Allen come out and walk around the deck, 'good at least he's still around' he thought. He walked on keeping the yacht in sight, two men walked along the quayside and stopped at the Sea Gypsy, one stood watch while the other went on board. 'My god' he thought 'they must be the Columbians they've searched and couldn't find the drugs.' He stood well out of sight and now he feared for Allen's safety. He couldn't go to his assistance, but sure enough he was one of them anyway. The fellow standing watch went on board and down into the cabin, he hoped this altercation might persuade them to give Kathie back. Allen couldn't do anything so they must realise it was useless trying to get information he hadn't got. He didn't realise these people didn't think like that.

Two men came walking up towards the yacht, they looked like tourists they both wore dark glasses and hats. My god they were going on board, it was turning out to be a right party. If only he could get closer to try and see what was going on, but it was too dangerous.

Something was happening, the first two came on deck and one of the other fellows started remonstrating with them, he pushed one of them and he nearly fell overboard. They left and walked up the quay looking back to see if they were being followed, the other two went below deck and must be talking with Allen. Which of them were the Columbians it was getting a little complicated now, and he couldn't go too close in fear of being recognised.

Approximately five minutes passed before the two emerged on deck and made a quick exit walking very fast up the quay. Cormack was undecided whether to go on board and speak to Allen. He held up his paper and glanced over the top watching to see would Allen appear on deck. Then he heard the siren of an ambulance, it drove fast down the quay and stopped at the Sea Gypsy. My God I wonder have they beaten him or maybe killed him. Then he saw a stretcher being carried up on deck and into the ambulance. This is getting very serious I will have to be careful, they know now I have the co-ordinates of their drugs.

Kathie and Chantal walked the highway hoping for a car to give them a lift to Georgetown. They walked slowly taking turns to carry the back pack when a pickup truck stopped and the driver asked where were they going?

"We want to get to the Treasure Island Resort."

"Well girls I'm not going that far but there's a small private house hotel just a mile up the road if you'd fancy staying there the night."

Chantal looked at Kathie and she was anxious to get off this lonely road, a fear still lurked behind those dark brown eyes. "I think we should stay there till morning."

"Yes we'll go to this small hotel do you mind taking us there?" asked Kathie.

"Come on," he said "get in the two of you and I'll have you there in a few minutes."

They were happy to be welcomed into a bright and comfortable house, and after some delicious local pastries and tea they retired to their room for a well deserved night's sleep.

Next morning Kathie was apprehensive about handing the lady of the house a hundred dollar bill but she explained she brought these dollars with her as they were acceptable in most countries. They had no problem and when their taxi called it took them to Treasure Island Resort.

Kathie was planning how best she could get Chantal safely home to France, and also continue with her own problem of finding Cormack if he was still alive. "Chantal here's some of the Cayman money the lady gave me in change, now will you go to the French Consul here and get a passport? They'll ask you a lot of questions so just tell them you were let ashore on the beach, and they can phone your father to confirm all."

"Yes I'll do that, I do want to speak to my parents, it would be better get the Consul to do that for me, and also arrange a flight home."

"When you finish at the Consul go to some bank and open an account, I'll tell you all about that when you come back."

Chantal left and Kathie was deciding what to do with all this money. She took what she needed for herself and brought the pack to reception and asked could they put it in their safe. She felt safer now but was in limbo without a passport if she couldn't locate Cormack. She decided to go to a computer and send an email to him, and she checked and he hadn't sent her one. He probably believed she had been killed or if not still a sex slave on that launch.

She left the hotel and went to buy some new clothes and a pair of dark glasses and a hat to disguise her face, to be on the side of caution. She walked to the marina and was elated to see the Sea Gypsy. At least she could go there and question Allen if Cormack didn't turn up.

Cormack decided he would have to go see what condition Allen was in, if he was dead he had no idea how to go about getting Kathie back. He walked the distance to the only hospital and enquired at reception could he see the man who was brought in by ambulance. He had to answer a lot of probing questions, and was told he could only see him for a few minutes as he was being prepared for surgery.

He wasn't expecting the sight of what he saw, he was bandaged around his head and his left arm was strapped up, his lips and eyes were swollen dark black and blue. He sat beside the bed, "Allen how are you feeling?" A stupid question he realised looking at his condition.

He turned to see who was there and fear was spread across his terrified face. "They would have killed me only for the two Cuban fellows came along."

"Those two fellows were Cuban? I saw them going on board after the Columbians."

"Yes they were looking for you and Kathie."

'Christ,' Cormack thought when he looked at Allen's hands, his finger nails on one hand were gone and the tops were a bloody mess. "What did the Cuban fellows want to know about us?"

"You give me the co-ordinates and I'll tell you, if you don't give them to me they'll kill me next time."

Cormack was in a quandary, he'd lose the bargaining chip for Kathie's return if he gave them. "I'll give you one co-ordinate when you tell me what did that Cuban fellow want, and what did he look like? I'll give the other one when Kathie is safe."

Allen closed his eyes, the pain relieving injection wasn't sufficient, he obviously needed another one.

"Do you want me to call a nurse to give you more pain relieving injections?"

"They won't give me any more until after the operation, the Cuban fellow had a scar over his right eye it was staring and half closed."

"What did he say?"

"Give me the co-ordinate and I'll tell you."

"Ok I'll give you one and when Kathie is safe I'll phone you with the other."

"Please give them both to me."

"What did the Columbians say when you asked about Kathie?"

"They said they didn't know but will try to find where they put them ashore."

"What did the Cuban want?"

"I told him Kathie was taken so he was going to shoot the Columbian fellow. Then he asked were you gone ashore and what luggage you had with you."

"What did you tell him?"

"You had a backpack and I didn't see what was in it."

"Right your first co-ordinate in on page 100 of the nautical almanac in the chart room. If you get some news of Kathie I'll phone and tell you where to find the second one." He got up to leave as the nurses came to bring him down to the operating theatre. He passed two policemen coming up the corridor turning into his ward. He moved quickly as they might want to question him if they realised he knew Allen.

Chantal arrived back at the hotel room and was greeted by Kathie who was unpacking her purchases.

"Well how did you get on at the Consul?"

"Great they gave me a temporary passport and booked a flight to Paris this evening. They phoned my parents and I spoke to them both, I couldn't describe their happiness and mine, oh Kathie I'll ever be so grateful to you."

They hugged and cried until all the pent up emotion had abated between them.

"Chantal I must tell you I got a lot of money from the safe on the launch and its down in the hotel safe. Now I'm going to give you a share and I want you to go and lodge it in that bank account you opened."

"Kathie there's no need for you to give me money you see my father is very wealthy and I am their only child."

"Oh my god Chantal you are all they have in this world."

"Yes I am all their life."

Kathie picked up a shopping bag and they went to the lobby, she got her back pack and took out packets of the dollars and put them into the bag. "Now Chantal just something to spoil yourself with, can you come over here to this computer. I want you to send me an email and here's my address, so I will not lose touch with you."

She sat and wrote to Kathie and pressed send, "please don't read it till later or we'll both cry again."

Chantal left on her journey home and thoughts of telling her parents about her ordeal at the hands of the Columbian monsters was causing her small panic attacks. How could she tell Emilie's family about what happened to her?

Kathie went to her inbox and saw Chantal's message but decided to open it later, no message from Cormack so she decided to write to him.

'Cormack I have arrived in Cayman and am staying in room forty seven at Treasure Island Resort, hope you have made it safely. I will tell you all when we meet. Love Kathie.'

CHAPTER 19

Cormack made his way back to the hotel and his thoughts were in a quandary, if he didn't give Allen the second co-ordinate and they killed him how then could he go about getting Kathie back safely. He would have to be vigilant as Amadeo was out there with one of his henchmen looking for either Kathie or him.

He showered and tried to think straight, he sat with a towel wrapped round his waist and took out the laptop. Maybe some news from somebody, home seemed a long way off now. It was only three weeks but seemed like a lifetime and a different world. He almost shouted when he saw the email from Kathie, room forty seven. He jumped up and pulled on some clothes and ran down the corridor to room forty seven. He knocked on the door and couldn't contain his joy and relief as he waited.

"Who's there?"

He was breathless and overcome with emotion just to hear her voice.

"Kathie it's me Cormack."

She opened the door and he almost fell into her arms.

He looked at her to be sure she was his Kathie. "God Kathie I thought I might never see you again, what happened?"

She pulled him over and they sat on the bed. She related the full story including Chantal and the money she said she stole from the safe, but lied about killing the men and burning the boat.

"I must phone Allen now with the other co-ordinate and that should get them off our back. Kathie what do you think Amadeo would try to do if he did catch up with you?"

"He might try to get me back to Cuba maybe by yacht, the same way we came here, or get me to someplace where he could torture me and make me hand over the security box."

"Well they are both safe in the Bank H.S.B.C. 68 West Bay Street, so if you want we could go there now and get them out?" He picked up the phone and dialled Allen's mobile, he had committed the number to memory. It took a while before he answered, "Allen is that you this is Cormack how are you now?" He made a face to Kathie trying to relay the bad news. "What did this Cuban fellow with the scar want from you?" a pause! "To know if I had visited you. Well I won't be visiting you and now here is the second co-ordinate. Pull out the small drawer left side over the chart table turn it over it's on the underside." He put down the phone, "well Kathie you heard that, Amadeo is very serious about finding anyone of us, especially you."

"I know," she said "he is a dangerous man and he's not going to give up, he's getting information and we'll have a job to get clear of him." She kissed him full on the lips. "I missed you so much Cormack and I want you to love me now and take all the pain away."

He slowly unbuttoned her blouse and she removed her bra, standing up she slipped down her skirt and pants, he was standing naked and unashamedly erect. Their lovemaking was slowly deliberate and teasing. The scent and taste of her erogenous region was like nectar, and when she climaxed she screamed gripping his hair and holding his head to her open rose petals. They lay exhausted and silent until a knock on the door brought them to reality. She stood out and pulled on a gown, she asked at the door, "who's there?"

"Room attendant, if it's not convenient I'll come back."

"Yes please do come back later." She was back in her fugitive skin again, "Cormack we will have to make plans. That was wonderful," she provocatively put her hand between her legs and lifting a damp palm blew him a kiss. He joined her in the shower and strictly no touching she commanded, and when both were back in their attire she outlined what was going to be their next move.

"Have you got my passport?"

"Yes it's over in my luggage what little I have."

"Right we must go to the bank and I will open an account and you will also open one. I will have to lodge that money and get rid of it, so you can take a part of it and lodge it to your account. Then we can decide what to do about the security box and paintings. Now I'm going to book a flight for us to London, maybe we can get one in the morning."

"Do you really want to leave that soon? It's wonderful here."

She threw her arms around him, "what am I going to do with you, my romantic Irishman, it won't be wonderful if Amadeo gets sight of us and he may even be watching the airport as it is."

"Okay come on I'll get our two passports and we'll go to the bank, and then book our flights."

The flight was for noon next day and with the money safely away in the bank and Cormack richer than ever before in his life, things didn't look so bleak. She insisted the safety box and paintings be put in her name, and when they asked for a next of kin she didn't mention Cormack but, put the name of some relative. He didn't ask who.

They were leaving the hotel and Cormack went to pay the bill for them both, she was annoyed when she came down behind him. She scolded him. "You shouldn't have paid for us both I want to be an independent woman now."

He smiled at her, "you are very independent, I was only being a gentleman."

"Well I'm sorry as I haven't met many of your kind I appreciate what you've done."

She went to see had the taxi arrived and Cormack noticed on her bill a phone call lasting ten minutes to Teheran in Iran. He crushed the bills and threw them in the litter bin.

"Come on," she called, "the taxi is here."

He jumped in and she threw herself over on him and kissed him full on the lips, "sorry for being cross with you but now we are heading for freedom, where is my hotel bill?"

"I threw it in the litter bin I didn't think you'd want it." He said hesitantly.

She closed her eyes and sighed. "No I don't this whole business is just so strange, give me time to adjust."

The flight landed at Heathrow Airport and a taxi drove them to the Kensington Thistle Gardens Hotel.

"My, my, Kathie this is luxury I'm only a poor Irish lad and not used to this affluent life style." as he looked around the opulent furnished room.

"I'm only a poor Cuban girl and a fugitive at that, and not used to this life style but could easily adapt. I want to spoil you Cormack, so now ready yourself and come on down to dinner."

Back in their room the cuisine and luxurious suite was an aphrodisiac, and their nakedness lying together was blissfully magic, Cormack slept like a newborn.

He awoke and heard Kathie in the shower, he went to the bathroom and she came out drying herself. "Oh I didn't mean to wake you. I couldn't sleep so I thought I might go for a walk in the beautiful park before breakfast."

Cormack looked out the window and the view over Hyde Park was stunning on this summer morning. She cajoled with him pushing him onto the bed. "Have a little sleep and I'll be back for breakfast."

He went to the bathroom and while wondering why Kathie was so excited, he heard the door close and he dressed quickly. He noticed her small bag was gone. He ran to the elevator and was at the front door in minutes.

Outside he saw her cross the road and go into the park carrying her small bag. He followed out of sight and could see she was looking for someone as she'd stop and look around. Then he saw him, well dressed handsome, a dark tanned man with black hair and moustache. She walked up to him and they exchanged words. He pointed to a woman wearing Muslim clothing her face covered, only her eyes showing. She had a young fair haired boy about four years held by the hand. Kathie ran to the child calling his name Jacob, and bending down she kissed and hugged him. The child knew her as he threw his little arms around her neck. Cormack stood transfixed, now he realised she must be married probably to this dark haired man. This man ordered the woman to take the child and ordered Kathie to follow her. As they walked to a gate where a big limousine waited for them Cormack walked over to the man.

He confronted this stranger. "I've been friendly with Kathie and helped her to get out of Cuba and now she goes away without even a goodbye."

He turned to Cormack with a look of distain, "so you're the romantic Irishman she used to break the Castro shackles, and now she comes to her family, I her husband, and her child. You should take my advice now and go home, your little romance and adventure is over. Don't meddle in affairs that don't concern you as you are way out of your depth. You are a young man with plenty of potential to prosper and find new women, so if you value life go now and forget all this."

Cormack was stunned and as he turned away he noticed the bulge behind his left hip, a gun no doubt. He looked back to see could he get a last glimpse of Kathie as the man got into the car. He was shattered as he saw the car drive away, I only wanted an 'auld bed in Havana' and look where it got me, another broken heart. Yes he thought the word she uttered in her sleep 'Jacob' a mother's love knows no bounds. He sat on a park bench deciding what to do next, it seemed home would be his only option.

The big car pulled into the reserved park of The Athenaeum Hotel. She had a separate room from Jacob his nanny and husband Frederico, as he knew she would not leave without Jacob.

He came into her room smiling and welcoming. "Great to have the family back together again, pity I couldn't persuade the authorities to let you join me in Teheran but now that you're here I'm sure they'll agree. We have a flight booked for this afternoon you'll love Teheran, and Mahvash, Jacob's nanny, she is so good to him really a second mother."

"You must realise that they could send me back to Cuba to stand trial for illegally leaving. You expect Amadeo and yourself to get your hands on my family's wealth. Will you torture me to tell you where the security box is hidden? Then as next of kin when I'm dispatched you'll legally inherit everything."

"You have a fertile imagination I will not touch a hair on your head, and if the authorities force you to go back to Cuba to stand trial, I will have to look after Jacob. Of course your family's wealth is rightfully his."

"What did you tell Amadeo and what arrangement have you with him?"

"You realise Kathie if you disappear everything goes to Jacob, legally that is, now make yourself comfortable as we leave for the airport in an hour's time. Don't want to miss our flight, Teheran awaits you."

She could escape but would have to leave Jacob, and to get him out of Teheran would be almost impossible. She would have to think of something, she had to be careful that small gun he carried behind his hip he would surely use if he was pushed.

Amadeo had the good news from Frederico that Kathie was in his custody and on their way to Teheran. "You won't have too long to wait until you have her back in Havana where she belongs." He gloated, laughingly.

Cormack back at the hotel booked an evening flight to Dublin, it seemed the carousel had stopped and he had to get off. He couldn't believe she could go without a word of goodbye, he took out his lap top and when he flipped it open a written note fell out.

"Cormack forgive me but I will explain all, keep email open will need your help today, don't forsake me I need you now, Love Kathie."
My god she is in danger I will have to keep my in mail open she's going to try to escape with Jacob. That man her husband is armed and could kill her or the child, should I tell the police?

The nanny Mahvash and Frederico came to her room with Jacob they sat while she spoke to the child and tried to rekindle some of the memories they had, it was only eight months but a child's memory is fragile. She was disappointed when he told her about Mahvash and how she brings him to school and takes him to play in the park.

"Now Jacob," Frederico catching him by the hand, "let's go with Mahavash we have to get ready for our flight back home."

They left her and she looked around to see was there anything she could use as a weapon, she was desperate now. She opened a desk top and there was a computer, she got to her mail box and saw where Cormack had got her letter. She wrote to him hurriedly to say she would meet him in Hyde Park same place. She was sending her love when Frederico walked in behind her.

"Didn't realise you had a social network contact, new for you Cuban girl." He snarled.

She clicked send, and he struck her across the face knocking her to the floor. He stood over her prone body looking for a flicker of eye movement. A little panic caught him as she was so lifeless; he bent down to feel the pulse in her neck. She felt the cool fingers and opening her eyes slightly she struck like a cobra, two fingers into his eyes. He fell back with a scream and sightless, she struck him at the base of his neck and he collapsed. "Really thought you knew me better" she said. She looked around for something to tie him, yes her under ware, a pants was okay for a gag and she thought the scent and taste might ease the pain and bring back happier memories. Her stockings were for hands and feet, great to thrust up nice and tight, she gathered her bag and left.

'Now this Iranian hag shouldn't be too much trouble,' she thought. The door was open and she walked in, Jacob was playing a game on his consul. She heard the shower in the bedroom, walking in she could see the figure through the frosted glass. As she approached the figure came out dripping wet and put her hand out for a small towel. Kathie was shocked at what she saw and she exclaimed "AH."

The naked woman screamed and pulled a large towel wrapping it around her.

"What do you want you shouldn't see me like this," she began to sob.

Kathie said "I am very sorry to surprise you like this but I am taking Jacob with me now."

"But you can't, Mr Frederico your husband will be very angry."

"What happened to your body those scars are horrific."

She had burn scars from below her right knee right up her body to just under her right ear.

"I was being married to an Iraqi man and our wedding was in Iraq in his home town. He was Sunni Muslim and I am Shiite Muslim so someone didn't like our union and they planted a bomb at the wedding reception, killing twenty five including my husband and both our parents. I can never let anyone see my ugly body again and I was so grateful to be a nanny to your Jacob. I love him so much but I'm glad if you can take him back again you are his mother."

Kathie told her about Frederico and they decided to tie her up, as she couldn't be implicit in the taking of Jacob. They used some scarves and tied her, laying her on the bed and covering her with a sheet. Kathie went and kissed Mahavash on the cheek and thanked her for looking after Jacob. "I will be in touch with you when this is all sorted out."

Out in the lounge she emailed Cormack and told him to be in the Park in ten minutes. She gathered up Jacob's little belongings and they left. She told reception to take tea to her room in one hour. She thought 'it would then be time to release the hostages.'

She walked with Jacob and holding his little hand she felt for the first time since he was taken by his father, that she was a mother again. She kept looking down at him to be sure he was still there walking along with his little steps.

"Mammy when will we see nanny again, there was something I forgot to tell her, she must feed Jogo for me when I'm gone."

"Who's Jogo?"

"He's my pet rabbit and he'll be hungry."

"Don't worry she'll feed Jogo for you. "

"Kathie, Kathie," he was running now and was a little out of breath, they hugged and little Jacob looked on in dismay.

"Jacob this is our good friend Cormack, he helped Mammy come here to get you."

"Hello Cormack, you a good man to help my Mammy."

"Yes Jacob you will be with your Mammy now."

"Cormack we have to get away from here immediately."

"Where should we go to? Kathie your eye is bruised and your face, did you fall?"

"No I didn't I had a run in with you know who, he caught me sending you the email."

"We better get something cold to put on that."

"I have some makeup that will cover it and take the bad look away. You needn't feel embarrassed if you think people are looking at you and wondering the worst." She kissed him on the cheek and pinched his bottom.

CHAPTER 20

Twilight was mystic as they arrived at Cormack's apartment, and Kathie marvelled at the light change as the sun sank over the Dublin Mountains. Jacob like all children enjoyed the adventure and soon fell asleep in his mother's arms; she tucked him into bed with a big kiss. Her joy and appreciation for this day that often seemed so elusive and unattainable was radiant and palpable as she climbed onto Cormack's knee, she threw her arms around him.

"Now my dear I have so much to tell you and where to start, I'm sorry I didn't tell you I was married as I thought you would just leave me. My husband Frederico is a nuclear physicist, and when he was loaned to Iran for their nuclear programme, I was supposed to accompany him and of course Jacob. Then all changed, and I was refused a passport. I was then informed I could not leave the country until all financial affairs concerning my family were cleared by the security department. I could not believe how this could have arisen after so many years, and I began to piece together how they got their information. The only one who knew about the security box and its contents was Frederico. Then Amadeo came on the scene and I realised that between them they were trying to wrest the information from me. How much of Amadeo's investigation is official and how much personal is debatable."

"Kathie I thought when you left the Hotel I had lost you forever."

"I'm so sorry about that but I didn't want you to get involved with Frederico as he could be armed and dangerous. I had to thrust your love for me and my love for you that we'd overcome that trauma." She smiled and putting out her tongue she poked it between his lips, "we have haven't we?"

He kissed her, their tongues probing and passions arousing, "Kathie I love you."

She took him by the hand and led him to the big double bed, "tonight is for love, tomorrow for plans."

Having undressed and standing naked together he pulled her onto the bed, "I couldn't agree more."

They spent a leisurely day confident of their security walking the streets of Dun Laoighaire and of course the beautiful East Pier. They sat in the warm bright sun watching the yachts sailing round the harbour and the larger ones heading out to the Irish Sea. Looking at one of these Cormack remarked. "That one reminds me of Sea Gypsy."

With a wry expression she said, "I want to forget Sea Gypsy and our treacherous Captain Allen who got us into the clutches of those Columbians."

"Yes of course you're right it was a terrible ordeal for you, hope we'll never hear from them again."

"I'd say not, we will have to try and forget it happened and be thankful we got out of it with our lives."

"Of course you're right Kathie."

Jacob was playing with a football and she turned to Cormack, "look how happy he is. Now we will have to find a good safe place for him for about a week while we retrieve the information from that security box in Cayman, and then go to Switzerland to sort out our finances."

"I have a sister just finished college and hasn't got work yet she could look after him, she lives in Galway with my parents."

"Cormack that sounds just fine! Where is Galway?"

"Oh sorry it's a county on the west coast, a nice rural area about two hours drive; I have a car so no problem. My parents will just love you."

"Really sounds wonderful, when will we go?"

Frederico was in hospital in Teheran with damaged eyes, his phone call to Amadeo who was back in Havana relayed the news she had gotten away. "I've no doubt she has taken up with that meddling Irishman, and would say they are in his home place."

Amadeo was devastated, "I was confident it was Teheran and job done. I suppose I can travel to Dublin and do some investigation if I get the okay from the chief here. It should be easy to track them down in that small country."

"Yes I believe you should be able to find them and arrest her for the crimes in Cuba, no need to take her back if you can get her alone, she'll talk if you have the child."

Amadeo's voice was harsh and unforgiving, "It sounds easy but you had it all sown up and lost her, how could you have been so careless knowing her capabilities?"

"I was too thrusting I thought she was hurt."

"Do you know if she had the security box with her, or maybe they left it in Georgetown?"

"I don't know but she had little or no baggage so I would imagine she hadn't it in England."

"Doing this type of job in another country could be troublesome, I will decide if it's going to be possible. Good Bye." He slammed down the phone and cursed under his breath, 'educated idiot, no end force.'

The drive across the Irish countryside was idyllic on a bright summer's day. Kathie fell in love with the country and its fresh green fields and hills. The few people they met in stop offs in the small towns for refreshments reminded her of Cuba, when growing up as a child. Cormack's home was situated in West Galway with a view out over the Atlantic. She and Jacob were warmly welcomed by Cormack's mother Alice and his sister Mary.

Alice showed them to their rooms, and Cormack had to tell Kathie that his mother would not condone them sleeping in the same room as they were not married.

She laughed, "I didn't think such strict moral rules still existed, but don't get me wrong I respect and also love it."

"I am back in my old room with my teenage toys and books and posters, I'll show you later, but we have to behave ourselves when mother is around. Tell me Kathie, why have you to go so soon to get the security box and then go to Switzerland?"

She sat on the bed and caught his hand and seated him alongside her, "if anything should happen to me all the property and wealth would automatically go to Frederico in thrust for Jacob. Now Amadeo and Frederico could do as they wished with their new found wealth. But if I have it all signed over to me then they know I am so wealthy I can employ personal body guards and security for Jacob and me. Also I will have to divorce Frederico as soon as possible so they are going nowhere, but I have to move quickly."

"Will you leave Jacob here while we go on this mission?"

"Yes! Is it possible for Alice to look after Jacob for maybe a week or a little longer?"

"We can talk to her about it, she has Mary who has qualified from college but has no job yet, so between them I'm sure it would be a labour of love."

Kathie was so reluctant to leave Jacob after having him for such a short time. She sat and explained as best you can to a small child, but he was happy around Mary and Alice, so she was happy he would be well taken care of.

They left early next morning to drive to Shannon Airport for the first leg of their flight.

"Cormack I didn't meet your Dad, and I didn't like to ask."

"I should have told you his job takes him away quite often as he's an engineer control manager for an American Company based in Dublin. His line of work takes him to countries around the world for short periods of time, but on the plus side he gets long periods of leave and can work from home."

"So Mary is company for Alice when your Dad is away?"

"Yes but for how long as she's anxious to get a job and be independent, just like us all I suppose. When you get out into the big world you just never know what's round the next corner." He looked out the window of the plane and could see the Atlantic through the broken cloud. He caught Kathie's hand and squeezed it, "just look at me now, and I was only looking for 'an auld bed in Havana.'"

They both laughed out loud.

"And I came with the auld bed and just look at us now, I love you so much."

As they landed in Georgetown they looked over the twinkling lights and the silhouetted palm trees against the mauve and purple sky. They were happy to retire to their hotel room and a comfortable bed.

Amadeo reported to his seniors about Frederico and how he was injured by his wife, and how she was wanted for an unprovoked attack on a man in Cuba, and stabbing him. He emphasised how much would be lost to the Cuban government if Frederico couldn't continue his work in Iran on the nuclear programme, as his sight was so badly impaired. The money paid for his services was huge and badly needed in the present time of drying up funds from Russia. He said she was wanted back in Havana to get her finances in order, as she was in control of huge resources that should have gone to the Cuban government. His senior was in agreement about getting this woman back to Cuba but working in a foreign country was going to make it difficult. He consulted with his two colleagues and when all three agreed he took Amadeo into his private office. "Sit now and we'll go through this in more detail."

Amadeo seated himself across the desk from his elder master and spoke in a conspiratorial tone, "I have information from her husband about wealth that is in oil shares and also property in Europe and cash in some Swiss Bank, also precious stones. All this is concealed in a security box now believed out of the country. If I can arrest her I can take her back here and she will give over to the Cuban government what is theirs. "

His senior spoke in measured tone. "How do you intend to get her out of say Ireland if that is where she is?"

"I will get her on a yacht which shouldn't be too difficult; also her young son may come in useful if I can get him away from her, she will do as she's told then."

"You know you will be working as an independent agent when you arrive in Ireland. The Cuban government will not help you or admit they know you if you are arrested by the Irish police."

"I understand but I will need the help of the Cuban Consul in Dublin to get established and find my contact, we have a contact in Dublin I believe?"

"Yes we have and you will get the name from the Dublin Consul, but leave there as soon as you get this information and funds. Don't be seen or don't be in touch with them after that. Understand that clearly as they will be under orders to say they don't know you."

"I am prepared to work under those conditions and I believe I can be successful."

His senior stood up and shook hands with him, "I wish you luck and I hope to see you back here with this captive, I will look forward to interrogating her myself."

The H.S.B.C. Bank gave Kathie and Cormack a private room to open the security box. It was laid on a polished wooden desk and they both looked at it and then at one another. The atmosphere was like as if you were going to rub the magic lantern, and this famous genie would appear. The combination figures were dull and the lock itself seemed to be seized with grit and dust. Kathie took out a white handkerchief and wiped the face of the lock. She put the handkerchief under Cormack's chin, "spit on that." She cleaned the lock and now you could see the figures clearly. "Good spit, now the part we've been waiting for."

Cormack sat close to her and could feel her trembling; he caught her hand and held it. "You're shaking, call out the numbers or have you got them written down someplace."

She pulled her hand away, "I must do this now, I have the numbers in here," tapping her head.

She spoke to herself and moved the dial, it wouldn't move at first but Cormack tapped it with a hardwood ashtray and it did the trick.

She spoke the numbers as she turned the dial and after the fifth one she stopped. A small lever alongside the dial was waiting to be pushed down. They both looked at one another. She put her hand on the little lever and pressed down and couldn't believe her eyes, as it worked. She spoke to Cormack, "I give you the honour of opening it."

The little hinges squeaked as the lid was lifted and both stared into the treasure chest with a gaze of wonderment. She lifted the contents out one by one. The precious stones were first to be assessed, a diamond studded tiara with four very large diamonds and two large emeralds. Two solitaire diamond rings with blue tinted stones as big as small bird eggs. Then a black leather pouch containing a couple of hundred gold sovereigns and another pouch containing diamonds, all these she laid on the desk. She took a deep breath as if this was some kind of trick that was being played on them.

"Cormack" she threw her arms around him, "is this real or will I wake up."

"Kathie this is your family's life savings for a hundred years, and you deserve all of it, and Jacob, after all you suffered to get what is rightfully yours."

Her voice was trembling. "You are so calm and down to earth but yes you're so right, we must look through all these papers next."

The papers were wrapped in chamois leather and sealed with wax. She broke the brittle wax and pulled out the papers. They were surprised to see them in such good condition, the deeds to the plantation in Cuba, the deeds to the estate in Eastern Europe, and oil shares which they could make out as issued in nineteen twenty two, there was two million of these five cent shares. The numbers to Swiss bank accounts were written in very heavy indelible ink on parchment, with the bank address in Zurich. She gathered all the papers and put them together, "we will have to leave the precious stones and jewellery and sovereigns here in a safe deposit box we couldn't chance bringing that stuff through customs."

"Yes you're right;" Cormack rang a bell for someone to come into them.

The bank manager came in and asked, "Everything okay can I help you?"He was staring at the diamonds, "what will you do with all those precious stones?"

Cormack looked at Kathie; she nodded to give him permission to make the arrangements. "We want to put them back in a safety deposit box and could you give us some heavy leather case to carry the paper work. Also I want to bring the paintings which are in the deposit box to a proper art storage facility. I believe they should be stretched out not rolled."

The bank manager thanked them for their business and gave them an address where to store the paintings and also get an evaluation on them.

The art dealer had secure storage and also could ship art around the world, so if, and when they wanted he would ship them to Europe. Happy with their morning's work they went back to the hotel and booked a flight to Zurich. The flight was mid afternoon next day so Kathie was happy she could be back with Jacob soon.

Amadeo arrived in Dublin and a visit to the Cuban Consul was his first stop. The senior person was somewhat taken aback at the audacity of this man to attempt to arrest a Cuban citizen in a foreign country. "I can tell you we will be of no help if you get yourself involved with the Irish Garda. You must remember we have excellent relations here in this country, and we cannot have that jeopardised or compromised in any way. "

Amadeo was visibly uncomfortable, "I can assure you I will not put you or our country in any compromising position."

The Consul handed him an envelope, "here are funds and the person who is to be your contact. Remember just a little advice you may get the impression these people are easy going and might be a pushover for what you intend to do, but don't underestimate them. Or be it at your peril." He stood up and shook hands with Amadeo, "I wish you every success."

"Thank you I'm confident of success, I know this person and her weaknesses."

He met his contact in Bewley's Cafe in Grafton Street next morning. He knew from speaking on the phone it was a woman, he wasn't too pleased as he never worked with a woman before. He knew her from the arranged colour scarf and cotton top, she recognised him from the description given her. She sat opposite him at a table for two and introduced herself, she already knew his name so formality was waived.

"Pleased to meet you call me, Angela." She spoke with a well educated British accent.

He was a little surprised at her beauty; she was fair skinned with a mane of beautiful red auburn hair. Her green eyes were mesmeric and when she spoke her ample ruby lips opened on white even pearly teeth. His observation of her was professional, he guessed her age at about thirty. He also took note of the wedding finger with its thick gold band and the sparkling solitaire diamond ring.

"Angela I have the name and address of a man here I want you to find out as much as possible about him, and if he has a woman and a young boy aged about four years living with him? The woman is blonde and fair skinned but she is a Cuban national. I will meet you here tomorrow at the same time, if that is suitable?"

She chewed a mouthful of a cream and strawberry filled croissant, her sensuous lips moving as if caressing the delicate confection. Amadeo wondered 'how could such a beautiful porcelain creature be a secret agent.' He handed her a slip of paper with Cormack's Dublin apartment address on it, "I may want to hire a car and if so could you recommend a reliable company?"

She took a drink of coffee and wiping her mouth with a napkin leaned over the table, "a car hire will have to be in your own name but otherwise it shouldn't be a problem." She stood up and flaunted her hour glass figure with a little tug on her tight skirt. "Enjoy your day and I will have news for you tomorrow."

He put on his dark glasses and left, he disappeared among the shuffling Diaspora of morning Grafton Street.

Switzerland from the skies was a most magnificent sight and Kathie turned to Cormack and got him to lean across her to look out the window. "I have a feeling of coming home; those mountains and valleys seem to be calling to me. Tell me am I being silly how could I be affected like that?"

He could taste her breath and feel her heart race as she held him to her, both faces against the small window. "Your whole being senses something you cannot understand, this is your primeval place on earth and for a hundred thousand years your ancestors lived around here."

"That sounds wonderful even if it may not be true I would like to believe it, oh I'd love to sing out loud now a song from the *Sound of Music*. I feel so happy and silly like a teenager on her first date."

Cormack gave her a peck on the cheek and sat back into his seat, "your happiness is contagious and I'd like to hold your hand and run through a summer meadow with the sun highlighting your hair, and the breeze blowing your skirt. Kathie you're my wonderful lady."

Their hotel room had a view over the city's awe inspiring architecture, and they looked forward to their itinerary next morning.

Kathie was sitting before a generous size mirror putting the finishing touches to her hair and eyelashes as she spoke to Cormack's image. "We must inquire how far it is to the Lawyers offices, our appointment is for ten a.m. and then we have the bank."

"Do you want help with your hair?"

"No thank you just finished."

"We will enquire at reception how far it is and maybe we can walk and take in the sights."

She stood up brushing her hands over the pale blue taffeta skirt down her shapely hips. She pouted, "I'm ready."

He put out his hand to her, "come my beautiful princess, your carriage awaits."

Amadeo was secretly looking forward to meeting the attractive Angela as he seated himself with his coffee and daily newspaper, every bit the normal business man. A little while passed until she arrived, and with a radiant smile she stood while he came around the table and held a chair for her to be seated.

"Thank you I'll have a cappuccino and peach souffle please."

He ordered; and laying her elbows on the table she leaned over to speak in a barely audible voice. "Your man with the girl and child were at this address but according to close neighbours left two days ago."

His look was grotesque with his staring eye half closed. "Have you any idea where they could have gone?"

She looked past him. "The only other location I think they could have gone to is his family home, which is in Co. Galway in the West of Ireland."

"Do you have an address for this house?"

"Yes I do, excuse me my coffee and desert has arrived." She sat savouring the delicious confection and sipping coffee.

Amadeo was agitated folding his newspaper and not daring to interrupt while she ate. He moved his chair in an effort to contain his frustration, frowning as he watched her wipe some cream from her ruby coated lips.

"Now" she ventured, "I can give you the address but I doubt if you will be able to find this house easily, as it's in a rural setting."

"How should I go about finding it then can you supply me a map?"

"No I think a guide would be a better idea." She comfortingly smiled.

"A guide?" he looked mystified, "have you someone in mind?"

"Yes I have the only person available at the moment, me."

"Will you travel to Galway with me and find the house? It would be very helpful and I would be very grateful to you."

"I will travel and find the house but grateful will not be enough, what considerations can you offer? You are in this for more than just bringing a girl back for a petty crime. There's a lot more involved and I want a piece of the cake."

He pushed the coffee cup to the side and leaned across to her, "I can promise a decent remuneration if everything goes to plan, but if we mess up and don't get our woman we get nothing."

"What are we talking here in money terms?"

"I promise you a villa in Spain, no money."

She blinked and touched the napkin to her lips. "Right I'll go along with that, so we need to make plans. I have a car we can use, and when we get there we will have to rent a house which I believe would be better than staying in a hotel."

"What will your husband say about this or should I ask?"

"Yes you should ask as a jealous husband could be trouble," she held out her hand with the rings. "I suppose you observed these so you couldn't but presume I was married. Well I am very much a single girl, but by wearing these most men presume like you and come on nice and strong. I pick and choose, and believe it; the most eligible are mostly married. But they believe they will have no responsibilities as I'm also married, so I have a good choice of wealthy studs."

He was shocked but didn't want to show his vulnerability to this worldly woman, who sat smiling at him. "When do you think we should leave?"

"I'll pick you up at your hotel at 10am tomorrow, will that suit?"

"Fine that will suit me just fine."

Cormack and Kathie left their hotel for the short walk to their lawyer's offices, they had time to spare so they window shopped, and enjoyed the wonderful ambiance of this busy but very conservative city. They arrived minutes before their appointment time and were shown straight into the office. A cordial welcome from a senior grey haired man who introduced himself, and bade them to sit in front of his desk.

"Welcome to Zurich and I'll just have your name madam in full, you are the person who requested this appointment."

"Yes that's right and I hope you don't mind my partner Cormack O' Gara sitting in on this with me."

"No as you wish, so let's get down to why you are here?"

She related the full story and showed him the large envelope with all the precious deeds and papers and asked could he deal with all that.

He smiled and she realised he was human, "I don't want to know anything about your wealth and I want you to forget you spoke to me about it. Your first priority is to get a divorce as soon as possible. You may not have realised that if you processed all that material you have here with you, it would reveal your material wealth. In substance your husband would be entitled to claim a lot as a divorce settlement. If you have not shown any wealth your husband's lawyer cannot prove you have any, so subsequently can't claim on your estate. Now I suggest we fill out divorce papers if that is what you want."

Cormack looked at Kathie who turned in her chair to face him, "we want this divorce."

He held her hand in his, "yes Kathie we do."

"Now that that's settled let's get down to business and fill out all the relevant forms."

It took almost an hour before they finished, and Kathie asked "how long will it take to be finalised."

"I should have all completed in two to three weeks and if your husband doesn't comply I will go to our courts here and have a formal injunction taken out which will be legal and complete. Now you take all that paperwork to this bank "he handed her a slip of paper with the name of Bank Sparhafen, take a deposit box and put it safely away. Good bye now and I will be in touch as soon as I have news, this address in Ireland," he waved the paper with Cormack's home address.

"Yes that is where to find us," Cormack shook hands and Kathie gave him a little peck on the cheek.

After visiting the Bank they enjoyed the city and its famous cafe's and coffee houses.

"Cormack how would you like to spend a few days here, just swanning around? As you Europeans call enjoying the sights."

"Kathie my dear I couldn't ask for anything more it's the nearest thing to pure bliss just being with you."

"I hope the divorce will go through without too much bother, I would never have realised how serious it was to declare the family wealth, and then look for a divorce."

"It pays to get a good lawyer and he seems to be one of the best, come on now forget all the nasty stuff and relax." Cormack squeezed her hand.

"Yes your right I want to explore my primeval territory where my ancestors walked around in hairy bison skins, and had just about enough communication with their women to keep the tribe in existence."

"Well put and now here we are, and thanks to them."

Amadeo sat as passenger in the black Ford Mondeo as Angela gave him a verbal tour of West Galway, he seemed to be enjoying the scenery with the soft Irish Mist floating through the valleys and clinging to the hill tops.

He spoke in an undertone, "there are not many houses in this part of the country and the roads are so narrow and bumpy, it will not be easy to keep surveillance on this house."

She slowed the car and then pulled into a gateway off the road. The view was stunning as the ocean was cerulean blue beyond the heather rocky cliffs of

Connemara. She pointed to her right, "there; you see that house sitting in a green patch between the rocky hillocks?"

"Yes I see it, and it will not be easy to pass there without being noticed. There are not any other houses for some miles near it." A worried frown wrinkled his forehead.

"Yes" she agreed, "and I will have to be sure it's the right one, so we'll go down and see what we can see or find out."

She parked about twenty yards up the road from the house and got out. "You stay here and I'll go to the house and have a little look." She could see a child playing on the front lawn as she walked in, and as she approached the little boy a woman came out and quickly took the child up into her arms.

Angela smiled. "It's a lovely day, he's a handsome boy your grandson?"

"Yes he is that," she put the child down and turned him towards the door, "run along into Mary now Jacob."

"What a lovely name Jacob it's not common in Ireland."

The older woman was wary now and started to walk away from the house towards the road, "and what is your trouble are you lost on these back roads?"

Angela put on a profound show of charm, her smile bordered on a laugh, "yes you could say we are lost in a fashion, I was looking for a family named O'Loughlin and I presume that's not you?"

Alice walked out onto the road with her glamorous enquirer and seeing the car decided to accompany her to it. "No" she spoke in a terse tone, "we are not O'Loughlin, and I don't know anyone by that name in this parish. I'd say you are way out with your directions, who told you come here?"

Angela stopped to try and keep Alice from approaching the car, "I must have misread the directions I'll go back and start again it's been a lovely drive anyway."

"Yes and you can continue on this road and it'll take you back to the main road after about two miles. Oh I see you have a companion so I'll give him directions, is he the driver?" Alice kept walking to the car.

"No it's okay I'm the driver I'll follow your instructions." She began to panic.

Alice put her head into the window of the car, "good day sir I was telling your good wife here that you are lost but carry on and you'll be on a main road soon."

He tried to turn his head away but she saw the scar over the rim of the dark glasses.

He uttered a "thank you," in his audible Cuban accent.

Angela thanked her and drove away.

Alice got the number of the car.

Amadeo was visibly shaken and angry, "what did you bring her to the car for? And the nosey bitch put her head close to me."

"I couldn't help it as she followed me to the car; it's the right place I saw the boy and she called him Jacob."

"Did you see his mother?"

"No there was a girl I presume her daughter named Mary I didn't see any of the other two."

He looked around as if he somehow might see Kathie, he spoke with agitation. "We will have to rent a place near here where we can continue our surveillance, what do you think?"

"Yes for your plan to work we need a place with privacy."

CHAPTER 21

Cormack and Kathie were lost in a whirlwind of sightseeing and togetherness their idyllic world seemed to be coming to fruition at last, all the pieces falling into place. After dinner they retired to their room, and Kathie picked up the phone handing it to Cormack, "call Alice and see how are they, I want to speak to Jacob he won't be in bed yet with the time difference it's only six pm."

Mary answered the call, "Oh Cormack Mam has some news for you, don't worry it's not about Jacob it's some woman and man who called today."

Cormack held the phone down, "Mam has some news for us and Mary is gone to get Jacob, he's fine and enjoying himself."

Alice came on line and related the episode of the woman Angela, and the man with the scar.

"Thanks Mam I'll tell Kathie put Jacob on."

He handed the phone to Kathie and she spoke to Jacob who was delighted to speak Spanish, and was breathless telling all his little adventures especially with the golden Labrador.

"Bye Jacob see you very soon, Mammy loves you too." She handed the phone back to Cormack who spoke to Alice for a few minutes.

"Yes Mam we'll be home tomorrow." He put down the phone.

Kathie was visibly shocked when she heard this. "What has gone so terribly wrong?"

"Sit down" he held her hand in his, "Amadeo has arrived." He related the visit of Angela. "We have to go back tomorrow, how could he find us so quickly? His intentions are very serious."

"Oh god will we never be rid of him, Jacob will be in danger."

"Mam will not let Jacob out of her sight she is taking him to sleep in her bedroom tonight."

"We must book a flight immediately," she phoned down to reception and asked them to book a flight for two for the next day.

Angela and Amadeo looked at some properties to rent and found one some two miles from Cormack's home. It had the isolation and privacy he wanted.

"If necessary I can walk to the house and hide in the fields and do some surveillance to see when the two arrive back." His cell phone rang, "yes it's me, how are you, are you out of hospital? Good. I am in Ireland, you what! Pause; Divorce proceedings from Switzerland today. What can you do to prolong this? Pause; nothing it will come into force in three weeks, pause; good Jesus anymore good news, you know when that becomes law all is lost. Pause;

yes you can't do anything about it, so I have less than three weeks to get this job finished. Goodbye! Call again if you have some good news."

Angela knew immediately from what she'd heard all was not going to plan. "What's the good news now, was that the husband from Teheran?"

"That was him and you heard she has filed for divorce so we have to work fast, when it becomes legal all is lost for us."

"I heard you say about three weeks, that should be enough time if only they came back. To me the only way is to snatch her not the child."

He rubbed his closed eye and seemed to be agitated, "she recognised me you know. And you're right it's not going to be easy, he won't leave her side, will you get some of those gas canisters sent from your connections we may eventually need them."

She took out her cell phone and pressed a call number, "I'll get onto it right away," she said, as she was connected to her caller. He heard her order the canisters with urgency.

He walked around the house and began to plan 'this room' he thought would be his interrogation cell, 'small with a high window'.

She called out, "we can collect those at the bus station in Galway tomorrow, I'm going to shower and retire to bed you should do the same."

He awoke alongside her in the big double bed her voracious and demanding love making had left him exhausted. She turned and threw a leg over him pushing her damp font of desire against his thigh and her ample breasts onto his shoulder. He slipped out of bed. "I'll get some breakfast ready and then I'm going to do some walking around the countryside, I've taken up a new role, I'm going to be a bird watcher."

She purred like a large cat "a girl's needs should be foremost."

After breakfast he took his binoculars and wearing dark glasses and hat he set out on a cross country hike. Turning round he said to her. "Will you go to Galway later and get those canisters?"

"Yes I need some shopping too," and in an admonishing tone, she said. "You need to be careful if you meet any of the locals, try not to engage them in conversation they are a curious lot."

Cormack and Kathie arrived home at midnight and after a long day travelling they got a quick update about Amadeo's visit and the woman Angela.

Next morning after breakfast they all sat down to discuss the best and safest way to handle this nefarious situation. Going to the Garda didn't seem to make much sense as they had no proof of any threatening behaviour from either party. Also Kathie's story might be taken lightly and of little concern in this jurisdiction. Alice was baffled by the threat until Kathie told her and Mary the full story. She hugged Kathie who was visibly upset and assured her they would all help her. She came out with the news that seemed to all to be the omnipotent solution to all their woes. "Dad will be home tomorrow and he'll know what to do."

Cormack put an arm around Kathie, "that's great news Mam, what would you all think if Kathie and me and Jacob took the campervan and drove away on a holiday. They could never find us once we were off on the road."

Mary clasped her hands, "we should wait until Dad arrives he'll know what to do, what do you think Kathie?"

She looked over to where Jacob was playing with the Labrador, "I'm not sure, will we wait until your Dad arrives?" Looking from one to the other, and then Cormack, they all seemed to agree.

Amadeo spent his morning hidden behind some scrub on a hilly outcrop of rock from where he caught sight of Kathie in the garden with Jacob. Cormack and Alice came into his binocular sights and Mary driving away her car seemed to be the full complement of the household. He went back to his house at mid afternoon and found Angela gone, he was happy to get a couple of hour's undisturbed sleep before she arrived back.

Well he greeted her, "did you get the stuff?"

"Yes" she threw a parcel onto the table, "two by the feel of it."

He picked up the packet and took out the two canisters, examining them and reading the instructions he said "yes one would probably be sufficient."

She put the canisters on the top of a high dresser, and she also took hold of the small gun she had hidden there, "hope we won't have to use this." She put it back out of sight.

He put his arms around her waist helping her down off the chair she was standing on. As she leaned against him her flimsy dress rode up her thighs, he took a firm grip of her shapely buttocks.

"Which do you want first," she spluttered, "food or fuck?"

"I will go for the latter."

She led him to the bedroom and he related his day's bird watching as they undressed.

"I have a fluffy bird here now that needs attention," she fell back onto the bed with her legs open, and a foxy bush of damp down parting to reveal dewy rose petals.

Alice was serving breakfast when a jeep drove into the front of the house. "Oh" she said as she dropped a plate in front of Cormack, "your Dad is here." She rushed to the front door and the big man swept her off her feet and swung her around, with arms around his neck she kissed him on the lips. "Jack it's great to have you back," she whispered, "put me down what will anyone think we're like teenagers."

He was the full of the room as he walked in and was introduced to Kathie, and Jacob who eyed him with a mixture of apprehension and curiosity. Alice was fussing around. "I'm sure you didn't have your breakfast sit in there and I'll get you something."

After breakfast while Alice was busy in the kitchen and Mary had Jacob outside playing ball, Cormack and Kathie were with Dad who insisted Kathie call him Jack, as they sat around in a kind of huddle. Jack was a big imposing man of six foot two, a tough rugby player in his day and still at fifty eight very formidable. His soft grey eyes revealed his inner self, a caring selfless man whose only concern was the welfare of his family. Now it was easy to see Kathie and Jacob came under that canopy. He listened to their story and thought it incredible that this Amadeo could follow her and Jacob like hunted fugitives. All for monetary gain which Kathie could only guess at, and was her rightful inheritance.

He spoke calmly with an authority, "I think you're going away in the campervan is a good idea, he will never find you around the seaside places this time of year."

Cormack suggested leaving late at night so if they were spying on them they would have a good start.

"Yes" said Kathie, "I think it would be a good idea and we could both look after Jacob, he'd be with us all the time."

"I'll keep a good eye around here and now I know the car and its number and colour I'll do a bit of investigating, and if I think it of any use I might talk to the local Garda Sergeant. Now get what you need into that camper and I'll tell your Mam what's happening."

Cormack and Kathie sorted out the camper and began to fill up the water tanks and stored some small necessities, the rest they would buy in transit. It was twilight when they pulled out and headed off on their itinerary, Cormack had the first stop pencilled in which was just an hour and a half away.

Kathie and Jacob were thrilled with this new adventure and they slept fitfully waking to a view over a beautiful sandy beach, completely deserted but for themselves.

Kathie couldn't wait to get in for a swim, "have we some bathing costumes?" she shouted to Cormack.

"Yes try the bottom drawers."

She pulled out some clothes which looked like ladies swim suits and held them to her for size. 'Oh my god, she thought 'who could wear this.'

He was standing with a big smile on his face, "kinda suits you."

"Goodness who wears something like this it has pads and things and it's almost dress size."

He laughed out loud "that is Mam's but she hasn't worn it for years, try again there may be some belonging to Mary."

She pulled out a bikini. "Oh lovely, who could ever have thought there'd be such a beauty." She held it to her for size but needn't have it was so skimpy. "A polka dot bikini I just love it, out you go now until I change."

They went to the water's edge in their swim wear, Kathie a picture in her little bikini.

"Right says Cormack you stay with Jacob and I'll have a dip." He ran out and between uhs and ahs he dived in and swam around. He came back in and took charge of Jacob. "Now my dear you go."

She walked out and squealed. "It's freezing oh my goodness," she splashed and dived when it was waist high and when she surfaced you could hear her scream reverberating back from the cliff face. She swam to shore quickly and stood shivering, "how could you enjoy swimming in such cold water?"

"It's cold but refreshing, but Jacob seems to love it look," He was trying to catch the small white waves and he couldn't understand when they disappeared just as he had it.

She was shivering "you look after Jacob I'm going to change."

He smacked her on the bottom, "pity, you look so wonderful in that little bitsi teeny weeney outfit."

"And you're a handsome bit of okay yourself, just as well they're no young girls around or I'd have to stay and mind you both."

"Get along with you they'd be nothing to compare to you."

Jack took the dog and went across the rough scrub land with its little stone hillocks. The dog chased a few rabbits and came back panting looking for a pat for his efforts. Jack stopped when he saw a figure squatting down behind a boulder leaning on it with a pair of binoculars, looking in the direction of his house. When this figure saw Jack he got up and began to walk quickly away. Jack followed until he got to the little laneway leading back to the road. The man with a brown type of sunhat was moving faster now and he climbed a fence and almost ran across the little field. Jack knew this country so he stood on a stone fence and watched him disappear in the direction of the village.

Alice was outside calling him for lunch when the dog bounced up to her, "where's Jack she said to the dog?"

He came over the garden fence in one vault, "I'm here."

"Lunch is ready had you a good walk?"

"Come in and I'll tell you."

"I saw a man with a pair of binoculars up in Casey's field and he was looking down this way. He moved off quickly in the direction of the village when he saw me. I wonder if it's the same fellow spying on Kathie, I'm going to go for a walk to the village and find out if any of the houses around have been rented lately."

"Yes Jack that would be a good idea, its well they are gone away, he has nothing to see now so he might just clear off, and good riddance to him. He has some cheek spying on that lovely girl and her beautiful son."

"Alice you're right but I'd like to get to the bottom of it, and if I met him, or the woman with him I'd have it out with them."

"You would Jack and no better man to put him in his place, but not to do too much harm to him."

"You know me now force would be a last resort but never ruled out."

"Jack would you like me to come with you?"

"No my little fire cracker you might be too hard to handle if we met them."

"Finish your lunch and I'll make a cup of tea." She coddled.

"A black Mondeo you said and I want the number, I might come across them on the road." said Jack determinedly.

Amadeo was out of breath when he arrived into the house.

Angela was standing with a towel around her having come out of the shower. "You're out of breath were you running?"

"Yes I had to run a bit, the fellow in the house, not Cormack I'd say it could be his father, came up the field and saw me with the binoculars. He followed me for a bit but I lost him, now we have to move out today. I see the camper van is gone and so are the three of them."

She was standing naked drying her hair, "how do suggest we are going to find them now?"

"Would you put some clothes on I can't concentrate looking at you naked."

"Oh" she said drying her left breast, "I didn't think I could have that much of effect on you." She sat and covered herself.

"If we leave immediately, you can study the local map and try to assume as best you can where they might go."

She began to dress, "yes I'll do that, pack some things we might need, how long do you think we'll be gone?"

"Until we find them and get them back here, I'll pack those gas canisters and the plastic ties, the gun we will leave but I need to hide it."

They were on the road and Angela had marked out a route by the coast going south which she believed was the most obvious route to take. She marked in a lot of small coves and beaches where they could stop besides the main caravan sites, these she believed would be their best chance of finding them.

She drove and he studied the map, he looked up as they came onto the main road, "the name on the camper van is RIVIERA and it has a distinctive red yellow and green type of decoration, so it will be easy to identify if we see it."

Jack set out with the dog, and as he approached the village he met Peadar Quilty the postman, although it was mid afternoon Peadar was only half way through his round.

"Good day Peadar are you heading out my way, if you have anything for me I'll save you the bother?"

Peadar tipped back his peaked cap, "Tis you're looking well Jack I haven't seen you for a while, hold whist now I have a couple of one's here with the windows, bills what have ye."

Taking his mail, Jack looked around. "Thanks I was wondering if any of the vacant houses around have been let lately, you'd notice people coming and going in them."

Peadar stopped walking and leaned the bicycle against a telephone pole. "Let me think now Jack, do you remember the young Sean Duggan lad who went off to Australia with the wife and two kids?"

"I do, Sean is a builder and a good one at that."

"Well the ould Celtic Tiger done him, and a lot more besides, so sign he had to go away foreign to earn a living."

"What about him Peadar is he back home again?"

"Not a bit of it what makes you think that, he'll not be back for a long time I do be thinking, but his house you were asking me about. I saw a car parked there on a couple of days, but I had no letters for them whoever they were, that were there."

"Tell me what colour car was it, and sure you'd know the make too."

"I would that, I know the maker of every car that's driving the roads, although I never drove one of them myself. It was a black Mondeo I can't vouch for the number but it was fairly new. I'm going out that way now if you'd like to come along and we can have a look."

They stroll along the dry dusty road, and Peadar brought Jack up to date with all the local gossip. The summer flowers were blooming on the hedgerows and young birds offered thrilling notes in free competition. An ass brayed a loud and primitive sound. Peadar stopped and listened for another one, "there now you hear that Jack?"

"Yes of course I hear it. It's Murphy's auld jack ass above in the field there, probably an auld mare ass in season somewhere."

"Naw Jack it means there's a Tinker dead in Kilkeran an auld saying but true."

"Do people still believe in those ould pishogues, I thought that was gone with the Banshees and Leprechauns?"

"I wouldn't laugh at them at all at all, it's only last week Bridget Darcy heard the Banshee and next day she got a phone call from Boston her brother was dead. So how do you account for that, I hears those stories all over the place. Anyways here we are, there's no car there today, so what do you think will we go in and see are they gone."

Jack opened the gate and walked up to the front door, he wasn't sure what he'd say if someone answered his loud knock. There was no movement inside so he peeped in the window and saw some clothes. He went around the back and tried the kitchen door, it was locked. He looked in the window and saw two mugs and a pot of jam and some bread on the table. 'There not gone too far' he thought, 'and will surely be back.'

Peadar was leaning on the bicycle, "what do you think are they gone or just away for the day?"

"I don't know but there are people living here."

"Sure I told you that, and what are you wanting to know about them, they're probably strangers? You wouldn't know them anyway or would you now, is it a kind of a mystery?"

"It's not a mystery at all. It's a friend of mine in Dublin asked me to look out for a couple who were coming to stay around here, and I said I'd show them around, part of the job you know Peadar."

"God tis strange you don't know their name or where they were to stay, strange Jack like the auld pishogues, odd auld things happen. I'll be off I have a few to deliver and tis getting late, good day to you now."

Jack watched him go as he pedalled away on his auld bicycle. He put his hands in his pockets and strode the road. 'Cute auld whore that fellow he's a clever auld fool but nobody's fool, I hope he doesn't talk about this but he surely will, it'll make no difference anyway.' He looked around for the dog, "there you are come on we'll head home."

They moved on after staying three days in this lovely secluded cove, and after five hours driving they stopped at a little beach near Black Head. Cormack took down the fishing rods and began to get them ready, "now Jacob will you help me with these?"

"What are they for?" he picked up a colourful lure, "that's nice."

"Oh be careful that hook is sharp." He put them into the box realising how dangerous these lures with their sharp hooks could be for a small child.

"Kathie" he called out "we're going to go fishing and catch some mackerel for dinner."

She was spreading some small clothes out to dry, "I'm coming with ye."

"Okay I have two rods, can you fish?"

"No but you'll teach me, is it very difficult."

He smiled, "not really for men that is, I don't know about the fair sex, take Jacob by the hand we have to go on the rocks."

The edge of the rock where he stopped was ideal for casting a line, "right we'll give it a try here." He rigged two rods with line and lures, "I'll try a few casts, stay back a bit with Jacob I'm always a little nervous when swinging the cast not to catch anyone with the hooks."

"How big are the fish we're trying to catch?" Kathie enquired.

"Mackerel are about maybe twelve inches, but pollack if we caught one could be anything up to thirty or forty inches long, and heavy. We probably won't be lucky enough to catch one of them. Here goes, "he cast the line out and watched it sink, then slowly reeling it in it started to bend. "Got one, look at him."

Kathie and Jacob came close to see the fish sparkling as it came to the surface in the clear blue water. "Oh my it's beautiful look Jacob." He became excited as Cormack swung the silvery blue mackerel up onto the rock,

"Mammy; Mammy he shouted."

He showed Kathie how to cast and he held Jacob back to give her plenty of room. The second cast brought a shout of delight, "I've got one" and as she reeled in she got animated and squealed I've got two, look Jacob, Mammy has two fishes."

They decided to stop when they had a dozen and Cormack filleted them in the sea water and they headed back to cook dinner. Kathie believed she never ate anything as delicious in her life as the feast of fresh fish was enjoyed.

They stayed in this small cove for two days, one other campervan came while they were there, and they mostly had the beach to themselves every day.

Jack took a walk up to the house every morning with the dog and saw no sign of life, the car wasn't there either. He decided to try a little detective work he'd read in some paperback. When he closed the gate he put a small bit of twig into the catch, so if it was opened the twig would fall out. He was pleased with this little Sherlock Holmes trick. He stood looking at the old ruined cottages dotted around where people from the famine time had been evicted, and families had been wiped out with disease. He was listening for what, he didn't know, the insects and bird call seemed mute, he had a strange feeling he couldn't explain. Peadar's auld pishogues seemed to have a presence, like a weird ethereal grip, gently coercing confused strange thoughts. The people who lived and died here were good god fearing people and would mean no harm, only maybe give a warning. He called the dog he was sniffing around the garden, "come on home the two of us now."

"Alice there is no sign of anyone up at that house I'd say they're gone, I was thinking should we phone Cormack and Kathie and let them know?"

"Sure I wouldn't be bothering them if they are worried they'll phone us. But again do you not think because they are not in the house they might be gone looking for the campervan?"

"Good Jesus Alice it never struck me, you could be right, but if they do find them what could they do?"

Alice wiped her hands in her apron, and clenched a fist. "I don't know, what did he intend to do while he was up at the house, he surely wouldn't attempt to try and kidnap either Kathie or Jacob."

Jack paced the floor. "Do you know you are right he's up to some dirty business, but Cormack is no push over and neither is Kathie for that matter. I can't see what he could do without using a gun or having some more help besides the woman Angela. His chance of finding them is very slim with all the small coves and places they could stop at. I think we are being a bit over dramatic, I'd say they're surely gone away."

"Well now Jack I have that feeling and call it women's intuition if you like, but I'm still fearful for the three of them, they might phone, I'd like to talk to them."

They sat in the bedroom of the bed and breakfast before setting off on another day of searching. She laid out the map of the area which had pencilled in the route they had covered. "Look here now" she scrolled the pen over the area going north from Galway and into Connemara, "I think we have come far enough this direction we should head back on the south side."

He took note of the map and said. "Yes I'd say you are right we will drive quickly back until we come to here," pointing out a small cove near Oranmore.

"Let's go she commanded we have a lot of driving to do."
The drive back to where they had originally started took them into the afternoon and they quickly searched coves and beaches until night fall, with no sign of their quarry. Angela got out of the car to stretch her legs she walked the sandy beach it had been a weary day's driving. The sun was dipping below the pink and mauve Atlantic, 'I don't know if this is going to work they could be anywhere,' she thought, 'I'm tired of him to, with his selfish attitude to quick sex, seems like he's just trying to get it done as a favour to me. He's like most of them they get careless about fore play after a few weeks, Bastards.'

He came up alongside her and put his arm around her waist. "You are in deep thought, what are you thinking about?"

"I am wondering are we wasting our time looking for these people, and do you believe you will be able to take the girl and the child with him there?"

He stopped and faced her, anger and torment etched on his face, the sinews in his neck tightened as he spoke. "Listen to me I know what I'm doing if we can find them, I am depending on you for that."

"What are we to do with them when we get back to the house are you taking them both with you?"

"You let that to me, you may have to take the child for some time, it depends where I have to take her, but as long as you have the child she will co-operate with all I want her to do."

"What will happen if we are reported to the Garda? Kidnapping in this country will get you a long prison sentence."

"We will have to move fast before any authorities are alerted, and once she is separated from the child she will do what she's told."

"I am still apprehensive about keeping the child, what will I do with him?"

"Come on back to the car, will we sleep in the car it's a bit late to look for a guest house?"

"God almighty" she groaned, "this better end soon, look there's a campervan in the parking lot, could it possibly be them?"

"I certainly hope not."

"Why not what are we looking for if we don't want to get close to them?"

"Look it's not a Riviera it's a Hymer great, if that was them they would have us spotted right away seeing the car, and they probably have our number plate. When we see them if we do, we will have to make sure they don't see us. This whole thing is about surprise."

He bedded down on the back seat and she leaned back the front seat and tried to sleep. Her brain grasped at nodules of unconsciousness as she surfaced and dipped in restless sleep. His soft snoring behind her brought back resentment and now she began to actually dislike him.

He woke at four thirty and the first streaks of dawn were poking like fingers from the eastern horizon. He opened the door and got out to relieve himself, getting into the driver's seat he looked at her, softly breathing like a child. He started the engine and she sat up, looking bleary eyed she asked. "What time is it why are we leaving so early?"

"I couldn't sleep so I thought we might get an early start, this could be our lucky day."

She turned back to sleep, "could we be so lucky."

Cormack was eating breakfast after an early morning swim, "my goodness" she put her hand on his wet hair "that sea is so cold how you could swim in it?"

He pinched her bum" it wasn't that cold, you could have come in, do you think we should phone home and let them know how we are?"

"Yes I do and see if they have seen that Amadeo or the woman around."

Alice picked up the phone, "Oh Cormack it's great to hear from you, how is Kathie and Jacob?"

"Fine Mam enjoying the break I'll put her onto to you in a minute; tell me have you seen those people around?"

"I'll put you on to your father, here Jack you speak to him."

"Cormack it's great to hear you are enjoying your little holiday, now I found the house that the two of them rented, its Sean Duggan's house you know the man who left for Australia with his wife and children. I went up there each day since ye left and could see no sign of them, but I couldn't be certain if they have left for good or just gone for a few days. I don't want to alarm you but could they be looking for you and Kathie and Jacob?"

"God Dad I would hate to alarm her but it's a possibility, if they are looking for us he is a very dangerous man with bad intentions."

"Cormack your mother wants to speak to Kathie."

"Kathie; Mam," he hands her the phone.

"Hello Alice we are having a great time would you believe I caught two fish, I cannot go swimming the water is so cold."

"Kathie don't let Jacob out of your sight especially near the water, and I am looking forward to you coming back home."

"I suppose we will be back in about a week I think Cormack has to go to Dublin about his job."

"Great Kathie enjoy yourselves see you then, goodbye."

She handed the phone back to Cormack, "Mam I'll phone you again soon, and if you have anything to tell me you phone me, you have my number. Good bye for now."

Kathie was staring at the little phone as if it held all the answers, he put it down.

Kathie's voice was anxious, "Is there something wrong Alice seemed a bit how can I say worried for us, telling me not to let Jacob out of my sight."

"Dad said he knows the house Amadeo and the woman are renting, and he has gone up there each day since we left and there's no sign of them. He says they have left, whether for good or maybe a few days, he wonders if there's a possibility they could be searching for us?"

She caught Jacob and held him to her, "good god Cormack what do you think we should do, I feel very worried now if he has found us he could be watching our every move."

"We'll move on and keep vigilant if he is following us he'll surely slip up and we should see him. I will go and confront him and tell him I am going to report him to the Garda and that will stop him."

"Yes I think we should do that if we see he is following us."

It was early afternoon and Amadeo was driving, "we better pull in here for fuel" he saw a Statoil sign ahead. As he approached the station he suddenly saw a camper van filling up, his first reaction when he saw the logo on its side was drive fast. "Look back and see is that a Riviera he shouted to Angela."

"Holy Christ that's them" she shouted "keep going fast."

He took the next left turn and parked a few hundred yards down that small road. He jumped out and ran back to the main road and waited, hiding behind the high scrub by the fence. They drove past and he confirmed the registration number and the coloured logo.

Waiting some minutes he drove back to get fuel, "now we will have to go easy and wait and see where they park for the night."

They studied the map and marked two likely locations where they thought the camper might stop overnight. The first one was about fifteen miles on so they drove slowly after turning off the main road onto the coast road. Traffic on these small coast roads was busy and campervans plenty, so when they came behind one they slowed to let it get well ahead, just to be sure they didn't slip up and be seen. A sign post showed they were two kilometres from the small beach, so Amadeo pulled into a small lay by cum gateway to a field.

Angela was scrutinizing the map looking to see were there any small coves they had missed. She lifted her head, and lowered the window looking out around her, "you will have to walk from here and wear your dark glasses and hat," sarcastically she muttered, "shame if you were seen; they might recognise your handsome features."

He spoke with venom, "If it wasn't for those American pigs I wouldn't have this scar and half blind eye."

Feeling remorse she torte, "I wasn't referring to your eye I was being a little sarcastic, you are actually handsome in a rugged way, have your girlfriends never told you so?"

"Girls where I come from know their place and are happy and grateful to have a man to look out for them. I will go and see if they are gone to this place."

She watched him walk away with his hat pulled down over his face and dark glasses covering his scarred eye. 'Who would like to be his wife or girlfriend in his home country, besides poverty, and party censure for speaking out, his robotic personality, and selfish cock? He is contemptible.'

She got out and went into the field to pee, 'a villa in Spain' a lovely thought. Some cattle in the field seeing her and out of natural curiosity ran to get a closer look. "Oh Jesus" she jumped up and ran trying to pull up her pants and fell face down in the high grass. The cattle came and ran away again as she got to her knees and shouted at them, "you bastards." She had pee down her legs and pants; she took it off and wiped herself. "Fuck there's nothing easy today, can't pee in comfort."

Back in the car she listened to the radio and sipped from a bottle of water, 'this child what does he expect me to do with him? I'm not going to take care of him for long, children are not my scene.'

She lay back and closed her eyes she must have dozed off. His hand on her leg awoke her with a start. "Oh Jesus it's you."

"Who else do you think it might be, hardly any of your studs around here."

"Well are they there?

"No; two other campers there but not our one, we better move on. How far is the next stop?"

She looked at the map, "there are a lot of likely places in the next forty miles, at least six."

He started up and drove on, "we should be able to see them all before dark."

"Yes we should; we have five hours of light left."

Cormack drove on as Kathie played to amuse Jacob in the small lounge area. She looked out the rear window and saw a black car close behind, she ran forward to Cormack. "There's a black car following us, could it be them."

He looked in the rear view mirror but couldn't see the car as it was right behind, he indicated to pull in and let it pass. As it passed he saw it was a Nissan. "Okay dear false alarm, it's a Nissan but we need to be vigilant."

"I'm becoming paranoid every black car I see I think it might be them."

"Well you're right and if we do see them we'll do as I said, we'll confront them or at least I will."

"No; you will not go on your own I'll go with you, and between us we'll demand to know why they are following us. Of course we know why, so we'll threaten them with the law and see how they respond."

"Yes we shouldn't be afraid of him, only if he produces a gun, then we might be in trouble if we're on our own with them."

She held Jacob on her knee. "How far is it to our next stop?"

"We should be there very soon it's a popular place so we'll have lots of company."

"I'll start making something to eat," she took Jacob into the back of the van and began to make up a salad. She sliced some fruit for her little man putting him sitting with his seat belt on.

"I don't want to be tied Mam."

"I know pet it's only for a little while we're nearly there now and we can go out in the water and make sand castles." She looked out and saw a big car park with lots of campervans and cars; 'good' she thought 'this is better with all these people around.'

Cormack found a nice place among some other campers, "right kids we're here." He took Jacob out of his harness and picked up his sand bucket and shovel. "We're off to build a huge castle, how long before tea is served?"

She turned wiping her hands and placing plates on the table, "I'll give you two twenty minutes and if the castle is not complete we'll finish it after we've eaten."

"Great come on," he held Jacob by the hand and they went bouncing away to the beach.

She stopped doing her chores and looked out the window at the two of them, and her heart was filled with love and a life she had only dreamed about. 'I'm so sure now she thought but how can I tell him, will it ruin everything? Oh god what will his reaction be?'

She had everything laid out ready when she called out to them. Cormack waved and stood up to go but Jacob pulled him back down to finish the top of the magic castle with small white stones. They both admired their crude art especially Jacob who turned to see was it still there as they walked away.

"Will it be there tomorrow in the morning when I go out?"

"Yes it will still be there and we can build another one and I'll get flags we can fly on it."

"What are flags can I put them on?"

"We'll make flags after dinner and have them ready for the morning."

"Mammy we are going to make flags for our castle tomorrow, will you make some to."

"Yes if you eat all your dinner I'll help you and Cormack make flags for your magic castle."

Angela was getting restless as they drove to a small cove. There were only two cars with couples in them waiting for the twilight to turn to dark, before engaging in contortionist passionate love making, with possibly a leg out an open window. She looked at them with a certain disdain, and a little envy, and the thought of 'how she actually enjoyed her unbridled shameless passion in similar circumstances and positions.'

Her voice had an edge, "they're not here and we better get a guest house before it's too late I'm not spending another night sleeping in this car."

He turned the car and drove back to the coast road. "Get the map out and see where we can get some place to stay."

"We'll find a place on this coast road there's plenty of guest houses and hotels." It was dark and she was keeping a lookout for a nice small hotel or guest house.

"That sign there," he said as he stopped the car and reversed back thirty metres. "Look a beach and caravan park five kilometres." He turned the car and drove down the small road, "this will only take twenty minutes and we'll get a hotel then."

"I have cramps in my arse sitting in this car all day I need a shower and a decent bed, so just hurry and get us back out of here."

The area at the back of the beach was shrouded in dusk and shadow, the white camper vans were parked in orderly fashion and they were both surprised to see so many of them. He stopped on the road well out of sight in the evening darkness and he turned off the car lights.

"How many of them are there?" He asked her.

She opened the car door and stood out. "I can count eleven, and three caravans, pretty busy spot. Which of us are going to go and investigate? I think it should be me. I'd be less recognisable than you if they did happen to be there and maybe out around."

"Do you think?" he said "we should wait another half hour until it's properly dark, there are lights on in most of them now, and shortly they'll be going to sleep."

"You are a silly man I would be more suspicious looking when all was quiet down there than now when there is a little activity, I'm going down." She walked away and became a moving shadow against the western sky and inky ocean.

He walked around the car and a cold sweat prickled his body. 'I know they're there.' He opened the trunk and picked up one of the canisters, he touched the nozzle and it sprayed, he took up a handful of the plastic ties and threw them back again. 'I'll get her this time, and no slip ups. It's at times like this I'd like a cigarette a few wouldn't do any harm. It's been ten years since I got that scare with my lungs I still get breathless though when under stress.'

She came back breathless, and got into the car motioning him to do the same. "They're there; no doubt but in between two other vans so whatever you're going to do you'll have to be very quiet."

"Great; will you be able to drive the car close to them, say twenty metres at least?"

"Yes I'm sure I can get that close."

"Good; we better get out of here for a few hours, we passed a bar and restaurant so we can stay for a while in their car park without any notice." He spoke with authority, "I'll go over all the details when we stop, we have no room now for a mistake or a slip up of any kind."

She spoke indignantly, "don't lecture me about mistakes, if there are going to be any cock ups it'll be your planning not my execution of your plans. I'll need a lot of know, about what's going to happen if we do get them?"

He drove to the top of the car park and switched off the lights, "I think we should stay in the car we have to wait about four hours before going back there."

"She pulled the lever and the seat fell back, "I'm going to have a sleep call me when you're ready."

His voice was stern "forget about sleep for a while I want to go over the details of what we're about to do."

She folded her arms across her chest as if she was cold, "go ahead I'm listening."

"At two am we're going down there and we'll park in the same place. I'll go and do the business with the canisters and then come back to the car, we'll drive slowly down as near as possible to the camper. When we have them back at the house I have to find out from her where she has deposited the contents of the security box. Now your job will be to look after the child, while she's separated from him she will do as she's told. Now I might have to take her to

Switzerland to get the documents out of the security safe, as with these new types of security she will have to give a palm print before they'll open them."

"What am I to do with the child while all this is going on?"

"You keep the child until I give you the all clear that I have everything under control."

"When I get the all clear from you, then, what happens to the child?"

"I'll leave that to you we don't want him around, you decide, you can abandon him in the centre of some big city like Manchester or just get rid of him I'm sure you have enough experience to do that."

"For this type of job I might have to get help, and I'm going to need two hundred and fifty thousand Euro lodged into a Maltese bank account the number I'll give you, and when you've completed this I'll look after the child."

"You are a tough bitch to deal with but I'll do it."

She retorted, "Do you realise what you are asking and how serious a crime it is, you are getting this cheap."

There was a trace of malice when he spoke, "get your sleep I'll wake you when I'm ready to go."

CHAPTER 22

He looked at the car clock two thirty, he had slept a little but the time was about right. He started the car knowing it would wake her.

She sat up sleepy eyed looking around. "Are we going down there now?"

"Yes" he growled "I hope you are ready for this?"

"As ready as I'll ever be, it's you're the one who can fuck it all up, I have to depend on you."

He stopped the car and switched off the lights, "right I'm going down."

The area was quiet except for the sound of the lapping waves on the sandy beach. He stopped to listen and looked around to see were there any lights on in any of the campers; he was happy all were sound asleep. He moved stealthily like a predatory cat and was sure he had the right camper. The vents were easy to find and he put his hand over each one in turn to feel the air being drawn in through it. He pressed the button and sprayed the gas into each of the vents in turn, he looked to see how flimsy the lock on the door was, 'easy picking' he thought. He got back to the car and went round to the trunk; he threw in the canister and took out a small jemmy bar and a fist of plastic ties.

"When I walk back down you give me five minutes and drive slowly without any lights on, as near as you can to the camper."He sat in and held the bar and ties in his hands, his injured eye was twitching and paining now. Time was passing slowly as he watched the car clock, he closed his eyes.

"Where in the car are we putting them when you bring them out?" she said sarcastically, "or have you decided?"

"We'll put her in the trunk and the child in the back seat with you. I'm going now, five minutes remember, I'll be ready."

He crouched at the side of the camper and listened, the silence except for the sea was palpable. 'I hope this gas works'. He was sure he had allowed enough time but where they were positioned in the camper would make a difference, he was sure he had sprayed in enough. He put the jemmy bar into the side of the door against the lock one hard leverage and it was open. He ran round to the back of the camper and crouched under a bicycle rack and waited a few minutes. He heard the car slowly approaching, and could see it barely outlined against the hilly backdrop. He went in and approached the large bed where Kathie and Cormack were sleeping luckily she was on the outside. He caught her two hands and put on the plastic tie, now he lifted her up and was surprised to find she was so heavy. Angela was standing behind him, he beckoned her to help, and they lifted her between them easing their way out. They put her into the trunk closing it softly. He went and got the child and handed him to her in the back seat. The car engine was still running, 'good thinking on her part' he gave her credit.

He drove slowly until they got to the main road to Galway, she directed him and he now drove at the limit, he didn't want to be pulled over for speeding.

It was dark when they arrived at the house the child was waking up, so Angela took him straight to a bedroom and locked him in. When they opened the trunk Kathie had her eyes open and stared with incredulity at the faces in the dark.

"Who are ye, what are you doing to me?" She struggled but the ties held her firm.

He nodded to Angela to take her legs and he caught her under the shoulders. "Co-operate and you and the child will be let go," he squeezed her soft flesh to emphasise his point.

"You bastard Amadeo you have Jacob, you'll not get away with this, you're not in Cuba now."

Angela pulled her legs roughly, "shut you bitch you'll do as you're told, or you'll never see that kid again."

She was tied onto something in a room she wasn't sure where as they never turned on a light. The last thing she heard before they closed the door was Jacob crying.

The door of the camper was open as the lock was broken, the air circulated from a fresh sea breeze. Cormack put his arm across the bed, and half consciously felt an empty space, he had a throbbing headache. He opened his eyes and heard the door moving with the breeze and tipping the side of the van. He sat up and saw the door open, Kathie was gone, he called her name. He jumped out and checked for Jacob, 'oh Christ they're both gone, Jesus Mary and Joseph how could this happen.' He picked up his phone and dialled home, after what seemed an interminably long time Jack picked up. He screamed into the phone "Dad they're gone he's taken them."

"He's taken Kathie and Jacob, how could that happen?" he sounded incredulous.

"I don't know but they're gone, go up to the house quick and see are they there, I'll be home as soon as I can."

"I'll be there right away and if they are there you can be assured he won't take them anywhere." He looked at Alice who was sitting up and had switched on the light, she thought she was dreaming. "That was Cormack" he said, fear now evident in his voice, "they've just taken Kathie and Jacob." He jumped out of bed and grabbed his clothes, "I must go up there immediately, you can drive me some of the way."

Alice ran with him to the jeep, they jumped in and she drove. "Jack what can you do if they are there with Kathie and Jacob? You can't get them on your own they are dangerous people they could kill you."

He held a short round stick in his hand and he tightened his grip on it, "I'll just watch until Cormack comes, and make sure they don't leave with them. You can be ready to drive back up if I need you. I'll phone in an emergency. Stop here and I'll walk the rest it won't be daylight for an hour so they won't see me."

She put her hand over and held his arm, "Jack be careful don't do anything until Cormack arrives, do you think I should phone the Garda?"

"No Alice we'll handle this, it would be better for Kathie and Jacob if we can sort it out."

She turned and drove back to wait for Cormack who was speeding over the limit his body tensed with worry and fear, and disappointment that he couldn't look after them.

Alice put on the kettle and made a cup of tea, 'Cormack should be here soon.'

Jack crept up the outside of the fence; he climbed over and got to the corner of the house. The light was coming from the kitchen window he crept along bent low and listened.

Angela was agitated, "come on we'll make her talk this time, I'll threaten her I'm going to harm the child."

He pushed the table in temper, "I know the bitch is lying the documents are in Switzerland, not here in some bank in Dublin."

They left the kitchen and Jack thought he might go in and take them both on; but what if he failed they'd get away and he might never find them. He went around to the front of the house and out onto the road, He was looking to see was there a way he could stop them if they decided to go before Cormack arrived. If he had a knife he could slash the car tyres, he never carried a pocket knife only when going fishing. He could hear Angela shouting "you Cuban whore you'll never see the brat alive if you don't come clean and tell the truth."

'God what are they doing to her, I'll just have to go and stop them, I'll be able for the two of them if I can surprise them.'

His phone rang, "Jack, Cormack is nearly here we should be up to you in ten minutes."

"You park the jeep in the same place and come on quietly."

There was a slight tint of lemon in the eastern sky, he heard the man shouting "drown the bitch."

He was crouched at the side fence when he heard a child crying. The woman came out and got into the car and reversed up to the front door. Jesus their leaving I'll have to stop them. She opened the trunk and went back inside.

He saw the lights of the jeep coming over the little hillock and down into the dip switching off the lights. 'Thank god they're here.' She came out carrying a bag and threw it into the trunk. He heard a crunch on the dry dusty road then he appeared alongside him out of breath.

"Cormack thank god they are about to leave, the woman has put a bag in the car, we'll go up outside the door and when the man comes out we'll grab him."

"Right; are you sure they are inside Kathie and Jacob?"

"Yes positive I heard Jacob crying." He looked behind him. "Where's Mam?"

"I'm here right behind the two of you." She whispered anxiously.

"Alice; wait here until we catch the man first then come up to us." Jack started walking, "Come on Cormack."

They crept up to stand each side of the door out of sight of whoever came out. They heard footsteps and Jack looked at Cormack and nodded. Amadeo came with a bag and when he bent to push it into the trunk they both grabbed him. Jack stifled a vociferous grunt as he caught him round the neck and pulled him to the ground. He swore and swung out catching Cormack a blow to the head. Jack knelt on his back pushing his face into the gravel driveway. Cormack saw the plastic ties in the trunk of the car, 'just what we need,' he took out a fist of them and tied his hands, then went to tie his feet, and as he had him trussed up Angela came out. She screamed and ran back through the house. Cormack stood up and ran after her; she grabbed a small gun from the kitchen table and ran through the back garden. The light was shadowy as he saw her stop and turn, she fired the gun and the bullet went through the kitchen window.

"Holy Christ" he dived onto the grass, he heard Mam screaming in the house. He jumped up and sprinted after her as she tried to climb the fence at the bottom of the garden. She half turned and aimed the gun but just as she pulled the trigger she lost her footing and fell off the fence. The bullet went harmlessly into the ground. Cormack grabbed her hand and twisted until she dropped the gun.

She lashed out with the other hand catching him across the face. "Let me go you ignoramus I'll report you for attempted rape." She brought her knee up and just missed his groin, he caught her other hand and she struggled like a vicious cat. She spat into his face and tried to kick him on the shins.

"Hold her I have some ties here." Jack was standing alongside them.

Cormack caught her by the hair and pulled her to the ground, "you vicious cruel bitch, just in time Dad did you find Kathie?"

"Mam is doing that."

Alice ran around the house and she heard Jacob crying, the door was locked but the key was in the lock. She pushed in the door and the little fellow ran back afraid until he saw who it was. "Come here my little alanna (Gaelic for baby) what have they done to you," she bent down and he threw his arms around her neck sobbing big tears, "Mama, Mama."

"It's alright now my pet it's all over now we're going home."

Cormack was frantic as he ran back into the house. He opened all the doors to bedrooms and the last was the bathroom. She was in the bath tied up with plastic ties and her legs tied up to the taps so she couldn't move; there was a cloth over her face. He removed the cloth and saw she was gagged, her eyes told all as the look of relief was just magic. He pulled off the gag and she couldn't sit up until he cut the ties.

"Cormack, Cormack thank you, where is Jacob?"

"Don't worry he's safe Mam has him outside what were the bastards doing to you?" He cut the ties and helped her out and put a bath towel around her.

"Oh Cormack I thought they'd kill me, they poured water on my face and I thought I was drowning. That woman said she'd kill Jacob if I didn't co-operate so I told them where the bank was in Zurich."

"Never mind Kathie it's all over now come on we're going home."

She screamed with delight when she picked up Jacob, "My little love what did they do to you?"

"Mama, Mama, Gran Alice found me."

Jack sat Angela into a chair in the kitchen, "you wait there, you haven't much choice have you?" He went and brought up the jeep and Kathie, Jacob, and Alice got in, he turned to Cormack. "Will you wait with these two until I come back we have to take them for a little sightseeing tour."

Alice took him aside at the house, "what are you going to do with them? For god's sake don't do anything foolish and get into trouble with the law. I know they deserve it but it's not up to us to punish them."

"I won't do anything foolish just teach them a lesson so they will never come back here again." He went into the garage and brought out a strong rope and a drum full of something, and went into the house and brought out a pillow from the bedroom. He drove back up to the front of the house and he called Cormack, "we better hurry its daylight and we don't want to be seen. Come on throw them both into the back here."

They lifted them into the back of the jeep and Angela was crying and pleading to let her go. He covered them with an old blanket and they drove away.

Cormack anxiously asked, "Dad where are we taking them?"

He looked over smiling, "I think a little sightseeing would do them no harm, as a matter of fact it would be a shame to let them leave the country without seeing our famous sights. It's early so there won't be anyone around."

Cormack looked out at the young day as the orange sun was slowly climbing through a haze of warm promise. "Dad they were water boarding Kathie, you know that terrible torture they go on with in Guantanamo Bay with the terrorist prisoners. She was terrified and thought she was drowning."

"Yes I've read about it and it's a terrible thing to do to any human being, let alone a young innocent girl. But this fellow might be suffering from vertigo before the day is through."

He pulled off the main road and drove on a small track which stopped at a gate into a field. "Get out and open the gate."

He drove up onto the cliff edge and stopped. "Right let's get them out."

The view out over the sheer cliffs across the wild Atlantic Ocean was majestic and primitive, as an infant day spread clawing fingers along this turbulent sea. The huge breakers pounding the timeless rugged cliff face were like Thor in his most violent mood.

They laid them on the damp dewy grass and Jack proceeded to tie the rope around Amadeo's waist and down through his legs.

The fear in his eyes was like a man going to the gallows, "please don't hang me, let me go and I will never bother her again."

Jack tied the end of the rope around the hitch on the jeep.

Angela was shouting obscenities, "You fucking bog men you'll pay for this."

Jack pulled her sitting up, "just watch because you're next you evil bitch."

They caught Amadeo and lowered him over the cliff head first, he screamed and whimpered. They jerked the rope as if letting him go.

"Please don't let go."

They dropped him some more and he urinated and it ran down his shirt and onto his face.

Jack went over to Angela and she was crying now.

"Don't do that to me I'm sorry what I did, it was all his fault please let me go."

"Take that stuff out of the jeep and bring it here Cormack." Jack tore her top and she was naked except for her bra, he pulled her skirt down and bared her pants. "Open the top of that drum; get the pillow," Jack poured the black tar over her head and down her body," now the pillow." He cut the pillow and shook the feathers onto the black sticky tar.

Cormack laughed. "Now you'll think twice before torturing a young woman and kidnapping a child again."

She opened her mouth to speak and the tar ran over her ruby lips and white teeth.

Jack went to the rope, "come on pull him up."
They got him up and his breathing was laboured.

Cormack half laughing said, "the bastard could die sit him up."

Jack took the rope off him and sniffed the strong smell, "oh god the dirty bastard has messed himself."

He poured the remainder of the tar over him and shook the feathers onto it.

"That's it Cormack we better be off it's been a long night."

CHAPTER 23

Alice was relieved to have Jack and Cormack back, "what did you do I hope you didn't hurt them, although they deserved to be given a good lesson."

"Sit here the two of you and we'll tell you exactly what we did."

Alice didn't know whether to laugh with joy and relief, or chastise them for doing such a terrible thing to them. Kathie was so pleased and thought they got off lightly considering what they intended to do to her and Jacob.

The evening news had a story of two people found tarred and feathered on a cliff in west Galway. They were brought to hospital but later released, no motive could be found for this act. The two people a man in his fifties and a woman in her thirties were both foreign nationals. The man a Cuban was believed to be at their Consul, and arrangements being made to have him flown back to Cuba. The woman a Belize national was also having arrangements made to be flown back to her home country.

They laughed and assured Kathie that was the end of her being harassed by any more secret police from Cuba. She was so pleased to be with this family, and Jacob was enjoying every day being pampered and made to feel so loved. Cormack noticed how she would sometimes sit and stare not talking but her thoughts far away. He put it down to the torture she had endured, and tried to comfort and assure her she was safe and they would never trouble her again.

Jack was playing with Jacob and the Labrador when Peadar got off his bicycle and walked into the front garden.

"Good morning Jack I have a couple for you," he handed him four letters, "aye and one foreign one for the girl staying with you I suppose."

"Thanks Peadar; anything strange happening around?"

"Not much except them people that were staying in the house, you know Duggan's place that you were enquiring about."

"Yes I never met them after, I suppose they never came back again?"

"Aye that's where you're wrong, they did come back, and left in quare kind of circumstances. Missing a few days and then going in a terrible hurry, from what I hear from Michel Joe who saw them go."

"Ah sure maybe their holiday time was up."

"Oh I don't know Jack tis odd things happen up there you know, tis the auld ones who's restless and tormented spirits can affect people, they know who's good and who's evil. If they want you to leave they'll haunt you with trouble and sorrow, they have powers we don't know about. My mother told me of the young girl when they were growing up who lived with her parents in a cottage near them auld ruins. She was pregnant and all in the parish knew, and talked about her. The rumour was the parish priest was the father. Her people kept two cows and some sheep up in the fields around the ruins cause no one else would go there. She went up there to bring the cow's home in the evenings, and low and behold they say the auld people took the child out of her womb. They can do that, and bring the unborn to their spirit world for the children they lost. She looked pregnant and swelled up but when it came time to have the child she had nothing, this; Jack; they called *phantom pregnancy*. When I pass there I go quick and say a prayer for the poor souls."

"Peadar that's more auld pishogues, how could that happen?"

He walked out and as he went to get onto his bicycle he turned to Jack, "Be careful of them auld pishogues."

Jack took Jacob by the hand and went into the house, "Kathie I have a letter for you."

She looked at the envelope, "oh from the people in Zurich, please let it be good news." She took out the sheet of paper and read her divorce has been finalised and could she make arrangements to visit them to complete their documents. "I've got it," she waved the paper over her head, then bent down to kiss Jacob, "great news my little love one." She ran out to the back garden where Cormack was mowing the grass. "Cormack, Cormack, I've got it."

He ran to her and she threw her arms around him.

"Oh god Cormack I'm free at last."

"That's the news we've been waiting for, at last Kathie you're free from all that life you have left behind you."

"Cormack" she caught him by the hand, "walk with me to the end of the garden I have to talk to you."

Dejection dropped on him like a shroud, 'it's the end of the road now' he thought, 'but she has her life to live and Jacob is her life. I'll miss them both.'

"Let's sit here" she pulled him alongside her onto the garden seat. "I have something very important to tell you so brace yourself."

He closed his eyes, "I'm ready."

She caught his hand in hers, "I'm pregnant."

He almost fell sideways off the seat, "Kathie I'm going to be a father I can't believe it how long have you known?"

"I'm two months now but I didn't want to tell you until I was sure. I was so worried, that with the treatment of their trying to drown me I might lose it. But Cormack," she threw her arms around him, "I haven't."

"Kathie will you marry me, I mean just because you're pregnant you don't have to."

She kissed him full on the lips, "I thought you'd never ask, and we are going to get married in the little church in the village."

"How; do you know the church in the village?"

"Alice has taken Jacob and me up to the village a few times for a walk, and we always visit the church, where she says a few prayers in thanksgiving for our safety. I also say some prayers in thanks for everything especially my new family, you, Alice, Jack, and Mary, you are all my family with Jacob and our expected new arrival. Cormack I'm so happy, Alice and Mary will help with all the arrangements."

"God Kathie; imagine." He looked at her and thought 'how beautiful, dreams do sometimes come true.'

Laughing she said. "Imagine what?"

"I only wanted an auld bed in Havana."

"I promise you when things there change politically I'll take you back and share that auld bed with you."

He laughed out loud, "That's a promise you'll have to keep."

"Cormack there's one more thing I have to tell you."

"You just can't have anymore secrets or confessions, I don't care I want to marry you no matter."

"Just this one and I hope you won't change your mind."

She related how she had to kill the two Columbian drug dealers and about Chantal and her friend Emilie, and how they set fire to the launch and she stole the money, and how they promised one another never to tell anyone. "But now you're going to be my husband you have to know."

"You're the bravest girl and what you did was admirable, thanks for letting me into your confidence and it'll never pass my lips."

They broke the news to Jack and Alice, and they were so happy expecting their first grandchild.

Mary was restless in bed with the thoughts of a new daughter in law and a grandchild, she turned over and asked. "Jack, you awake?"

"Yes"

I can't believe it, and won't they make a wonderful and beautiful couple."

"Yes Alice they surely will but did Kathie go to see a doctor about her pregnancy, is she really sure she's pregnant?"

"Sure; sure she's sure, women don't make mistakes about things like that, what makes you say that?"

"Oh I don't know just all that she's been through she might be mistaken, I still think you should talk to her about going to a doctor."

"You're a worrier Jack, go to sleep I'll talk to her."

EPILOGUE

Kathie opened Chantal's email and read, 'I want to thank you for saving my life and will be forever in your debt, and please let me know all when you are settled, from your loving friend Chantal.'

She replied with a wedding invitation and her baby news.

Cormack and Kathie married in the church in the village and were later blessed with a daughter who they named Ruth after her grandmother who she loved so much. Chantal was a pretty picture with her young boy friend.

Alice and Jack were overjoyed with their new family and Mary became like a sister to Kathie whenever she was at home.

Angela and Amadeo were never heard of again.

Kathie true to her word made arrangements for Mahvash to go to a clinic in Switzerland and have surgery on her scarred body. It was successful, that her face and body was almost eighty five percent perfect. She became housekeeper and companion for Frederico who remained in Iran as a university lecturer.

Kathie's fortune when it was all unravelled came to over five hundred million Euro, and as stock markets fluctuated and oil rose and fell on world markets she never knew exactly how much her and Cormack's wealth really was.

Cormack sold the shares in his business and now worked with his accountants to help keep track of their huge portfolio.

They built a house not far from Alice and Jack and only went abroad when necessary.

As of writing they hadn't gone back to Havana to share that *auld bed*.

THE END.

I want to thank you for reading my book and if you have enjoyed it I would be very grateful if you could put a review for it.

Thank you.
John Molloy   (Author)